THE GREY COAST

19th Aug. '81

THE GREY COAST

By

NEIL M. GUNN

I ken a gloghole
That looks at the sky
As much as to say
'I'm as deep as you're high.'

HUGH M'DIARMID

SOUVENIR PRESS

First published by Faber and Faber Ltd.
This edition copyright © 1976 by
Souvenir Press and John W. M. Gunn
and published 1976 by Souvenir Press Ltd,
43 Great Russell Street, London WC1B 3PA
and simultaneously in Canada by
Methuen Publications, Agincourt, Ontario

*The publisher acknowledges the financial assistance of
The Scottish Arts Council in the publication of this volume.*

ISBN 0 285 62248 X   casebound
ISBN 0 285 62253 6   paperback

Printed in Great Britain by
Fletcher & Son Ltd, Norwich

to

MY MOTHER

CHAPTER ONE

BEFORE she had called her uncle to tea, she had drawn the cheap slip of window-curtain to one side, so that the last of the daylight might be made use of and paraffin saved. Now as her uncle pushed back his plate and cup, and sucked at a tooth, and cleared his throat, saying, 'Ha!' and 'Huhuh!' in husky, replete grunts, she observed through the darkening a figure enter by the slap in the dike at the foot of the potato patch. Her features stiffened perceptibly.

But her uncle's quick, crafty eyes did not fail to catch that look, that stiffening expression, and twisting his wizened neck he peered blinkingly through the window.

'Is that someone coming, Maggie?'

'Ay,' she said, laconically, for his long vision was as good as her own.

He sat stiffly for a little, sucking his tooth with reflective deliberation, his arms on the table. The dishes clicked and clattered as she scraped and gathered them.

But in these few moments of silence between them awareness became acute. Again the opening had been made. For all the calm unconcern with which she slid plate to plate, there existed internally, in spite of herself, a dumb expectancy. She saw what was passing in the old man's mind by the very set of his head to his shoulders, the twist of the neck, the stillness.

And without turning his head, and in as matter-of-fact a tone as though he were enquiring where the cow had been tethered, he asked:

'Has he said any word to ye?'

An artistry which was met by a plate clatter that did not cease, by no slightest suspicion of feeling disturbing the calmness of Maggie's indifference, as:

'No,' she answered him.

Thus awareness became articulate and the repression named.

He shifted his position on the board; a hand went feeling for his pipe.

'Weel, ye know fine he's going to.'

She did not answer. Watching her face now, he went on:

'The croft has for long been getting beyond me, as ye know. Withoot him we'd have been in the Poorhoose.'

His tone was casual. He sucked the hollow tooth twice.

'An' Tullach Farm is a place for a leddy . . . no' to speak o' anyone else.'

She carried the dishes through to the back-place without a word.

Hauling his pipe from a waistcoat pocket, he got up from the table. It was as well he had said what he had said. It finished it. Now she knew. He glimpsed the approaching figure and began to feel his pockets for his knife. The thought of Daun Tullach's golden-bar plug crossed his mind. Presently the door-sneck rattled and Daun himself entered the narrow, dark passage-way.

Jeems peered into the gloom, then his head lifted

8

and his voice rose hospitably as he appeared to recognise his visitor.

'Is that yourself, Mr Tait? Come right in! Here we are, no more nor finishing our tea.'

'I didn't think I was so early, Jeems.'

'Ye're no' early: it's us what's late.'

And Donald Tait of Tullach Farm, known inevitably as Daun Tullach, entered the half-light of the kitchen.

'Good evening, Maggie!' he said to the young woman who was gathering the tablecloth into a crumb-enclosing heap.

'Good evening,' she returned, with a small smile, and passed him to shake the tablecloth outside the back door.

He watched her go, then turned to the flickering peat on the hearth-stone.

'Ay, man,' he said, 'it's no' a bad night, after all the rain there's been in it.'

'It's no' that,' agreed Jeems. 'Sit ye doon, man; sit doon!'

Daun Tullach took the stiff, upright armchair with the feather cushion in the solid seat, the most comfortable chair, and normally that occupied by Jeems himself, who now scraped over the stone floor a simple wooden chair to the opposing ingleneuk.

'Maggie!' cried Jeems, 'come an' put a bit blink on the lamp, canno' ye!'

'I'm coming,' said Maggie evenly.

'Terrible mindful o' the rain it's been,' he continued, sitting down and scraping the dottle from his

9

pipe into a palm. Then he blew lustily through the pipe-stem, and began to hunt his pockets for a bit of twist, when Tullach offered:

'Try this plug.'

'I canno' think where –' muttered the old man, continuing his search as though he had not observed the offered plug.

'Here ye are, man – try this!'

'Ah – weel – ah – thank ye!'

Maggie came in and lit a paper spill at the fire, Tullach taking a swift, sly, appraising look at the finely made, lithe body as it bent to the blaze. Deep, dusky hair. The firelight gleamed in her eyes and danced impishly over her face, the faintly browned pallor flushing faintly to colour. Subtle, hypnotic riches of youth.

The lamp having been lit and hung from its central hook in the ceiling, she came to the fire again and lifted the kettle off the crook, retiring with it to the back-place to wash up.

When she had gone, Daun Tullach straightened himself and took out his pipe. In the lamplight he showed up the snodly dressed appearance of a man of about forty. His face was firmly cut, even stubbornly along the lower jaw, which protruded a little. The moustache was scrubby and ginger-coloured, the eyes small and restless. Out of their blinky restlessness, indeed, it seemed as though a certain cuteness kept flickering over the solid facial background, a twinkling slyness – capable of meas-ured restraint, perhaps, but ever ready. His dark homespun was snugly cut, the creases at elbows and shoulders showing at once the thickness of the material and the intention of lengthy wear.

Maggie took her time over the dishes, going through the business of washing and drying slowly, automatically, her eyes round and unseeing on the thick, cheap ware. The drone of the two voices reached her from the kitchen, her uncle's placating, agreeable, the other oracular, first-personal, and punctuated every now and then by three or four quick barks of a gusty laugh. At each recurrence of the laugh a momentary hardening caught at her eyes or lips, a coldness as of instinctive withdrawal. But plainly not a conscious emotion at the moment. In the vague eye-gazing there seemed no consciousness at all, as though the mind had got plunged in a grey vacancy, where reality was a matter of muffled and fateful echo.

The last dish dried, she remained gazing at it fixedly for some time; then, sighing, suddenly stirred.

Having put the dishes away and taken stock of the back-kitchen – or back-place, as it was invariably named – she began tidying up. With the floor swept, the place could have borne any inspection; and having nothing further to do, she opened the door and entered the kitchen.

The kitchen looked cosy and inviting in the yellowish lamplight. The two brass candlesticks gleamed by the tea-caddy on the mantelpiece. The rows of old blue-patterned plates, on edge in the racks above the kitchen dresser, were a note of clean colour, and were fittingly supported by a rather large soup tureen of the same pattern, which rested on the middle-back of the dresser itself. In the space between the dresser and the wall-corner, and at Daun Tullach's back, a wag-at-th'-wa', yellow with age, tick-tocked with metallic deliberation.

From these two walls, she turned to a third, against which stood the large boxed-in kitchen bed, with looped-up curtains and scalloped green fringe of paper along the top edge. Stretching in over the multi-coloured patchwork of the counterpane, she picked up a half-knitted woollen sock of hodden grey. As she took her seat on one of the chairs by the bed-side, she glanced quickly at the wag-at-th'-wa', noting the time to a minute. Then her needles began clicking a pattern of dry sound in and out the personalities of the fireside.

'So ye said that til him?' was nodding Uncle Jeems appreciatively.

'I did! What's the good o' a man on the County Council, if ye canno' get him to stick up for yer own bit o' the parish? That's what I would like to know!'

'An' what did he say?'

'What could he say? He hummed an' snottered aboot an' said the road wasn't this or that, wasn't exactly a first-class road. So I took the word from his mouth. "No," says I, "it's no' a first-class road – an' that's certain!"'

'Man, ye had him there!'

'Eh! But that wasn't all. I says to him: "What are ye paying Geordie Grant in the year by way o' contract for the whole road? Do you think I don't know?" . . . I tell ye, I soon let him know all aboot it! Ha! ha! ha!'

Ould Jeems removed his pipe and spat with bullet-like precision into the heart of the fire.

'It's no' right,' he said, ' – on ye.'

'They think they can do what they like; they think – an' they say, too – that it's no-but a bit private road o' mine. But it's nothing o' the sort – an' I'll haud them to it. I won't put a penny piece intil it!'

'Ye're quite right –'

'An' I'm telling ye, if I break an aixle or have a coup or any damage, all I say is – Look oot!'

The voices droned on interminably, ould Jeems ready chorus to the importance of the other. For Daun Tullach was a farmer in a fair way: decidedly a man of substance on the strip of grey coast, where the rule was the small croft with its low grey dikes built of the boulders which the land in labour never failed to give forth.

The voices settled to a drone again in the margin of Maggie's consciousness. Now and then, as she drew out a needle and prepared for another row, she would glance from under her black lashes at the wag-at-th'-wa'. The glance, returning, would take in the figures by the fireside, and for a moment a subtle appraisement would gleam in it and die. The expression on her face, however, never varied from its indifferent calm: as though the secret life of the mind could go on of its own accord, without touching immediate material existence at the surface at all; indeed, so remote from it that even the gleam of appraisement betokened rather a criticism by the unconscious than a disturbance in her positive reflections.

13

Silence, the long brooding hours altogether too long to be filled by thought, the wakefulness wherein no word is spoken, the vague self-hypnosis: it may be that under it all the mind of its own inscrutable volition pursues hidden ways of dream and thought, to be revealed outwardly in a gleam, an unconscious gesture, a decision positive as unexpected.

And of all places, such a grey strip of crofting coast, flanked seaward by great cliffs, cliffs 'flawed' as in a half-sardonic humour of their Creator to permit of the fishing creek, was surely the place for the perfect growth of this duality of the mind, whereby the colourless, normal life becomes at once a record of the stolidly obvious and of the dream-like unknown.

But as the minute hand went on, an indefinable quickening came to Maggie's expression. The calm was still there, but the flesh was drawing on the deeps. A moment came when out in the gathering night beyond the gable-end there was the sound of a heel being sucked out of a wet, clayey soil. Faint, scarcely audible the sound, yet it focussed Maggie's attention as though it had been a pistol-shot. The colour receded from her cheeks, but her needles never stopped. Heart beating, she listened with painful intensity to the voices by the fire. They droned on. They had not heard.

Roy, the collie, who had curled himself under the table when Tullach had entered, came out, however, came over to Maggie and laid his long nose on her knees. His eyes looked up at her with an intelligence that brought the colour back to her face. His tail wagged slowly.

14

Her knitting needles stopped. She looked down upon, bent over, the long head.

'Well, Roy – what is it?' She sat up suddenly. 'It's no' milking time surely?' She stared at the wag-at-th'-wa' with consummate surprise.

Her uncle spat in the fire expertly.

'Ay, it's that; an' be ye going.'

She did not require to think of what passed in his mind to prompt so ready a response. There were milk customers from the fishing village of Balriach who came nightly with their pennies, and she had better see to it.

She got up, went through to the back-place, where with rattle of pails and lighting of lantern she busied herself. Presently her voice was heard: 'Come on, Roy!' The sneck of the back door clicked behind mistress and dog.

For all his talk and short gusty laughs, Tullach had listened to every sound from her first movement. He listened still to the perfect silence without. Not even a dog-yelp betokening stranger. Of their own accord his hands came for a moment to the wooden arms of the chair and ettled to heave him to his feet. But he hesitated.

And he hesitated because of some subtle forbidding sense of the dignity due him. He was no farm hand, no penniless, jaunty young fisher fool. What he was doing he was doing solidly, with the dignity of a man of substance, and the end was inevitable. His position and his person preordained it, apart from other considerations such as the croft's dependence in vital ways on his generosity, and the obviously ingratiating welcomes of ould Jeems. The welcome of Maggie not so obviously ingratiating, perhaps; but for that he could go the more warily. The something retiring, uncertain about her held a queer, teasing, sometimes even maddening attraction.

He licked the scrubby edge of his moustache, while his eyes concentrated on ould Jeems, who was telling some personal experience at length. But his eyes did not see ould Jeems. . . . She was out there in the byre with a dim lantern and the milk going hiss-hiss into the pail – and nothing else.

The picture became very vivid. He saw himself looking down on her as she sat on the wee creepie, the milk-pail between her knees, her hands pulling rhythmically at the teats, with a squirting of milk at each downstroke, her face turned sideways so that he need not remove his eyes from it, or with forehead pressed against glossy hide when the nape of the neck became a glimmering paleness of indescribable allure.

Passion moved, surged slowly. He could have the feeling, looking down on her, that he was looking down on the woman who would be his to do with as he liked. To do with as he liked. A desperate fore-tasting that filled the senses with a gluttonous delight. His breath came a trifle noisily through his nostrils as spasmodically his lips tightened.

Yet his hands slid off the chair arms and began to slice the golden-bar plug. As he spat in the fire, his face suddenly puckered in a slyness that might not easily be overcome by impulse. His time would come and he could bide it. Realisation would be the

more absolute and crushing – then! His eyes blinked
and brought ould Jeems within focus again.

Instantly his glance surprised a searching puckishness on the face of the old man, whose eyes
appeared to be glinting curious and secretive understandings, personal understandings; and Tullach's
glance steadied and stared abruptly, penetratively.

But in a moment ould Jeem's eyes had switched to
his pipe-stem, from which he proceeded to whisk
juice into the fire. He laughed, a low husky laugh,
full of enigmatic, fleshy humours.

'So, as I was saying, Sandy stood there looking at
her, and she wi' scarcely a stitch on her at all. He
was a big set-up lump o' a chiel from Stoer beyond
Lochinver yonder. They used to call the West
Coasters "fair weather sailors," because they might
do a season on the yachts at Oban or Glasgow or at
the fishings, but would go home for the winter to
their crofts. It was Sandy's first trip abroad. He had
signed on at Stornoway – the first time ever he got
drunk it was – after nearly killing a man. Wi' two
glasses in him he would be that quate an' raw,
mooning aboot as though trying to come up on his
shadow for want o' any other provocation, as ye
might say – oh, fight! No, ye steered clear o' him
till he was sober, an' when he was sober he was just
like a mess o' brose, that soft, an' ye could lead him
like a lamb. He was Gaelic spoken an' had English
that would make some o' the other fellows laugh –
when they were by themselves, or he was sober!

'Weel, we thocht we'd get Sandy on to this ploy.
There was a devil o' a fellow from Stranraer way –

17

Jocky Bendie by name – an' Jocky was – och! och! Jocky was the gey laad!

'He knew his way aboot them Eastern toons as well as ye might the roadie from Tullach to Balriach. He made sure that Sandy had gotten a good shot in him. Then we went doon a street wi' red lamps in it.'

He paused to peer knowingly at Tullach. Tullach's face creased to a sardonic, measured puckering of the left corner of his mouth – the eyes remaining penetratively steady on Jeems.

'She was a fine woman wi' black eyes glittering on ye an' wi' paint an' scent on her, an' no' much forby. Jocky spoke as though quite at hom', an' made by way o' introducing Sandy. Then he gave him a bit putt wi' his elbow. "Now then, Sandy!" says he.

'Man, Sandy had gone stiff. His face had a flame in it an' his eyes were staring as though the scarlet woman had come oot o' the Bible an' the memory o' his upbringing an' the church at hom' had come upon him like the hand o' Gode! He sobered stark staring! Then withoot a word, withoot as much as a grunt, he whirls roond an' catches Jocky one welt that the sole wonder of it was that it didn't kill him stone dead on the spot. Sure as death, ye'd've heard the skelp of it beyond Balriach. It knocked two front teeth oot o' him an' split his lip. It was the greatest skelp ever I heard in my life. It was a terrible skelp.'

Jeem's eyes glowed. He stooped forward animatedly and spat in the fire; then turned to Tullach again.

18

'It was a terrible night that! I'll never forget it. Man, queer things happen in places like yon.'

'No doubt,' said Tullach.

'Man, ye've no idea o't. The queer things.'

Tullach smoked steadily.

'It was two nights after, maybe, or three. The sea was calm aboot us as a great pool; no' a breath – an' hot. Sandy had been quate an' never speaking to anyone; quate an' dour an' as though the drink had never gone off him at all.

'I was on watch – how I can see the night now! – when I beholds a figure coming towards me. I said never the word, for it was Sandy. Maybe there was something between us, seeing we both came from up north in a way, an' I had a little Gaelic from my faither. But I was taking no risks wi' Sandy, ye might be sure!

' "It is a good night," he says, sort o' offhand.

' "A fine night," I says. An' I knew from his voice there was something on his mind. But it took him a little while to come wi' it, as though he was haudin' himsel' in to let it oot easy. An' then his voice, cracking a little:

' "Will we be going back to yon place?" '

Ould Jeems laughed his thick throaty laugh, and looked sideways at Tullach, eyes glistering.

But if Tullach's face creased again, his quick barking laugh did not follow. Nor did he reason out the cause of the enigmatic hostility that now floated perversely in his mind.

No exception could be taken to Jeems's reminiscences, which, if in a certain sense grotesquely apt

19

so far as certain secret processes of his own mind were concerned, were yet all too plainly but incidental part of an inexhaustible whole. It was almost as though he could not allow himself to imagine that a certain silly, puckish glance had been a prying, a leering, into his dark inner privacy, a prying that, were he but sure of it, he would crush with brutal swiftness.

He cleared his throat and suddenly laughed, the laugh of self-assertion, of self-assurance.

'Funny!' he reckoned. 'I jalouse he was anxious to go back.'

'Weel, ye see, that was the joke!' said Jeems. 'That was the joke! Actually, we never went back as it happened. Nor did Sandy ever have dealings wi' women, on that trip anyway.'

Twisting over on one hip, Tullach regarded him with a superior, tolerant smile that masked his subtle uncertainty, that was even a final effort to dissipate it.

'So ye could never be sure what he meant, eh?'

'No, man,' said Jeems. 'No. . . . But it was like the thing!'

And between them, it felt to Tullach, the enigmatic puckishness floated still.

CHAPTER TWO

WHEN Maggie had clicked the back door behind her, she immediately stooped to Roy and fondled an ear. 'Well, then, Roy, lad!'

A shadow moved over against the byre, but Roy barked no acknowledgment. Not that there was much fear of this happening in any case, for beyond a neck-bristling growl at intrusive tramp or tinker, Roy had been brought up in strict reverence for the poacher's manifold ways of quietude.

His tail wagged, however, as he trotted across to the shadow and had the same ear scratched, if a trifle more boisterously, more pleasurably.

'Hallo!' said Maggie, with sufficient gay astonishment, but on an obviously hushed note of caution, as she stretched a hand to the byre door.

The limber young fellow into whom the shadow had resolved itself stiffened visibly at the undernote of caution, hung poised a moment, then:

'Hallo!' he acknowledged, with a caution subtly less.

Her hand hesitated on the byre-door clasp. His hand covered hers by chance and lifted the clasp. The fumbling of hand on hand sent her heart racing and she slipped in through the door quickly, with the suspicion of a suppressed laugh following the whirl of her body.

That liveness of the body with its whirl and suppressed gaiety, its elusive, nameless gaiety, banished for the moment all thought of the underbreath

21

of caution, and he closed the byre door behind him.

He watched her stretch for the creepie into the corner shadows, turn round again with the lantern light flashing on her face, and going up to Nance, the cow, slap her mildly on the flank.

'Round, Nance; round!'

Nance turned her head in the stall, regarded the two of them, then turned away again, chain ask rattling indifferently.

'She's that stubborn when she likes!' said Maggie.

The young fellow in a stride or two was beside her, and with a couple of weighty slaps made Nance instantly give ground.

Maggie tucked the creepie under her, and, getting hold of Nance's tail, tied it by its own whisk to the near hind leg.

Then forehead pressed against glossy hide, she stretched to her work and immediately a thin thudding sound was rhythmically beating the bottom of the shining tin pail. Maggie's head turned sideways. Now that she was secure she was ready.

The half-conscious invitation was as half-consciously accepted, and Ivor Cormack, stretching a hand to the young calf in its boxed-in stall, began a trifle boisterously:

'Well, what's doing?'

'Same as usual.'

'That's exciting!'

Maggie's smile broke on a note of banter:

'Excitement's bad for the heart!'

22

'Oh! Who said that?'

'The doctor!' said Maggie.

Ivor sniffed a laugh through his nose. Maggie had a feeling that the thin joke was not only foolish, but, in some way, a sort of insensitive indecorum; yet feeling, too, the exciting necessity for a weapon. And possibly at such a moment the byre fork may be given the shining and glamorous properties of an Excalibur; certain, anyway, that the rapier of a nicer wit, attempting educated 'mannerism,' would have drawn only ruthless laughter.

'You're getting a fine edge on it!' considered Ivor.

'Amn't I?'

'Ay. Maybe your education these nights is well taken in hand.'

'Don't flatter yourself!' said Maggie.

He threw her a quick look; then his lips curled in a slow irony.

'It's no' myself I was flattering.'

'No? Then it's bad form to flatter anyone else.'

Her use of the superior expression 'bad form' held that pertness of affectation which she did not recoil from. She did not want to think of Daun Tullach now.

But, growing tormented, with the counter craving to torment, he had to make her think of Daun Tullach, as though that first cautious whispering had to be dissected openly and to a point of unavoidable understanding.

So he laughed.

'I understand,' he said enigmatically.

It was with difficulty she restrained herself from

23

immediately asking him what he understood. But instinct warned her that that would be merely to help the 'draw.' She had dismissed the question and was searching for another, when involuntarily she asked:

'What do you understand?'

The young calf had got hold of his hand, was sucking at it.

'His teeth are coming through.'

Maggie turned her head quickly.

'Oh, that calf!'

He met her eyes.

'What did you think I meant?'

The question searched the silence idiotically, but the laugh which had jumped too readily to her throat was suppressed as she got forehead to glossy hide. In some way, he was having the better of it. He would manœuvre her into a blind corner, if she was not careful. And if he manœuvred her into a blind corner – what then?

'I think it is time,' said Maggie, 'that you were cutting your own wisdom teeth!' A happy stroke, and defiant laughter could afford to gurgle.

'Do you think so, now?' Yet in a moment it was seen that he could ask even that with the persistent undercurrent of innuendo darkly in evidence, dourly.

'Don't you think so yourself?'

'Perhaps you're right,' he agreed perversely.

There was silence, a live tense silence for Maggie in which her heart beat not unpleasantly. The calf's slobbering and whisking on the one hand and on the

24

other the hiss-hiss of the milk muffled now by the froth; otherwise silence, with the vivid animal reality of life touching the senses, with the doubtful equipoise of dark emotionalities and future obscurities touching the spirit. Decidedly not a time for thought, for explanation, both hated of this irrational, iridescent foreplay.

Yet he must persist in thought, in tormenting her for an explanation, as though the future obscurities had to-night got an undue fillip in the knowledge that in three days he would be leaving Balriach for the West Coast fishing. Not at the moment that he actually wanted certainty, that he wanted any relationship to be defined. Still – that underbreath of caution . . .

He laughed, and even his laughter, usually an open infection, had a twist to it.

'You're not saying much!' he bantered.

'You're not saying much yourself, are you?'

He wiped the slavers from his hand on the calf's neck and scratched the hard forehead. In love with this tickling the calf tried ineffectually to put its tail up, and then boxed the hand.

'When are you selling the calf?'

She did not answer, but settled the pail more uprightly between her knees, for the froth was mounting. In spite of herself, she felt this touch of perversity, of dourness, getting at her own spirit, dimming the iridescence to the everlasting grey vagueness of the croft and of the coast.

'In a week or two, I suppose,' he answered for her. 'Dave sold his at the sale last Thursday at Oulster and got three pounds for him. It was a pretty fair price.'

She gave all her attention to the pail. The squirts of milk were growing shorter. She was nearly finished.

'Though three pounds is no' very much when you think on it,' he went on. 'Money – money is everything.' There was a craving upon him suddenly to talk, to go on talking about things that did not matter at all – except by way of dark and mocking innuendo; and now everything he would say would gather this mockery of its own accord without any effort on his part.

She got up.

He hunted out the calf's coggie, and she poured into it a frothy rush of the warm milk. He lifted the coggie over the partition and set it down inside the calf's stall, taking care that the excited young beast with its instinctive head-buttings and sprawling of spindly legs didn't upset it.

'Hits! ye brute!' he admonished; then turned a quizzical glance on Maggie, whose attention, however, was entirely taken up with the calf.

'It's a good calf,' he said.

'Ay,' she acknowledged, not looking at him, face stiffening perceptibly.

He smiled and turned to the calf's dish. It was nearly empty.

It was nearly empty, and in another couple of minutes they would be outside, their meeting over, and he would be going home! The sense of emptiness in life, in the byre itself, of the appalling, almost

26

gawky futility of himself, of his actions, the sheer silliness of his words – got him in a moment at the throat and choked him.

Maggie's eyes were clouded vaguely, their gaiety having faded back into the film of inevitable endurance. It was as though his perversity had filched the moment of opportunity, the golden sweetness, leaving the byre the cowshed it was.

What a fool, what a senseless fool, what a bluidy idiot! The knuckles of his left hand stood out white on the partition ridge as at last he heaved himself upright and swung the coggie from the calf's stall.

Yet he could not break through and touch her; he could not – he could not; every muscle was netted in his perversity, his emotion was netted, strangled. He could not break through to take her in his arms, to crush her.

Actually he smiled as he swung round, his voice casual:

'Well, Maggie, that's that!'

'Yes, that's finished.'

She got hold of the milk pail and turned to the door. Three or four paces and they would be outside; it would be all over. Three or four paces – one, two, three – Shadows danced impishly, swung grotesquely with the lantern.

His hand fumbled at the latch while she stood by him. It lifted with a click and the door swung open. They were outside, and behind them he clicked the door shut.

She could not move off all at once. Something had

to be said, even of good night if not of good-bye. An awkward moment with its subtle denial of speech, with personal consciousness painfully alert. It might be a last night.

But she was not quite prepared for the remark he suddenly let drop with an attempt at flippancy that did not come off, that even had an undernote of sudden bitterness.

'I suppose he's in?' he said.

'Yes,' she replied at once, altogether now beyond dissembling, beyond questioning whom he meant, though the matter had not been a subject of discussion between them before. She twisted the handle of the milk pail as though to get a better grip of it. She could not lay it down.

'Let it down! You're no' in such a hurry, are ye?'

'Oh, I better be getting in.'

'Ay, perhaps you are in a hurry,' he agreed.

She winced. The silence curled about them.

She looked towards the back door of the house, but could not take the first step away. In another second she would go; then another second . . . A pulse was beginning to beat – up and up. . . . Oh, she must go. She twisted the milk pail.

'We'll be making ready for the sea to-morrow night,' he said at last. But he could not get lightness back into his voice, was beginning not to care whether he could or not.

'What time are you going?'

Her voice was more even, better controlled, than his. To him it seemed perfectly controlled, with no

28

trace of this black madness that was choking him. Of course, he was a fool. . . .

'We're going out on the first o' the ebb the following morning. That'll be about eight o'clock,' he said levelly.

'An' when will ye be back?'

'Depends. Seven weeks or eight, maybe. The fishing'll be over by then.'

That they were now merely making conversation they were both aware. The answers to her questions she knew already.

'But you like Stornoway?'

'Oh, it's right enough!'

'I've heard them saying you have good times there!'

He sniffed ironically.

'Fair to middling – what wi' the girls at the gutting an' the Lewsachs!'

She gave a little nervous laugh.

'In that case you'll no' miss the folk you'll leave behind ye!'

He knew that she did not mean it altogether in the first-personal sense, but he answered at once:

'Oh, yes. I'll miss you right enough.'

Something downright in his words sent the pulse beating up again. But now, after that personal note, there was nothing on earth to say, and nothing to do but go in. She had to go in! She must! If only she could move. . . .

'Well, I must –'

'Though maybe you'll no' miss anyone yourself.'

Never before had she known his voice like this,

dogged, flippant, bitter, his voice that had had ever a note of daring in it, of laughter.

'Yes, I will,' she said timidly.

'Oh, I don't know,' he answered at once, his eyes turned from her to where the yellow lights of the fishing village were clustering in the dip of the moor.

She did not take offence at the hardened voice, at the sudden harsh scepticism, for she understood only too well that hidden undertow of misery which sucks darkly at the sunlit things of life.

Stiffly they stood by the byre door, looking out on the young night, but seeing nothing of the pale stars, of the dim expanse of moor, hearing no note of the sea down over the cliff-heads. Staring fixedly at the yellow unwinking lights of the village, he saw only the utter and complete nothingness of himself in relation to life in any shape at all. A darkness, a bitterness, catching at the spirit and drowning it, so that no argument was left, no reasonableness, no hope.

Two little girls came round the gable-end.

'There's Jeannie for the milk,' she said evenly.

The intrusion startled him. His mind spun in a swift groping search for some sort of outlet from this unbearable black deadlock of the spirit. Something had to be said, something must be done, a word, a sign. . . .

As the little girls came on towards the lantern flare, he suddenly turned to her:

'Perhaps if I made some money at this fishing –'

As his own words struck on his ears, he stopped

dead, as though their thinness were a devilish sort of mockery.

'Good-bye, then,' she said gently, 'and – good luck!'

Without another word, she went.

CHAPTER THREE

WHEN the back door had closed, Ivor Cormack moved off down the ditch-side in the direction of the village lights. He moved to a jerking of feet and hands that was quite automatic, to a stark thoughtlessness, as though life at a stroke had shorn through the smoothness of youth to the skeleton-frame.

Tripping on a sudden grass tussock, he pitched by the left shoulder into the shallow ditch. The violent jerk sent a fierce blood current surging through his body. Picking himself up on the crest of it, he gave vent to a torrent of curses.

His mind got going furiously. It suddenly hated with a black bitterness the village lights, the croft, life. He swung off the ditch path to the right, passing by the back of the village and making for the shallow strath which, at a little distance, gave on either hand to the slow-rising moors.

A small wind came from the moors, blowing to the sea. The stars shone clearly in a vast expanse of dark sky, cumbered by scarce-moving masses of gargantuan cloud, as though a week's rain had not sufficed to exhaust their bloated possibilities. But the changling wind escaped the sodden indifference of earth and sky and blew between with a freshness that was keen rather than soft, that was unscented and yet tanged as by a reminiscence of bog myrtle. No longer a destroying wind, and yet but subtly less.

It blew on his face, whipped with tonic coolness the bitterness of his spirit, so that the bitterness

32

quested and cursed spasmodically, whirling and eddying with as aimless a searching as the wind itself.

He came to rest after a time, at first no more conscious of the night mysteries about him than the boulder he sat on. But by degrees that unreasoning thunderstorm of curses blew itself out; and presently in the stillness there drifted down his mind the grey mist of soul weariness. An utter weariness of self; a self-mockery. He counted for as little as the boulder he sat on; he owned as little, landless, penniless, a fool – oh, a most utter bluidy fool! His body writhed a moment in a resurging thin spasm of personal futility. It passed. Of no more substance or weight in the eyes of men than a boy at the school.

No accent of self-pity intruded; only the accent of withering realisation, the accent of fact. There it was, plain enough for him to see; mockingly plain. No wonder he could not break through that perversity which had dogged him in the byre. It had kept the rein on him, the rein of fact, the fact of what he actually was. Had he cared less, had he been philandering only, had it been any other of the nights within his experience. . . .

He glared fixedly, his vague bitterness resolving itself to a point, to a visualisation – Maggie. Then in an instant he saw her with a clarity so intense that his fists knotted up, his muscles flexed rigidly. He glared on her, on the whirl of her body, her neck, her face. . . .

That was why he had not been able to break through. At one blow loose love had finished its

33

love-making, its thoughtless, beautiful philandering, and come up against the possibility of unfulfilment.

Not that he consciously reasoned it so. The unconscious did the reasoning, as at such deeps it did with most of them on the grey coast. Accent, mood, action were its reflections and, to a certain extent, its outlet.

So that to the vision of Maggie there succeeded the vision of Daun Tullach. His body instinctively recoiled a little from Daun Tullach, gathered itself, like an animal preparing to spring. He watched him warily, with a malignity that was acute and clawed. His fingers curved and stiffened.

He spat from him the bit of heather he had been grinding between his teeth and jumped to his feet, leaving the strath behind him and making for the moors.

He walked the green rankness of his physical humours out of him in the next couple of hours, and by the time he was again by the burnside in the shallow strath he was quieter, more collected, more deadly.

Stretching himself on his stomach, he dipped his face in the burn and drank in round gulps. Then he rubbed his dripping face with his cap and, sticking out his legs in front of him, felt for his pipe.

He lit his pipe, puffing slow, deliberate blasts of acrid twist upon the cool night air. The burn's monotone was a background of reverie, of which he was unconscious, but which may have had in it a virtue prompting to reflection.

To a certain jaunty, defiant reflection to begin

with. He was not finished! By God, no! His body, smoothly at rest, strengthened his assurance. His arms, his legs, his youth – his bitter powers of endurance. Not beaten, by a long 'take'!

There flitted across his mind the figure of the Irishman with the wooden leg who had come to the door selling studs and laces the other day. This country, he had told them, was nearly as poor as his own – all grey boulders an' sodden turf. If it wasn't for America that kept the wind off their backs . . .

At that they had all looked at him, as though the vision of America as a grey, sheltering dike was novel and surprising, compelling a smile by its truth.

If it was America that kept the wind off the Irishman's back, it was Canada that did it for the men of the grey coast. Five had gone this spring. Nine altogether last year. Fellows of about his own age.

He could always go to Canada.

He looked at the map of Canada, the red map on the school wall, with the Atlantic Ocean between its vastness and the speck that was Scotland.

A sardonic twist came upon his assurance. He could certainly go to Canada. Ay, damn, he could go to Canada all right!

His heel ground the shingle apart.

He could not as yet bring himself to the point of considering any action in its bearing on Maggie. He could not do it. His heel dug a hole into which the water soaked. He could not just say to himself that if he went to Canada – what then?

Yet in a moment, without touching the implication, his mind jumped to that 'what then?' He could ask 'what then?' without any meaning holding on to it at all.

If he went to Canada – what then?

He would go, of course, like the other fellows. When they went there they hunted for work. They mostly got it. Sandy Swanson was a car conductor in Winnipeg, getting good pay. Others were working on farms, on new road construction, on the railways, in stores. They were all more or less getting steady pay, and some remembered the old folk at home and sent dollar money orders on the post office, and some didn't. He might make enough money at the fishing to pay his passage.

And – what then?

The map slid before his mind's eye; distance, time. . . . He crushed it back. His teeth closed harshly on his pipe. His lips thinned.

After some years . . . But no, his mind suddenly balked, then tore the tissue of impossible make-believe to shreds. Going to Canada was no damn use; going to Canada was no solution; going to Canada was – going away from this – *now*. That meant . . .

He had to face it. That meant – throwing up Maggie. That meant – Daun Tullach!

He glared now in earnest, and his breathing quickened and hissed in his nostrils. The shank of his pipe suddenly snapped in his fingers. Cumulative moments of vision. Maggie – himself. . . . Maggie – his wife! God!

His mind spun wildly, so that no thought came

out of it; only a warmth over the body, shivering over the body, his fingers clawing and shutting on the broken pipe.

For a long time he remained unmoving, stiffened in the grip of that thought which turns youth of any years – and he was twenty-five – into a subtly different stuff of manhood.

And thus at last he faced the problem, seeing it as in a sustained high-flashing of the mind, so that the admission of it was not rationally absolute. The thing was too white for that, too overwhelming. It was hedged about by a lot of small pertinent considerations on which he could get a hold, must get a hold. One could not go on thinking and living in the thing itself. One could not – with nothing on which to stand, nothing but Canada, futility!

He had the sensation of savagely smashing out the white light so that he could get a hold on the pertinent things that hedged about.

And impelling itself through the flimsinesses of Canada, fishings, crofts, was the figure of Daun Tullach. The solid figure with the boned face, the scrubby, ginger moustache, the restless, cute eyes. The eyes probed at him now, raked him. The eyes saw that there was nothing in him at all; emptiness, wind. The mouth, below the searching eyes, laughed – three short barking laughs. So vivid was the visualisation that Ivor's fingers closed involuntarily on a stone. He could have brained him with it.

And all the time there was no blinding himself to the fact that Tullach was right. His mockery was warranted.

37

At home there were six of them. His mother, his oldest brother, Dave, who worked the croft and did carting and other jobs that came the way, to keep the place going; himself bred to the sea and doing what he could in the off times at land-draining or road-mending; his two sisters, Jessie and Anne, both at home, with prospect of Anne becoming a dairy hand at Tullach next term; and the youngest, John, still at school. His father had died five years ago.

And the fishing, at one time the great industry of the coast, was dying, visibly dying before the eyes of a single generation. Even in Ivor's childhood every little creek or fault in that dark precipitous sea-wall had been a hive of pulsing life. Good fishings and the land smiled, the shopkeepers throve, money flowed with a generous freedom; for the sea, ever changeable and treacherous, and as much a matter of luck as war, breeds a clear-eyed self-reliance, a silence, a grim courage, which has its reaction in an openhandedness that not infrequently slips into a spendthrift recklessness.

In the sea lay danger and uncertainty, lay money and romance. And the crofter, ever tearing with gnarled hands at the lean remorseless soil, looked at it with feelings which varied from envy and greed to prayers for drowned souls and thanks to Almighty God for even the security of a roof. The sea had been the dominant motif in the grey-woven symphony of the coast.

And now all that was past. The fishings were dwindling, boat hulks lay rotting at their haulage. The day of the sail and the small fishing creek was

38

giving way before the ousting mastery of steam, the steam of the drifter and of the railway. The fishing industry was concentrating more and more in the big ports – Wick, Fraserburgh, Aberdeen – and the wealth of communal life that had enriched the bleak sea-board with a rare self-sufficiency was growing thin in the blood and cold, was dying without hope.

And of this communal life, Ivor felt himself a unit among the dying. The three or four boats which still fished out of Balriach were adding tale to tale of hardship and lost gear, with little to show when a season finished beyond empty pockets and despair, the despair that did not, perhaps, parade itself readily, but that bit in all the deeper for the restraint.

Little more than a deck hand on a sailing boat, for though he actually shared to a certain small extent in the profits because of the six nets which he contributed, yet he had no share or portion in the boat herself. And apart from this dying hazard of the sea – nothing. Had there been even a croft at his back, anything . . .

He saw the bleakness of his position with narrowing eyes and lips, its sheer empty nothingness. He was of far less account than one of Daun Tullach's stots. Far.

He shivered suddenly and got to his feet. The cold water he had gulped, the perspiration induced by walking, the searching wind . . . his teeth rattled. Laughing harshly, he spat on the earth, as though he spat upon its grey barrenness, its hungry meanness, a land of knotted rheumatism and dead things.

He strode on evenly, the laugh now turning upon

himself. What in the name of God had he been arguing about? What did he think he was? What a bluidy fool! . . . The contemptuous finalities shut off thought.

The light of the schoolhouse near the head of the village broke on his sight. He knew the schoolmaster. Often he had taken him out in his boat. A decent fellow, not many years older than himself – friendly – easy-going. There he was on a salary, a steady inflowing of money, certain in its coming as the day. . . .

A voice hailed him from the shadow of the gate.

'That you, Ivor?'

'Ay.' Ivor paused and the schoolmaster came across.

'For off – to-morrow, is it?'

'No, the morning after.'

'You'll be pleased at that!'

'Oh, well – there's not much doing here.'

'No. And it's fine, a trip away to the West.'

The way he mentioned 'the West' one might have imagined it a country of legend or dream.

'It's right enough,' said Ivor.

'You're lucky! I shouldn't mind taking your place!'

Ivor laughed a half-note through his nostrils.

The schoolmaster peered at him.

'How would *you* like sticking here to teach kids?'

'Well, I don't know,' said Ivor, not troubling himself with an imaginative effort. The thing was hardly worth it – as things were!

'I think,' said the schoolmaster, 'I often think that

you fellows don't know how well off you are – in a way.'

'Ay, in a way.'

The controlled irony, the uptilted seaman's head, an air of primal reality, got at the schoolmaster, but though he peered narrowly he could make nothing of the face in the gloom. Then he laughed quietly.

'I've just been reading about the West – Gaelic myth and poetry. I think I should like to take a trip there. Fellows like you set off there and think nothing about it! That's what I was thinking.'

'I suppose so,' said Ivor.

He stood nearly a head taller than the schoolmaster, to whom at the moment, indeed, his figure appeared not unlike one of those figures of strength and gloom moving with destiny on them in the shadow land of myth.

A natural echo from his reading. Yet possibly there was more to it than that, a subtle, basic comparing and contrasting. On the one hand teaching kids: on the other, the land, the sea, the struggle with elemental forces, the pitting of strength to strength in the old hazard of life or death, the raw stuff out of which all poetry, all legend, is woven. Here before him was a sample, looming at him in a primal self-sufficiency, even positively with the air about him of brooding emotion!

But no, that was overdoing it! And for the same reason he could not let it go at that.

'Come in for a little. You're not in a hurry, are you?'

'It's time I was home.'

'Oh, come away in, man! We won't see you for a long time again.'

Ivor hesitated. His nature was sensitive enough to make unpleasant the thought of appearing in any way ungracious.

'Come along!' The schoolmaster turned to the house, and Ivor followed him.

The study was cosy, smelling faintly of the peat that was burning in the iron grate. Books and periodicals lay scattered on a table, some open.

'Have a fill? – and sit down there.' He stretched Ivor his pouch.

Muttering his thanks, Ivor hunted for his pipe. A darkness flushed his face, passed, and he smiled with inscrutable innocence.

'I must have left it,' he said.

'Well, you're in luck's way! I bought two clays to-day. The way Sanny Ardbeg black-seasons them struck me as wonderful! I thought I'd have a try.'

Ivor accepted one of the white clays, and did not altogether force the smile that acknowledged Sanny's powers and the schoolmaster's easy naturalness. The schoolmaster was the sort of fellow who appeared to have no swank, who seemed to like to do a little of what everyone else did. Moreover, he never did it with the air of one who was playing at doing it, who was making a condescending pastime of another's grim reality. And that was likeable in a man in his position.

First taking the tobacco from the pouch on to his palm, Ivor began carefully to fill the clay pipe. The schoolmaster watched him, while appearing to wait for the pouch himself.

He noted Ivor's hands, the firmness of them with the full smooth wrists above; strength, flexibility, instancy. His eyes travelled to the neck, the set of the head. Was it in the set of the head or in the expression of the face that he sensed the elusive something of self-reliance and sensitiveness, a something not of the land so much as of the sea, the uncertain sea, older than myth itself? He had been reading that night some stuff of Fiona Macleod's. 'It is destiny, then, that is the Protagonist in the Celtic Drama' haunted him meaninglessly like an echo.

Receiving back the pouch, he began filling his own pipe, a small covering smile flickering on his face.

'Yes, I shouldn't mind a trip with you,' he said cheerfully.

'Oh well! . . .' said Ivor.

'You think I wouldn't like it?'

'I don't know what there's to like much in it!'

'I should imagine that now and then there would at least be excitement. You're always in the teeth of the sea – uncertainty – what!'

'Yes, there's that.'

'But not much more?'

'Not much more.'

'Not much money, anyway, I suppose, and that nowadays is the main thing.'

'That's just it.'

A flicker of hardness passed over Ivor's eyes.

'Yet I wonder! I must say I often wonder to

43

myself. Is money everything? I mean, aren't we inclined to overdo it? Here in the old days, now, I don't think money was so much thought of – and people were every bit as happy.'

'I suppose they were,' said Ivor, tone absolutely non-committal, detached, yet pleasant. That smooth secretiveness of the Gael, thought the schoolmaster.

'I think it's a pity that – that all that old way of looking at life has passed. There was a slow richness in it – and poetry. You know, all these old Gaelic tunes – milking-croons, and sea-croons, and death-croons. . . . You'll have heard them out in the West?'

'Oh, the Lewsachs have great songs sometimes!'

A numbing sense of bafflement beset the school-master. He knew, of course, that the young fellow was just a fisherman, of a certain schooling till he was fourteen, but with no consciousness of beauty, culture, developing in a continuous education.

Could it be that schooling, culture, was a sort of vicarious experiencing, and that he was prompted to his own questioning by a sense of his own insufficiency? And if so, why always hedge the questioning, and yet tortuously be driven on by it? Was it because the answer might require to be something in the nature of a personal decision rather than a solution?

Altogether an obscure sense of uncertainty that troubled, that now made him, with an inconsequential gesture, a slight smile, pick up a poem and observe:

'I wonder what you'd think of this now? It was written not long ago by an Irishman. It is supposed to be pretty decent stuff. Shall I read it?'

'All right.'

Allan Moffat cleared his throat, and, smile still flickering (he was giving nothing away) read:

' "I will arise and go now, and go to Innisfree,
And a small cabin build there, of clay and wattles made;
Nine bean rows will I have there, a hive for the honey bee,
And live alone in the bee-loud glade." '

When he had read all three verses, he looked up. Ivor met his glance, face properly smiling.

'Sounds nice,' he said.

Bafflement again gripped Moffat, and in spite of him his face stilled to rather more than an enquiring calm.

'Yes, but – isn't there something there, something that is real, like truth; something near –' the word would come – 'near the heart?'

A small hollow of silence, wherein Ivor's smile got fixed a trifle.

'Oh well! . . .' he said.

'You think it's just nice?'

Moffat's eyes were direct now, and the least bit appraising. Ivor's smile remained, but the eyes hardened.

'Ay, it's nice.'

'But actually far enough from the truth?' probed Moffat.

'I don't know,' said Ivor evenly.

Moffat suddenly threw the poem down.

'What I mean is this, Ivor. Is there any reality in

45

that stuff at all, or is it just visionary nonsense? Does the fellow really want to go back to that sort of thing – or is it all moonshine and sugar-candy – and he wouldn't go back if he could?'

The sudden note of sincerity in the searching was at least disarming. Yet there was involved the question of a literary criticism – a book question. As though divining the difficulty, but with sufficient subtlety to hide the divination, Moffat went on:

'Let us look at it clearly. It's interesting. It's the sort of thing big minds in the world of – of literature and so on get fascinated by. But, damn it, it must have some relation to life. If it has no relation to life – and we are the judges of that, for, as you might say, we live on the spot – if it has no relation to life, then the writer has merely hoodwinked those big minds that know no better. You understand me?'

'Ay.'

'Well, and what about the clay cabin and the bean rows and the bees?'

'Just poverty.' Ivor's smile twisted quite pleasantly.

'Besides,' said Moffat, 'we don't grow beans. Won't thrive. And no one keeps bees except the minister!' His tone held a perverse mockery. But in his mind stalked the thought: 'My God, how appalling this is!'

'That's true,' acknowledged Ivor.

Moffat could not look at him for the moment, and took up his pipe with a smile.

'These questions interest me sometimes,' he explained, 'and it's pleasant to get another's opinion.'

'I'm sure,' agreed Ivor.

'Ay,' said Moffat, studying with simple gaze the fitful flicker over the now smouldering peat.

'Well, I must be getting home,' announced Ivor after a little. 'Time is getting on.'

Moffat looked at the clock on the mantelpiece.

'I suppose it is. And you'll have to be up early.'

He accompanied him to the gate, shook hands.

'Well, good luck, Ivor! – in case I don't see you before you go.'

'Thanks,' said Ivor, in his pleasant way. 'Good night.'

Moffat watched his dark figure disappear; then, re-entering his study, started pacing up and down.

What a fiasco! he thought. What a fiasco! Great Heaven, how aimless, how empty! . . . If it's not real life it's nothing! What has beauty to do with reality? Eh? And is not Yeats even in such a snatch as that depending on fellows like Ivor there, on their ways of life, their stark, poetic habits! – just as in the Destiny-Protagonist business. . . . And that was the fellow himself! . . . Or was it? Don't I know I didn't see past his skin – except once when he thought I was going to dissect and be superior! He hardened then! . . . Yet he doesn't think. Yet the poets' thinking is about him. . . . Lord, what a maze! . . . I wonder what the devil was really in his mind all the time? Was it just the sort of wary blankness of a mind out of its natural element?

He continued to pace, to ask himself unanswerable questions, æstheticism tortured by considerations of the absolute value of life in action, tortured because

47

each consideration had to face a first-personal touchstone.

. And yet how he would like to be sure of the Ivor type, to make certain of *him* at all events! Yet not even of that – though the fellow had been sitting there! What was that about the girl of the canebrake? . . . 'These deep elementals are the obscure Chorus which plays upon the silent flutes, upon the nerves wherein the soul sits enmeshed. They have their own savage or divine energy, and the man of the woods and the dark girl of the canebrakes know them with the same bowed suspense or uplifted lamentation or joy as do the men and women who have great names and to whom the lords of the imagination have given immortality.'

'Know them just the same, eh? Good old word-spinning Fiona!' He dropped the book with a thud on the table and set to his pacing again. Wearying at last, he threw himself into his chair, and slowly his mind stilled, his eyes glimmered. Where 'Peace comes dropping slow . . . midnight's all a glimmer, and noon a purple glow . . . full of the linnet's wings. . . .'

CHAPTER FOUR

IN the back-place Maggie attended to her small clients, setting a sieve on the top of their milk pails and pouring into each such a quantity as, she considered, generously met the need. She had a word for each of them and the invariable enquiry: 'How are all with you to-night?' receiving in return the customary: 'Very well, thank you.' The needs of courtesy duly met, there might be a hurried, timidly expressed hope that 'Mother was wondering if you could give her a pound of butter on Saturday?' To which – 'No, Jeannie, I'm sorry. Tell your mother that the calf is not away yet. I have hardly enough for ourselves.' A further half-whispered 'Thank you,' and Jeannie, neat little business woman, would lay hold of her pails and be off.

At last Maggie snecked the back door and turned to the kitchen entrance. Her face calmed to a stillness that to the casual eye might well appear a stolid, half-weary indifference. She entered.

Tullach was standing now with his back to the fireplace. He had evidently got up to go, but had not apparently quite cleared his mind of its humours. Her uncle was sitting sucking at his pipe, eyes a-glimmer – probably pretending a momentary reverie.

With Maggie's entry, Tullach's expression changed to a light pleasantness, changed noticeably as by some inner dismissive gesture of the will. He hunched his shoulders, straightened his body.

49

'Got through with them, Maggie?'

'Yes.' A faint smile flickered courteously a moment, but she did not look at him.

'Your uncle,' he pursued, 'has been in great fettle, telling me about his foreign trips.'

Maggie felt the something questionably ironic in his tone.

'Has he? I hope you enjoyed them.' Her own tone was even, pleasant.

'Oh ay! He was a bit o' a gey lad, I'm thinking!' He turned and looked down on ould Jeems, small eyes twinkling and shooting.

'Wheesht!' admonished Jeems, with jocular deference, 'wheesht, man! You will be taking yer len o' me!'

'No len in it at all!'

'Och! och!' Jeems got to his feet. 'Won't ye sit doon? There's no need for ye to hurry off yet, surely!'

'Ay, there's need.'

'Is it early in the morning, then, for ye?'

'Well, no' particularly,' considered Tullach.

Maggie had taken up her knitting. With his head bent forward a little, Tullach watched her with the air of a judicial absentmindedness. He was conscious of the impression he was making, the impression of being the live, magnetic centre of things in this small kitchen at the moment. But beyond that impression – what? He watched her fingers sliding and slipping against the white-spotted, blue overall that curved with her breast until the throat-band was hidden under the down-droop of her chin. Her dark

50

hair, her fresh, smooth cheeks, the dark lashes masking the eyes. . . .

Unexpectedly, quietly she looked up at him. He did not start, his mind instantly commanding his eyes to a continuing absentmindedness, so that he appeared to be looking at her without seeing her. And Maggie's eyes moved from his face to the mantelshelf where they dwelt for a moment, without any visible change in their calm, upon a brass candlestick, before returning to the woollen sock.

Tullach suddenly laughed.

'Oh well, that was good!' he chuckled, as though he had all the time been turning over in his mind something that had been said. 'But I must be going!'

'Och, the night's young!' persuaded ould Jeems with due hospitality – bracing himself to the leave-taking.

Yet Tullach did not take a step away, but stood, head bent, still watching Maggie's fingers, the grin creasing on his face.

Maggie did not move, nor show by a flicker the slightest discomfort. The grouping for a moment became fixed, statuesque, around those restless hands, those weaving fingers. Nothing could come into Tullach's mind whereby he might smash the composition by a vital revelation of his own power, his overlordship; and trapped into impotence by the indifference of the weaving fingers, he remained unmoving, grinning from under his bushy, reddish eyebrows.

Maggie looked up again, and the almost placid unconcern of her eyes met now the deliberate, would-be-enigmatic scrutinising of his. Her look passed smoothly to the fire, lay emotionless a moment in its glow, then returned to her knitting.

Tullach did not move, but his voice, with its harsh, laughing inflection, remarked suddenly:

'Geordie will be finishing the Dike park by early on in the afternoon to-morrow.'

'Will he though?' said Jeems. 'Will he that? He's a good plooman if ever there was one.' His voice held a quick, ingratiating note.

'Ay, he's no' bad.'

'Oh, extrae, extrae!' His old body twisted restlessly. He scratched his chin noisily through the clump of short, grey whiskers. Tullach did not move.

'I believe he might be spared for a few hours after that.'

'I see,' nodded Jeems. 'Yes.'

Tullach took his time, face screwing up a trifle in its hardening humour. It would but repay the ould devil to make him beg for Geordie's harrows, to make him beg – now. His eyes were on Maggie's hands.

'Ay,' he said.

For a moment Jeems's eyes puckered at him, then he moved restlessly again.

Silence.

Maggie got up, and, quietly depositing her sock on the bed, turned to the back-place as though some forgotten business or preparation for the morrow had occurred to her.

With an inexplicable sense of being foiled Tullach

remained stiffened where he was a moment or two longer.

'I was just thinking to mysel' to-day there's that corn for that bit ground o' mine,' remarked Jeems. 'It's time it was doon.'

'Ay, it's getting on.' Tullach stretched himself. 'Ay, it's getting on.'

'I was wondering maybe –' Jeems paused to clear his throat.

'What?' enquired Tullach, as with half his mind.

'That perhaps if Geordie had nothing extra special to do for an hour or two –' He cleared his throat again.

Tullach waited.

'If you could spare him for an hour or two – after he'd finished the Dike park. . . .'

'Spare him? I see. Oh, surely,' said Tullach. 'I'll tell him to come doon an' do the job.' He gave the impression of waking up from a deeper thought. 'I suppose ye'll sow yourself?'

'Oh, yes!' said Jeems. 'Yes, yes!'

'I'll see to that, then.'

'Thank ye! Thank ye kindly! It's indebted to yersel' we are. . . .'

Tullach did not appear to hear. He turned to the wag-at-th'-wa'. 'Is it that time o' night?' He consulted his watch. 'You're a little fast. Ah, well, I must be going. Good night, Jeems!'

Jeems raised his voice:

'Maggie!'

'Never mind Maggie,' said Tullach. 'She's busy!'

Maggie appeared.

'Good night, Maggie!' said Tullach.

'Good night,' she returned, with her pleasant, polite smile.

'Maggie'll see ye over the door,' said Jeems.

Tullach walked on as though he had not heard. Maggie hesitated, until she caught her uncle's expression. By the time she reached the doorstep, however, Tullach was moving away into the night. She looked after him for a moment, then closed and locked the door.

Tullach heard the locking of the door, and his expression, freed from observation, glowered on the night, his teeth shutting on a husky oath. He had the sensation of a man with absolute power haunted by a maddening powerlessness.

Maggie came back into the kitchen. Her uncle turned to her a face in which there was no longer any trace of the ingratiating.

'It mightn't cost ye much to be a little more pleasant.' His eyes darted fiery gleams at her.

She made no answer, retiring to the back-place as though to finish what she had been at.

From the back-place she could hear him mumbling to himself. But the calm of her face did not break, as though all instancy of emotion had died within her. She remained staring at things with which her hands were trifling till she heard the clip-clop of his old slippers going ben the house. Then she re-entered the kitchen, and, going to the fire, raked it a little, smooring the kindling and sticking a whole peat on end in the midst.

When she had finished, she realised that she had

smoored the fire too early. Somebody might yet look in. She did not want anybody. But they might. She sat down by the fire.

A long time passed in a grey, hypnotic weariness. She stirred, got up, began undressing. She felt she could sleep for ever: a long, lost sleep; would sink down out of sight, out of mind.

But as she lay in perfect stillness in her bed, her mind began to come to life, to a restless sort of worming life.

Looking out through the looped-up curtains, she saw the two men who had sat there that night. She had lived long enough with uncle Jeems to know something of him, to be able to follow the secret ways of his mind to the final miserliness. Crafty, harsh, stupid, ingratiating, he could be anything by turns; but every turn lead to the same finality. His poverty was an obsession that, on the active side, endowed him with strange qualities of cunning, so that his brain, cuter and nimbler than Tullach's, was also more unpredictable in its impulses; and withal knew an undercurrent of fleshy humour that could indulge itself to a replete huskiness in human reminiscence. On the passive side, poverty was an obsession that desolated him to a bleak, slack-mouthed animality, with a voice muttering and mumbling. He would then go about the house, back bent, feet scraping after him. If anything 'kem at' Maggie he would be 'taken away,' for he had nothing, nothing, and was an old man. Of the Poorhouse he professed a profound terror, as, indeed, did Maggie herself. Sometimes she would listen to his mumblings as he pottered about intent endlessly, in every little action, in every lifting of a piece of string or a nail or a pin, on saving, saving; and then as the mood was she would suddenly be wearied and exasperated and full of rebellious despair, or just sorry for the old man.

Yet difficult altogether to pity him, even to be sure of him, because of a strength near the bone, a positive rawness of reality, as though the grey matter crawled along his skull bones in an inner dark tarn of the mind with a curious secretive knowingness that, however dissembled in outward expression, always left the observing mind uncertain of him; as Daun Tullach was often uncertain, as Maggie herself sometimes 'couldn't make a thing o' him' – even though the phrase might be the outcome of a half-petulant exasperation rather than a deliberate belief. For all practical purposes – which might be no further than youth cared – she reckoned she understood him only too well.

Yet he had not been always the miser. She could clearly remember a time when as a little girl of ten he had come upon her with presents and the glamour and importance of an uncle from foreign lands. He had been kind then. Was it not generally known that he had shown financial sympathy to his sister-in-law, Maggie's mother, and, on her death, had paid the doctor's bill and the simple funeral expenses?

She could remember her mother's death, very vividly the eye-daze from the drawn, yellow blinds, the hush, the unreality that hung about the dim, faintly tainted air in a stillness that kept the eyes staring so wide that they would not shut. . . . Moments of remoteness from sorrow – followed by the sudden choking spasm of realisation, intensely poignant, knotting the flesh, the salt of tears in the throat. Mother! Mother! . . . The eyes opening wide again, the body light-headed, queer; the veil over the world. . . . The hush once more, the unreality, the looking on at herself. . . . How vividly, how near . . . her mother!

Uncle Jeems had just got possession of his croft at the time, and before the funeral he had come for her. She had watched the long line of black figures following the coffin on the bier, had watched from this very kitchen window . . . twelve years ago, and she was ten then. She could not remember her father. He had been drowned off Duncansby, making for the west north-about.

Twelve years ago. Uncle Jeems had been almost open-handed then. He had bought his croft furnishings and stock outright. She remembered the rumours of his reputed wealth. He was taking over the croft because a man must take over something, but really he could afford to 'live on his money.' For one to be able to live on one's money never failed to give a pause to thought, a reflective moment to the eyes, to produce a certain nodding of the head. Old women, meeting and gossiping, could manipulate the phrase most effectively. Men felt the brunt of it as well as the pensive wonder.

But in these last twelve years – what a change in Uncle Jeems! as though the eternal misery and meanness of the land, the bitter struggling with it, the parsimonious scraping and saving engendered by it, had not only slowly filched away whatever ready money had been left to him, but had also gradually bitten into the very marrow of body and soul; warped him, twisted him, until every glower he gave, every ingratiating welcome, every cute response of body or mind, had, to Maggie, one dominating, almost instinctive, ulterior design: only saved from abjectness by that flickering, uncertain contrariness, that queer, puckish, fleshy humour which had in it something hidden, which, indeed, at certain moments seemed mocking, satiric; a raw inner refuge of the mind holding some unfathomable quality of personality that saved him from being dismissed.

There was that other figure by the fireplace – Daun Tullach. In the darkness of the kitchen her eyes could embody them both as heavy black shadows leaning over in their chairs, with something of the inescapable imminence of fate in their nearness, blocking her vision. Something also of secret understanding between them, collusion, conspiracy – not given shape and definition in words, perhaps, but underlying every greeting and parting, all droning talk of weather and stirks and ploughing.

For – they could hardly have bargained in so many words! Hardly that! Oh, hardly that!

Maggie stirred under the bedclothes. Her brain was now worming so actively in its hot sleeplessness that she knew herself capable of thinking anything, attributing any motive. Yet undeniably the cold facts were that for the last two years Daun Tullach had 'put down' Uncle Jeems's croft and harvested it, got his peat-cutting squad 'to give a day' to Uncle Jeems's 'bank,' and then had driven home the peats. In other words, Daun Tullach had done everything that would have required money outlay; he had obviated hiring.

How had he been paid? Or, rather, how was he going to be paid?

Hitherto, the question could always be dismissed, did it obtrude at all, with a toss of the head. It was not her business what Daun Tullach and Uncle Jeems might agree to do for each other.

Wasn't it?

None of her business. It wasn't! After all, she had always given two days of her own labour when the threshing mill had visited Tullach, not to mention other days in potato planting and lifting. Tullach had offered to pay. She had refused. She could do no more than that; couldn't do more than that; it couldn't be expected. . . .

Couldn't it?

She had the sensation of dashing herself against a blank wall. But with an effort she steadied herself, took a grip. She was used to facing things, facing life in the sordid, everyday aspects of an impoverished croft, from which any dribblings of romance, colour, were inexorably squeezed.

She remembered the day, a month or so ago, when Geordie had finished ploughing their corn patch. Tullach called in the evening by way of making sure that all the ploughing had been done, had stayed and talked, had gone home. Just as her uncle had been leaving the kitchen for his bed, she had suddenly asked:

'What's Tullach charging for the ploughing?'

She had not meant to be so bald as that, but the words had come of themselves.

Her uncle had paused, turned his face on her, eyes puckering craftily.

'What do ye think?'

She knew she had not shown any quick feeling; had, in fact, appeared to consider. Then quietly:

'I don't think he's the one to do it for nothing.'

'He's not, I'll a-warrant ye!' with a throaty pech of a laugh.

Silence for a little, then:

'Well, I don't know,' she had said dismissively, implying that after all to her the matter was one of indifference, and had moved to the fire.

Her uncle had remained as though there were something on the tip of his tongue. She had felt what was on his tongue and her whole body had tingled in a sudden anger.

'This is no' the world where ye get something for nothing!' his voice had scoffingly insinuated.

So much of the world she knew, and had not replied.

He must have caught sight of the anger in her face, for he had restrained whatever had sat on his tongue. Then he had turned away, mumbling to himself in his grey whiskers. As his feet went clip-clop, the sound had echoed a sinister amusement.

Then to-night at tea-time, he had spoken, spoken out of one of his moods of gloom and miserly mistrust, and what had been indefinite, and therefore capable of indefinite delay in expressing, became at once definite and expressed. She would be a leddy at Tullach Farm!

That she would work there, of course, as hard as she worked here was so obvious that she did not even think of it. But her position as mistress of Tullach would be one of such solidity and worth that hardly a girl in the district but would go pale with envy in contemplation of it. That Tullach had set his mind on getting her she could now no longer pretend to ignore. Once or twice she had been conscious lately of escaping a declaration by a ready use of her wits, an easy smile, a subtle misunderstanding of his mood, a polite expressionlessness – anything that she instinctively felt would stave him off. And she had staved him off, strangely conscious within herself of a certain power over him, which kept him from a suddenness of familiarity such as the swift encircling arm, the brutal earnestness with the jocular froth, the crushing of her. She knew how he would do it; had, indeed, imaginatively felt him do it, to the extent of being smothered by the unventilated smell of his clothes, of feeling her body constricted.

Yet once or twice near enough to be touch and go! And a time would come – soon . . .

She turned on her back, breathing heavily. She felt spent, and for the moment no longer cared. After all, however she argued it, she saw the ending of it all, the inevitability. Life was a grey onflowing, and poverty's skeleton fingers throttled all foolish notions.

Moreover, from any point of view in the world, except a foolish point of view, the alliance would be a fine one. She could understand Uncle Jeems.

And, when all was said, Uncle Jeems was the main concern. If she married Daun Tullach every material question would be solved for Uncle Jeems and for herself. If she did not, sooner or later there was the Poorhouse for him, and for her hired service in just some such place as Tullach Farm, till she, too, maybe, got old enough to be cast aside. For, though the croft would naturally revert to her on her uncle's death, what could she do with it alone – even supposing that everything were not sold up long before that? If by some unthinkable means they kept going until her uncle died and she got the croft – what then? She would just have to sell it up. Nothing else for it. She would have to sell up what, properly attended to and sufficiently stocked, would be at least a home and homestead. And with any little extra coming in . . . The broken sentence flashed on her mind – 'If I made some money at this fishing . . .'

The noise of the old man moving ben the house came suddenly to her ears. She listened. He must be thinking of starting the rabbits again – although they were small enough surely. But why didn't he visit his snares in the morning like any other sane person? Wearisome the way of him. No doubt he was frightened that someone might lift a snare or a rabbit! . . . He was getting ready right enough.

It must be the small hours. How the brain turned things over endlessly, endlessly! How one could stare at a grey thought, and stare, and keep on staring with nothing happening in the mind at all!

He came into the kitchen and put on his boots, seeming to move and feel in the darkness like an old dog. No word was spoken, and presently the back door clicked. Matthew's Woodie lay mostly between the off boundary of the croft outrun and the upland grazing of Tullach. In the lower edge of the part within the croft outrun stood an old shed, always carefully locked on account of the snares, trapping paraphernalia and what-not stored within. Thus operations were always easy and their secrecy complete. So he lost no time in leaving the house; but the sudden sucking of his old boots in the clayey soil as he rounded the gable-end brought the memory of an earlier hour to her heart.

She turned restlessly under the bedclothes; felt his near presence again as they had stood by the byre door and looked on the darkening moor, the grey sea. He was going away. Like so many others, he might not come back. What was there to come back for? There was nothing to come back for. Five had gone last month to Canada. There were no crofts, no homes, no money here; nothing but old thrifty people slowly dying, old decrepit people dying like the twisted stumps of the rotting trees in Matthew's Woodie.

He had nothing to come back for. Nothing. She felt herself for a moment borne on the undercurrent of unconfessed hopes and longings, not so much longings, perhaps, as dim gropings towards some fulfilment of heart's desire, some magical arriving at the place of heart's ease. . . .

But there was nothing to come back for. It was so true that, coldly and nakedly true. She realised it with that perfect fatalism of the grey hour bred of poverty and labour. It did not occur to her to think of herself as being something to come back for; something and nothing were economic terms swaying the personal factors ruthlessly. Only occasionally, when the surge of youth beat up rebelliously to the bitter sting of tears, did she think she was something, needing and demanding something, in despite of all the economic factors in the world.

CHAPTER FIVE

TURNING the corner of the house, ould Jeems with a sharp 'Sst!' brought Roy to heel. The precaution was unnecessary for the collie knew what was afoot with as much eager definitiveness as did his master, now plodding on with a humped stolidity like a creation of the night's darker forces.

The visible stars sparkled with a white brilliancy too defined, too clear, against a profound blackness of sky. The gargantuan cloud masses seemed visibly to swell rather than to move. The freshness of the night was a washed coldness, keen, like the shiver of wind on a naked body.

Down over the cliffs went the wind till it struck the grey-glooming floor of the sea and rose with it in a smooth race to the horizon. There was a figure on the cliff-heads, bent double, not unlike a boulder being weathered by the inexorable forces ever shaping to a pattern. Shaping Ivor Cormack body and soul at the moment. The fierce personal rebellions, the wild choking mirth at clay cabins and bees, the hot spasms of throttling angers, all the past hours' red riot – being beaten back, stilled, squeezed to an even greyness, leaving finally a lull of impersonality, the seaboard's impersonality.

And in upon this greyness flickers a pale night-moth of vision, a paleness that grows in light and still desire and is related with a sense of infinite remoteness to that recent white high-flashing of the mind when realisation of Maggie had been complete . . . until the flicker fades, time thins out, and

65

the body, uncurling itself in a cold shiver, slowly turns its back on the sea.

Eastward from Balriach and set some little distance back from the cliffs lie crouching together the farmhouse and steading of Tullach. The wind plays round it, leaving no nook nor cranny unsearched, and picks up on its clean wings a pungent reek of deeply rotted manure from the heaps disturbed these last few weeks in the process of feeding the soil.

Round the house whirls the pungent reek, and as though something of its revitalising animality touches the heavy sleep of Tullach himself, he snorts and pechs and stretches out a grabbing arm as the elusive forms in his slumbers lure or mock; then, still again, breathes heavily in defeat or conquest, or with the cunning instinct that, even in sleep, can bide its time.

Over his shoulder at this slumbering mass of Tullach Farm, ould Jeems threw an occasional look. He wanted no interference from that airt, and as he bore inland, with Tullach fading away to the right and Balriach far behind and to the left, he kept ears and eyes on the alert.

They were making for Matthew's Woodie and the shed. An inadvertent kicking of a stone or a stumbling produced a husky grunt with all the abruptness in it of an oath. Plainly he was as eager as the dog at his heels, plainly as given to the night's sport, with the eagerness that held in it not so much a fear of interruption as a spirited singleness of purpose, a delight in the adventure itself.

Into the dog's faithfulness to the old man may have been woven this comradeship of the night and of hunting, this singleness of aim and of understanding, with its haunting echoes down the dark ways of the mind from prehistoric partnerships on many a wild foray. From that allegiance Maggie could never seduce him, feed him exclusively as she did, and fondle him as she might. The most perfect courtesy and affection he showed her at all times, and did his duty about the croft with a will at her bidding. But let a word be spoken by the master — and it was the fiat gone forth.

The hut stood half within a light belt of hazel trees which curved in a semicircular outgrowth to the Woodie proper. Arrived at the door, he paused, a new keenness touching his figure to a stiffened listening. But the night held no unknown sounds, and he looked at the dog. Long nose uptilted, Roy stood mutely regarding him.

There was the thin tinkling of a chain as Jeems caught at the padlock. The key was produced from a certain waistcoat pocket and the lock snicked open. Letting the chain fall noiselessly against the wood, he pushed open the door and disappeared. A second or two and he was out again, clutching by one arm a black bundle. The chain was lifted, the padlock snapped shut. Turning to the Woodie, he faced it again, vigilant. Nothing.

Up slantwise through a clearing in the trees, breath coming a trifle thickly now, the old weak heart thumping and filling his breast. A steepish climb, a gasping and momentary resting on the upper edge, but with no thought at the moment for anything but the ploy ahead. Probably a useless ploy, but the time for snaring was not yet. A pity that. The setting of the snares in the darkening on Tullach land was a delicate business, the visiting them at this same early hour an exciting fulfilment, the whole an artistic affair with its beginning, its interval of troubled expectancy, and its ending. This netting job was crude in comparison. Worse than that, the once or twice he had tried it of late years he had drawn a blank. It was not so much, he judged, that the rabbits had got wise to the danger of the two drain-openings – 'cundies' – at adjacent corners of the rectangular, diked-in Caol park, as that they had come to form the unfortunate habit of taking cover within the stone walls themselves at danger's sudden signal. Digging them out of the stone wall was always a laborious business and at best a gamble; but what made it prohibitive was the resultant wall ruin which waited on the daylight to tell the night's tale to a glance.

However, everything to its season, thought Jeems; and to-night the craving had come upon him to have a shot at the two cundies.

But the approach to Caol park had to be up-wind if possible and certainly noiseless, with Roy to heel. It engrossed his whole attention.

It was a longish trek, for the Caol lay beyond the immediate upland with its perfect snaring ground; lay, in fact, well into Tullach land and with a bearing towards the farm proper that brought a ploughed field against one of its walls. Not the happiest position.

The last few yards he covered on hands and knees, finding this method of progression easier than a crouching stoop. A head moving above a wall can be caught against a horizon; can be seen by rabbits, it was judged, horizon or no horizon. Dividing his bundle, he opened out one of the two pieces of herring net and spread it loosely over the drain outlet beneath the dike. Then with small stakes which he drew from an inside poacher's pocket, he pegged the net all round, leaving a comfortably loose sack for the problematic rabbit to roll about in and truss himself.

It took time, and when the job was finished he wiped his forehead. There was nothing wrong with the setting of that net, he reckoned, taking his breath. He looked around on the night, peering into its unchancy darknesses with a grim humour. Something within him whispered that his heart was not so good as it was last year. He twisted the grim humour at it in a coarse flick. Here, with the night-shapes, defiance gathered a small warmth of exultation. He picked up the second net and started along the wall, stooping as low as his somewhat refreshed body permitted. The ground was broken, and when he stumbled and fell he could stick to it for a bit with hands and knees. There was no desperate hurry, the distance separating the cundies being less than two hundred yards.

With the second net pegged, he deliberately rested himself, back against the wall, letting the primeval night settle down again upon his momentary disturbances of it so that they might be blotted out from the hearts of all things. It also gave extra assurance that nothing was coming out of that night, tracking him.

At last he got to his knees, cautiously peered over into the ploughed field, turned his head to the crouching, quivering brute at his feet, raised a hand, 'Sst!' Silently, clean over, Roy launched himself and was gone.

Squatting against the wall, just clear of the cundie, he waited. The dog would slip up between the edge of the ploughing and the dike for a long way, then at a bound would be over the dike and in the grass of the Caol park. He would quarter the grass, all out, nose low, scarcely even swerving when a rabbit shot downward from his ghostly approach.

Jeems waited, reckoning out the dog's movements. He would be in amongst them now, cutting across and across, coming nearer. . . . He held his breath to listen. No sound. A good brute. Able. . . . Couldn't be far now. He crouched closer to the net. . . . Not a sound. Damn them, the old game – slipping into the dikes! Seconds passed. Not a move. Nothing would come out of this empty business. How could it! Yet a man might be pardoned for thinking that the juicy young things would know no better than come shooting out through the only two cundies for their true sand burrows lower down. Surely he might be forgiven for thinking that! But no! . . . If only it had been the snares on the upland above the Woodie, how the brute would have sent their white scuts helter-skelter – for the invisible golden nooses set so cunningly on their runs! It was an art that . . .

Suddenly he distinctly heard the swift padding of Roy's paws. So it was a blank. . . . And in the same moment the night was riven by a frantic rabbit squealing from the off cundie.

The wild music of the hunter's lust. He started for it at a shauchling trot. The stumblings started a deeper pulse, a keener expectancy, a fiercer joy. When he bit the earth he spat it out, cursing huskily. There was, however, this also about the squealing, that while it affected his hunting lust it also affected the night. There was no need to call the night to witness; for to give the night ears was to give it eyes. Fancy could too easily give it eyes at any time. Often enough he had felt them on him. And under the eyes of the night fear crouches with horrible expectancy. It was Tullach land, and in the business of protecting his rights no one could be more thorough or more zealous than Tullach himself. Young harum-scarum devils poaching there, and leaving behind them snares or other indication of their maraudings, were known to have been surprised on a succeeding expedition by a form heaving at them out of the night, wild shoutings to stand or be shot, gun-shot spattering about their feet, collie brutes launching at them. An exciting warfare, spoken of down by the boats of Balriach with boastful exaggerations, but indulged in with distinct infrequency.

The net was a black, living thing when at last Jeems fell upon it; full of rabbits, jumping and shooting with them. Would he never get his hands on them, would he never finish them! He had dropped his stick on the way and could not wait to feel about in the dark for it. Now here they were, squealings redoubled. . . . He finished them through the net, getting his gnarled fingers about their throats, one by one.

In all there were just four of them. A family of young ones, no doubt. Holding up each by the hind legs, he felt back and hips. Real fine stumps, surprisingly grown! This was luck of the best! His satisfaction rumbled throatily through his gasping breath. Even the skins, if, as they were saying, the prices were moving . . . Ay, the skins, maybe! Extrae stumpies! He felt about in his pockets for a piece of string wherewith to tie them in pairs by the hind legs. This was no place to waste time in.

The rabbits dangling and the nets bunched close, he reached the Woodie, his face and head sticky with sweat, his breath labouring asthmatically, but with eyes still alert, with satisfaction at his heart.

Once in the brae-face amongst the trees, he sat down. There was a trembling in his legs. The strain told on his lungs, on that ageing, uncertain heart. He knew it, but again not with despondency, rather with a crowing mockery that could overcome all things – old in the horn as he was! Age has its triumphs, and its reckless indulgence in them may approximate more nearly to youth's fine carelessness than does any intermediate period. He could still score off them! (meaning Daun Tullach, youth, life itself).

He rubbed his forehead with the inside of his bonnet and turned an eye on Roy who was lying extended at his feet, breathing rapidly. No intrusive scent disturbed the dog; there were no sounds in the wood beyond the swishing of the wind. He was secure. His violent exertions had at least cleared throat and nostrils to a keenness which caught at the earth scents. The smell of the old earth, the trees, the wind in them, the hunting, the rabbits, this dark loneliness shutting him off and shutting him in, the eerie, unchancy nature of it . . . He gulped it all down and his face twisted in a silent chuckle. He could have made squawky noises in his throat with contempt for he knew not what, with love of he knew not what. His old body responded to the old earth, earth to earth, mystery to mystery, humour to humour. The squawky noise came into his throat and ended in a full satisfying spittle.

Pushing himself to his feet, he spoke a whispered word to the dog, a pleasant word. At the unusual accents the tail wagged, a soft whine whistled in the throat. 'Come away, then!' and ould Jeems picked his steps carefully to the brae-foot, spanged the ditch, the crumbling dike which was the boundary between Tullach ground and his own, and, looking about the clearing between him and the hut, made for the hut door.

Once inside, he secured the door by means of a stout wooden bar pivoting centrally on an iron bolt and sliding an end into an iron staple on the door jamb. Thus securely battened against intrusion, he groped his way in the windowless blackness to a bench. Striking a match, he saw the thick stub of candle in its sprawling mess of melted grease on the off end of the bench, and lit it. He waited until the flame had died down and come again, then examined the rabbits.

A successful outing! Four. A good night. Blanks were known. And not every week would dare one night's poaching. In the candlelight his eyes gleamed craftily. A very good night. He lifted his head, went quietly to the door and listened. Yes, he could detect the vigilant Roy's breathing. Coming back to the candle, he made an effort at treading lightly, as though he were instinctively guarding against proclaiming his intention even to the night.

But arrived at the bench end, he hesitated. A new excitement was now working on his face. As he listened, his mouth fell agape, breath coming and going in short gulps. A far more anxious quality of excitement this than any he had shown that night. It drew and pinched the features, and the haggard hollows of age suddenly showed themselves pitilessly.

Once under way, however, he acted quickly. In the adjoining corner of the hut was piled a heap of valueless crofting lumber, from lengths of rusty barb wire to grass ropes and broken fence stobs. On the removal of this lumber bodily from the corner there was revealed a remnant of board flooring, the floor generally being no more than the trodden earth.

Upending this floor boarding, he stooped and heaved from a hollow in the ground a small but very stout wooden box. With both arms he brought it carefully to the bench.

His legs were now trembling again, as were his hands. Hauling from under the bench a broken-

74

backed chair, he sat down and proceeded to undo the hasp.

The money inside the box was tied up in two leather pouches, and it was all gold. Each pouch gave a smothered chink as he lifted it out and laid it on the bench. Then he cleared the box to one side, cleared the bench as far as his arms would reach around him, and, satisfied, lifted somewhat fumbling fingers to the knotted noose of the first pouch.

He let the coins come gently, spilling their golden trickle in a drawn-out, exquisite economy. The candlelight played its part with an effectiveness that would have been diminished had there been clear, all-pervasive light and no shadow. As it was the trickle held a darkling secretiveness, the taper-gleam dancing in furtive, impish points of starry gold to the clinking castanets of the slipping, sliding coins.

All too soon the stream ended. What a gorgeous dream – to have kept it running for ever! But practised at the game as he was – how soon the pouch ended on him! To have stopped the flow would have been to have destroyed the illusion of endlessness. . . .

He laid the pouch to one side without taking his eyes from the coins. There was still the second pouch, and the second pouch began its living cascade into an already existing pool. The music of it! There was no music like it. Gold to gold. Blood and fighting and red Jamaica rum. The life-blood of the world's body. The last coin slid down the heap to a slow intake of breath from its master, who

75

remained staring, fascinated, his hands clawed around the coins, leaving them as they lay.

They did not represent a fortune. There were just three hundred and seventy-one of them all told. A poor hoard, a slim enough bridge over the gulf between poverty and wealth. In his own case, it might have been, a possible bridge, some justification, at least, of the phrase 'to live on his money,' hardly more.

And in the beginning, perhaps, when he had come back from the sea for good, it had not been meant for more. Rarely does the sea breed miserliness even among the poverty-stricken, toiling fishermen of the creeks. There is too much of chance, of uncertainty, in the sea; its harvesting a game of hazard too swift in give and take for considerations of sly canniness to spawn and thrive naturally. Fronting the sea the body is essentially a naked thing swept clean of all encumbrances and winning in the treacherous game by reasons of inner qualities of instant readiness and courage. The passions and moods of the sea are passions and moods of instancy. And if stoicism, courage, readiness overcome them in a sudden trial of strength, the sea exacts by way of reaction a reflection of its own moods and passions. The sea is the eternal spendthrift.

Jeems had to come back to the land, back to the croft, to an endless, pitiless struggling with its stony impassivity, its lean, grudging soil, its drawn-out eternity of misery, before miserliness got its claw-fingers on his soul. And even as he sat there gloating, the greed in his eyes was subtly irradiated with

76

triumph. The gold was the sea's triumph, and held a satisfying curse in its throat, which, in an ultimate, could consign Tullach and the land to hell. That was its power, its secretive, glucking power. Not that he thought deliberately of Tullach at the moment, nor of the land nor of the sea; the magic of the golden pool was too potent.

Presently his clawed fingers closed in on the heap, touched it, grasped slowly, spewing coins between. One rolled off the bench, and on hands and knees he searched for it like a bereaved animal. Retrieving it, his head came above the bench and he caught sight of the gold afresh. The sudden vision of it from this new angle stiffened him in a momentary transport as though his eyes could hardly credit the wonder, the magnificence of what they saw. His! He drew closer, sat in to them, put his arms around them, nursed them, with harsh mumblings in his throat. Then, as if indeed fascinated, his staring eyes drew nearer, nearer, till the exquisite coldness was slithering under the pressure of his hot face.

He lifted his face with a jerk, and the light in it held a suspicion of fierce, daring guilt, as though something deep in him had jeered at the caressing action. Mouth puckering, eyes narrowing, he glared an unreasoning defiance, a sardonic ruthlessness. Like this, one of his roving race might have glared at a knife-point in a cantina.

It was with very uncertain fingers that he made his little glittering stacks of twenty. To have the old rebellions and passions evoked even thus mistily was a little too much for the ageing body. The wine of

77

youth was too strong, its savour too heady, let age dilute its red brilliance to a mistiness howsoever vague. Yet how the old heart throbbed to it, how life pulsed!

Carefully padlocking the door behind him, he started for home, altogether shaky on the legs now, played out, but with the note of exultation still unsubdued. The darkness, the poaching, the gold . . . the way of life's final hazard of all. The sea was dead. The sea lived. Curse them!

CHAPTER SIX

MAGGIE was up betimes the following morning, got the cow milked and led to pasture. The grass was coming green and succulent beyond and around the lower strip of Matthew's Woodie, along the dike-sides, and in the ditches. She tethered the hungry beast some little way beyond the hut where later the bracken would grow tall, driving home the small stake with the ubiquitous grey stone.

On her return, she did not muck out the byre. That, it was understood, was her uncle's job, and she was very careful to leave it to him. Fixing the byre door so that it remained open, she went to the hen-house. The boulder against the somewhat ramshackle door she rolled away with a foot, tugging at the same time with both hands at the door-edge. The door came grudgingly. Immediately she was smothered in a flying mass of feathers. They could not get out quickly enough to ensure that no peck of food be lost. Cluckings, squawkings, rushings hither and thither, but managing at the same time to contrive a mass formation behind Maggie as she made for the back door.

She had to be at some care to secure the door against their entry, while she got the tin dish with their food from an inner shelf. Presently, to the accompaniment of much snapping rivalry, and the stretching of necks half-choked by dry gobbets, they prepared themselves against a day given over to loafing or to red-combed industrious scrounging.

Maggie washed her hands and, entering the

79

kitchen, gave her attention to the fire which she had hurriedly raked together before going out, blowing the peat to a fine blaze. The iron porridge-pot was already on the crook.

While the pot was coming to the boil, she started in to make her bed, to sweep out the floor, to give a general tidy-up to the only living-room. While yet the porridge was thickening in soft explosive bubbles she heard her uncle stirring ben the house. She laid a plate and spoon at each end of the kitchen table on a cloth holed but white.

Her uncle entered without any greeting on either side, while Maggie was ladling the porridge into the plates. He sat down and, taking up his spoon, began pushing away the porridge from the centre on to the edge of his plate, helping this cooling process with much closely directed hissing and blowing of breath. Not until these noisy preliminaries were completed did he say a word. Then:

'It's like to be a better day.'

'Ay.'

'Where did ye put the coo?'

'Doon by the shed.'

'Fitch! Hiss-s-s! Ay, it's coming away a bit there.'

This reference to the growth of the grass, Maggie accepted without remark, her attention given to her porridge.

'Fitch, it's hot!' he exclaimed irritably, having betrayed himself into a premature assurance. Tear-drops came into his eyes. He blew on the porridge with marked vehemence.

'It got no time to stand,' said Maggie.

'I can see that!' Ding it, anyone in their senses could see it!

A drop of milk hung pendulous a moment from the rich redness of her lower lip before she retrieved it in a quick flashing of white teeth. Then her eyes filmed a moment in a half-indifferent humour, and again she gave her attention to her porridge.

She rarely 'answered him back,' hardly ever lost her temper with him, not out of any marked fear of or respect for him so much, perhaps, as out of an innate sense of what was due to herself and to him as an old man and her uncle. At difficult moments she 'maun e'en bear wi' him an' keep a calm sough in her heid,' as she had heard a Morayshire woman advise in a somewhat similar case. Anyway, her mind's natural bias lay that way. To quarrel with an old man and try to order him about held something in the thought of it both wearisome and unnatural, even if in her own case it could be done – which was doubtful enough! Not but that there were times when she had to bite her lips to keep them shut.

He pushed his plate from him.

'Weel, Geordie will be here wi' the harrows this afternoon.'

She looked unconcernedly out through the window at the patch of ground awaiting operations.

'It'll be in good time this year – an' it was no' unhandy the way it worked in,' he pursued.

The way it worked in! – had worked in last night!

'Have you the seed ready?'

81

'Oh ay. I was half expecting it might work in for any day.'

She could not answer him. At such times it seemed he had a perfect talent for this sort of searching innuendo that on the face of it was no more than the simple truth.

But, remembering last night, she was not to be got at, not to be drawn. The weariness of the sleepless hours was still in her flesh. She felt her mind too near the surface, a little raw and uncertain.

Gathering the plates and bowls, she retired with them to the back-place. When she returned for the kettle he was still sitting at table, his face in a fixed stare at nothing. But in a minute or two he passed her on his way to an outer shed, Roy at his heels. The door of this little shed was locked. Once inside, he stretched for the two pairs of rabbits hanging by their pads to nails on the back of the door.

To the skinning of a rabbit he gave much time and care, beginning after a fashion of his own as low as possible on a hind leg and finishing near the nose tip. He never risked a ruthless pull-over, working wherever the skin stuck with the point of a pen-knife.

Maggie left him at it, and with a couple of buckets, kept from her legs by a wooden hoop in the centre of which she walked, set out for the well, which was some little distance down the ditch-side towards Balriach. On the way to the well her eyes wandered over the houses of Balriach, which ran in a double line towards the cliff-head. Down in the invisible hollow beyond them, the strath ended in the harbour, and there, scattered about the brae-face, were some more cottages. Altogether a compact community, not so much on the land as crouching to the sea.

Her eyes came to rest on the roof of a house near the bottom edge of the off row. Beside it was a black wooden shed where Ivor stored his fisherman's gear. She could not see the roadway between the two lines of houses, but her mind's eye saw him easily enough. He would be busy with his nets and one thing or another, his blue-black guernsey sheathing the supple strength of his body, his black hair fallen over his brows, his voice ready and cheerful, his eyes —

She had a momentary acute sensation of them looking searchingly at her in an inscrutable, disturbing way, and her heart missed a beat. His eyes had at certain times a stormy blackness no more than half-veiled by any superficial humour of expression, as though in the depths of him lurked a dark vitality of the blood.

But Maggie did not give way to the look she had conjured up. Even as it was, her body had known a swift pulse, her hands gripping spasmodically at the pail-handles. Self-indulgence is not bred easily on the grey coast. Only in matters religious, perhaps, is it allowed free play, and then it might be said that from no peasantry in the world does such fervid fluency of extempore prayer ascend to Heaven.

She filled the pails and started back, a certain almost deliberate numbness having succeeded to her momentary visioning. She did not wildly accuse herself, nor rail at the ways of fate. Except at rare moments, and these moments intensely secretive, the luxury of indulging even a passionate mood must needs be instinctively inhibited.

The skinning of the four rabbits satisfactorily accomplished, ould Jeems emerged from the out-house carrying the small pink bodies by the hind pads. Catching sight, in a quick survey of the countryside, of a spring-cart proceeding up the road from the village, his eyes glimmered and he nodded. Entering the back-place, he dropped his burden on the wide deal shelf, observing to Maggie, who was stirring the earth off some potatoes in a small tub of cold water:

'There's that!'

She straightened herself and, looking at the bodies, nodded. Then as it seemed nothing need be said, she stooped to her task.

'I saw two boaties coming in from the heicht o' the sea this morning,' came his most casual tones.

She waited, knowing what was coming, but prompted by no desire to help him out.

'One of them would be Sanny Ardbeg's,' he proceeded. 'I thocht ye might go the length o' Kirsty's as soon as ye could an' take one wi' ye.'

She began stirring the potatoes, and it was some little time before she gave him an obviously reluctant 'Ay.'

There was silence. What could he be waiting for now? Looking up in her sudden quiet way, she caught his eyes going over the eggs she had gathered that morning. She kept looking at the eggs, too.

'They're no' going off the laying already, are they?' he asked.

'Two clocking,' she answered levelly.

He shuffled on his feet, grunted, and, turning, went out at the door, leaving it wide behind him. She closed the door and returned to her potato-stirring.

It was not that he tried to make sure of every egg which came into the house, of every pound of butter churned, of every pennyworth of milk sold, that disturbed Maggie as she steadily swirled the potatoes round and round; after all, to a certain limited extent she could have deceived him there: it was what his pursuit of the knowledge implied along the dubious ways of mistrust so that the buying herself some necessary bit of clothing became an essay in daring, in hidden mutinies, in secretive discomfort, in self-argument, which galled. And to know that it should not gall, that possibly his enquiries were not prompted by mistrust of her but by the sheer urgencies of his miserliness did not help at all.

However, that attitude to their inevitable way of life was always with her (reaching fine distinctions when the bit of clothing was of arguable 'necessity'). What galled particularly at the moment was the business of going to Sanny Ardbeg's house with a skinned rabbit, so that Kirsty, Sanny's wife, would present her in exchange with some fresh fish. That, shorn of discreet neighbourly formalities, struck her as very near direct begging. She was not altogether blind to the possibility that she was merely over-

85

sensitive on the point, that a rabbit would be welcomed, the fish given gladly. Still . . . Her gorge would rise, in spite of her.

Voices suddenly came from the direction of the byre. She listened and caught the sing-song whine of Beel-the-Tink's pleadings. Her lips twisted. They would be at it now for long enough!

The contest over the rabbit skins had indeed but begun. Jeems had paused on his byre-graip in negligent consideration of the inevitable, 'Hae ye ony rabbit-skins th'-day, mister?'

'Rabbit-skins? Oh ay!'

'Hoo mony hae ye?'

'Four, I think,' he reflected, scraping the cobblestones.

'Ye'll let me see them?'

Jeems thought that, well, he might let him see them for that matter of it, but he was kind of busy at the moment. However . . .

They reached the locked shed and the skins. Beel-the-Tink examined the skins minutely, but could discover no flaw. Howsomever, the fur at this particular time of the year was almost worthless, it appeared; a point which so strongly reflected itself in the matter of prices, that rabbit-skins were hardly worth the carting away.

'So that's the way o't! Uhm, I see!'

'Yes, mister – sure as death!'

'Ah, weel, in that case I'll no' burden ye,' said Jeems, hanging the skins up again.

And so the battle became joined. The tinker's whining and pleading, his scoffing, his retreatings –

and returnings 'just this once,' broke like so much froth on the unheeding stolidity of the old man.

Not that Jeems's stolidity was lifeless. The bold, black eye-flashings of Beel-the-Tink were countered by a sarcastic, humid gleam of blue-grey, holding an assurance of knowledge and power blending to a half-contemptuous indifference.

'No, no, my man!' He turned to shut the door.

Beel-the-Tink shot out a detaining hand.

'Wait ye!'

'Weel?'

'I canna afford a penny! Sure as death, I canna, mister! I'll no' get ma money back! Ye're hard, mister! There's Wullie an' Jamie an' Betty an' Makum an' Maryann an' the haill o' us. I canna, mister! I canna do it!'

'I'm no' asking ye,' said Jeems. 'Threehaepence each is my price. Ye can take them at that – or want them. It's all one to me!'

'Threehaepence! Oh, Gode, mister – threehaepence!' He laughed harshly.

'Threehaepence.'

'Threehaepence! Ye're makin' fun o' me! It's oot o' a' question. I never gi'e more than a penny for the best skins; never!'

Jeems began to close the door.

'Ye're a hard one, mister! But that's the end o't. I canna mak' money oot o' naething. There's no one in a' my roonds sae hard as ye are!' Then switching off the subject as though it were finally dismissed: 'Hae ye ony rags or bottles or a pair auld boots th'-day, mister? Ma spring-cairt is at the roadside an' I canna wait. I could swap the mistress a cream-jug or a bowlie.'

Jeems deliberately snecked the door, and took the first step back to the byre, throwing over his shoulder a gruff:

'We've nothing for ye here.'

But the tinker was after him.

'Mister! Mister! Sure as Gode, I'll gi'e ye a penny a skin, though it'll ruin me! Wait, noo! I'll tak' them wi' me. A penny, an' that's as muckle as onyone ever got from me for the finest skin. I'll mak' naething o' them at that!'

Jeems paused. He was aware he had been offered top price, was astonished he had been offered it, knew he would not get the threehaepence, yet hesitated, his soul craving the little more than the most. There had been that rumour about the movement in price, of course . . .

'I'll tell ye what I'll do wi' ye,' with a first suspicion of bargaining frankness in his voice: 'I'll let ye have the four for fivepence. No' a fraction less!'

They stood a moment fixedly gazing on each other, then with a dramatic gesture, Beel-the-Tink threw up head and hands and departed, exclaiming:

'Sure as Gode, mister, ye'd rob a blind bairn o' a broken doll!'

Jeems watched him go, his heart misgiving him. Other than Beel-the-Tink, he had no outlet for his chance skins. And fivepence was a goodly sum for a single night's work, not to take into account the flesh – and the fish. He should have taken his fourpence. He turned away stolidly, however, some subtle instinct forbidding him to call after, to give in to, the tinker. Besides, the skins would keep for a bit, and next time Beel came round and offered his fourpence, he would fling at him with impatience, 'Oh, take them wi' ye for any sake, oot o' my sight!' and would pocket the fourpence with the air of one tired of tinker's whinings.

He had not gone many steps when he heard feet padding softly to the back door. It was little Betty with her beggar's poke on her back. A second or two and she was followed by Beel-the-Tink, her father, as though he were looking for her. Beel, however, seemed suddenly to spy Jeems and, leaving his daughter at the back door, took a few quick strides in the direction of the old man.

'I hae the fourpence in ma hand, mister.' He chinked the coppers inside a shut fist. 'A haill fourpence for thae four skins. I canna gi'e more, mister — sure as death!'

Jeems took him all in, the humid gleam glazing in a withering search. But the tinker's black eyes were pleading, frank, almost engaging. Now was the perfect opportunity for flinging the impatience. Yet — the tinker had come back — and —

'Fivepence!' said Jeems, without flicking an eye.

The tinker revolted, stamped up and down, cried in his whining sing-song upon the almighty powers to witness how he was having the blood sucked out of him and out of the whole of his family. It took time, and, a trifle fascinated, Jeems watched him. He felt it coming, the flung impatience, but not from himself — from the tinker!

Beel-the-Tink stuck a heel into the ground, smashed the chinking fist into a cupped palm, tossed his head derisively, all in one sweeping gesture, and –

'Here ye are, mister! Fivepence! Take them! Take them! An' surely to Gode ye can hardly grudge throwin' in a pipefu' o' tobacco!'

Jeems hesitated, mouth opening in a curling of lips from the gums. Then he took a finger of twist from a waistcoat pocket, cut off about an inch and a quarter, shauchled slowly for the skins, and received in payment his fivepence.

As the tinker turned away muttering the curses of one who has been harshly dealt with, Jeems noticed Betty and her poke leaving the back door. A slow-gathering suspicion that Beel-the-Tink had adroitly kept him engaged while his daughter begged, now assailed him. Added to the four skins and the tobacco was possibly a 'puckle tea' or a 'puckle meal' or a 'puckle sugar' – a something that at least countered the unprecedented fivepence. He walked meditatively in at the back door.

'What was she wanting?' he asked.

'Oh, begging as usual,' returned Maggie.

'An' did ye give her anything?'

'Not much,' said Maggie.

'What?'

'Oh, I gave her something to eat,' said Maggie, turning away abruptly.

He hesitated a few moments, then returned to finish his byre job, with enough food for reflection until Maggie, later, announced that dinner was ready.

Salt herrings, with potatoes bursting through their skins. The staple dinner, varied occasionally by rabbit stew. Uncle Jeems ran his bare fingers against the scales, scraping the flesh clean; then taking a few potatoes from the heap on the plate in the centre of the table, he broke them open so that they might steam their heat away by his hand. The succulent saltness of the herring, sucked into the mouth from the fingers, invited a great quantity of potato. And the potato was dry and absorbent and flavoured most palatably. Like the morning dish of porridge, it was certainly more than a meal of poverty. Yet how short the step from either – to starvation!

The meal over, Maggie arose and scraped the potato-skins on to the left-over potatoes. Jeems sat with his elbows on the table sucking at his hollow tooth. He was still disturbed by the thought of what Maggie might have given to the tinkers. But he did not want to raise the issue and be foiled. After all, he could never be sure of getting at the real truth of the matter. Maggie, for example, sold her eggs to the itinerant grocer's van at the roadside – or, rather, bartered them for goods – not only a quarter of tea, or a pound of sugar, or a loaf of bread, but such things as baking soda, washing soda, and so on – odds and ends the real monetary significance of which he could never quite grasp. And sometimes she asked him for money. He had all of fivepence at that very moment in his pocket. Altogether it was a ticklish position. He sucked his tooth. A drowsiness was stealing to his brain. Getting up, he went over to the mantelpiece, and taking the lid off his pipe, lit what was in it, puffing clouds of smoke with a smacking unction. Then he composed himself in his armchair.

Over the plateful of potatoes and skins Maggie had spread a handful of oatmeal, and was now squeezing the warmish mess through her fingers, the better to mix it. The second and last meal of the day for the fowls. Her mind was on the afternoon's trip to the village. It was also on the very circumscribed question of her clothes. The question troubled her with such nagging persistence that the real business of trading flesh for fish assumed a secondary importance, a business which, after all, she knew she could get round well enough. There was no conceivable way of getting round the business of clothes. Normally one could accept with grey resignation that inevitable 'making the best of it.' One could not be blamed. What else could one do? Nothing one could do.

Now she could not accept it easily. Brush her shoes as she might, she could not hide their shabbiness. Her appearance walking down the village street passed in review before her mind's eye. Her heart cramped at the sight. She had an inner sinking feeling of futile rebellion, of tears starting. Only for a moment, however, and her expression stiffened again. She must make the best of it. Her mind concentrated on the faded ribbon round her hat. She entered the kitchen and, going to the table, slipped some spoons into the drawer. She did it quietly – having noticed that her uncle was nodding off. From a nail on the side of the bed, she deftly removed her hat and retired with it to the back-place.

Half an hour later, legs swinging from the deal bench, she held the simple straw at arm's length, turning it this way and that. Decidedly the reversing of the ribbon had done no harm. Her eyes were alight, her cheeks caught the red of a faint excitement. Oh, if only . . . But her mind did not stop at this or that once it started on a swift dreaming, and before the eyes of her mind her figure moved as something desirable. . . . Awaking, she gave one more look at the hat, a long penetrating look, then laid it aside coldly. Stooping for her bucket of water, she entered the kitchen, the eye-light faded, the cheeks pale.

When she had washed the blue paving flags from front door to back, she untied her apron and, securing the doors leading to the back-place, prepared to dress. When, later, she entered the kitchen, she found her uncle in a deep sleep.

CHAPTER SEVEN

SHE had come in to say, 'I'm off!' but the casual indifference of her expression was suddenly arrested by the sight of that old head lolling sideways, lips apart and puckered, breath a little stertorous. She had surely seen it often enough for familiarity to have blunted any possible sensation about it. Hardly a pretty spectacle! never an impressive one; to be dismissed out of mind with the unpitying, impatient gesture of youth, of youth somehow denied by it, on account of it. Yet now there came staring up at her something so immeasurably old about the face, so near surely to a final dissolution, that the usual vague distaste got caught by a sort of startled pity, the pity that is youth's instinctive recoil from the cold clamminess of the clayey husk that is Death. The deep furrows across his forehead and radiating from the corners of his eyes had smoothed somewhat their earthy, peering cutenesses and anxieties; and now running down for a little way from the lank, withered hair-wisps on his temples was a pallor curiously delicate, frail, almost transparent.

And as she looked on him, and the first instinctive recoil faded into startled pity, she saw how old he was, with the age that might fall before some simple ailment like a chill and be henceforth on her hands, bed-ridden, more useless and troublesome than a bairn. The thought appalled her, her eyes rounding starkly at the frail pallor.

She withdrew quietly, and closing the door behind

94

her, stood looking forth unseeingly on the great sweep of rock-bound seaboard that stretched from her feet to the far-distant, brooding headland, which always gave the impression of a head crouching upon the sea, the line of the backbone running inland against the sky and culminating in a mountain ridge like a series of vast spinal dislocations.

Across the vagueness of her steady-eyed gazing nothing moved in all that expanse; no noise broke the stillness of grey-glooming land and sea and sky. The atmosphere had grown humid in a heaviness as of imminent fog, the cloud masses having got smothered to an evenness of dark-grey. Yet woven into this heaviness was a curious warmth, a warmth of elusive awakening.

She stirred to it – but with an involuntary poignancy that immediately deepened the sense of the forlorn. And all at once she heard the larks.

Myriads of them invisible in aerial fields. Far as the eye could carry, seaboard and hinterland were a treeless land, and, from the interwoven ecstasy, which began with the first faint silver of the dawning, plainly a paradise for these singers of the wing and the wastes. Indeed, so endless the arabesques of song that often the ear heard them not – and then heard them with a suddenness of revelation which might not be endured long. Something rose into Maggie's throat, choked her, and on a little rush she made for the byre, where, crouching on the creepie, she wept.

She felt the lighter for her tears, and stealing in by the back door, made sure of her eyes and her hat.

Then she set out again, swinging a small pail in which were the dismembered portions of two rabbits.

Down by the ditch-side she went, eyes still smarting a trifle, a curious sense of warm colour about the heart like a rainbow from the storm of tears, an uncertainty, a foreboding touched by excitement. She might meet – anyone! If she met him, could she be sure of her bright, untroubled acknowledgment? – as she would have been sure yesterday or any day before. She did not ask herself the question; but a hundred visualisations and intuitions dealt with it of their own accord. But they did not tell her the answer and she went on, her navy-blue suit for all its threadbareness of texture, its indifferent cut and uncertain hang, moulded by her body to line and motion that caught the eye infallibly. A native grace of youth, not wild but tamed to the ultra-civilised restraint of country proprieties, with colour and form and line like guarded flames.

The path by the ditch-side gave on a cart-track at Alick Hendry's croft. Mrs Hendry was feeding her hens as Maggie came by. The old woman with her kindly if over-ingratiating ways, smiled her face into a myriad of welcoming wrinkles.

'Ow, how are ye?' crawled her voice.

'Fine, thank you. All well yourselves to-day?' responded Maggie.

'Alick is talking aboot having a touch o' the rheumatics – but I'm telling him that it's just that he's getting ould!' She laughed. 'Young people like mysel' have much to be thankful for!'

Her eyes glimmered with fun, then sobered in a

96

moment as she added: 'Indeed, it's thankful we should be! Yeth! Did ye hear yon aboot poor ould Peter Mackay's turn?'

'No,' said Maggie.

'Oh, I just heard it this morning mysel'. Seemingly he was oot yesterday doing a little at the tatties and something took him all o' a heap. Jeemsina was telling me. He groaned sort o', then took a stagger, and in a wheep was stretched his length on the ground. It gave her an awful start, poor thing!'

'Ay,' mumbled Maggie; 'it would that.'

'So they sent for the doctor.' She paused. 'He's no' that ould – I'm sure a year or two short o' yer own uncle, an' yet they're saying – I don't know and I hope it's no' true – but they're saying that most likely he'll never come off his back again.'

She looked at Maggie as though searching for a due appreciation of the dread intelligence. And Maggie's face had gone pale enough.

'That's terrible news!' breathed Maggie, with a note in her voice that held something more than the sympathetic fatalism normally demanded by the seaboard.

'Ay, it's that. We should be thankful! We should be thankful!' Mrs Hendry's voice, quickening to Maggie's feeling, caught the doleful, 'm'urning' inflection. 'For we never know the day nor the hour. No, we do not.'

Maggie was silent. The 'm'urning' voice, the voice of age before doom and the dead, always oppressed her with an inexpressible sensation of being stifled. And now the unfortunate allusion to the age of her

97

uncle, whose face she had seen a few moments since staring up like a death mask, gave Peter Mackay's seizure an almost personal significance. She looked past Mrs Hendry, past the gable-end of the croft to the grey sea, her spirit netted deep in the troubled gloom of her eyes.

It was befitting; it was well done: Mrs Hendry felt impressed, felt the urge to further murning; yet beyond a heavy sigh restrained herself, she did not know why. It may have been that the subtle insidious luxury of doleful gloom, so near to the heart of age, with its treasured gift of permitting a last wallowing abandonment of the spirit, found something in the stark poignancy of Maggie's youth so vital and wordless that it was subconsciously checked, headed off. Mrs Hendry could not sigh and murn — and receive sign and murn in return, as she could have, had it been a case of age to age. Then the theme of not knowing the day or the hour, with the involved element of thankfulness, would become one to expatiate upon, to intone, with an art highly developed in its aspect to the conventional decencies and not without its subtleties in expression. Of that art Mrs Hendry was a high exponent from the very first quiver of the voice to the final surreptitious wiping of an unchecked tear. Not, indeed, that it was essentially an insincere art, that it had no true foundation in the feelings. On the contrary, it breathed of the feelings with such expert facility that everything of grief but its heart trembled visibly before one.

Now, however, fronting that pale quickening of

youth, Mrs Hendry hesitated. She hesitated long enough to permit a decent dismissal of inevitable gloom. Then with an engaging effort her face broke through the gloom into a smile.

'But ye are young, my dear! It's no' for the likes o' ye for us ould bodies to be singing our sorrows!'

A wavering, awkward smile flickered on Maggie's face, leaving the eyes the darker.

'Hardly that, Mrs Hendry!'

'Ay, it's true. Ye have yer life before ye. An' it's ither things ye'll be thinking of besides the ills o' ould folk. An' quite right, too!'

Maggie's smile deepened.

'Indeed,' pursued Mrs Hendry, eyes brightening rarely, 'a birdie will be whispering things til me,' and she engaged Maggie with those same brightening, challenging eyes.

In her deep despite, a touch of colour came to Maggie's cheeks, but she bore up with a tolerably impersonal:

'Indeed! That sounds interesting!'

'Ay, it's all that!'

Maggie waited, but Mrs Hendry left it there. Maggie could not leave it there without affecting either superiority over, or indifference to, the whisperings to which Mrs Hendry had given ear; and such affectation would be anything but neighbourly.

'Well,' said Maggie, smiling upon Mrs Hendry in an obvious preliminary to departure, 'I hope it's the truth that the birdie told ye. One can't always believe what's whispered like that!'

99

'Maybe no', but there is the ould saying that there's aye a little water where the stirkie drooned!'

'Ay,' countered Maggie, 'when there's a stirkie in it to droon!'

'Weel, as to that,' replied Mrs Hendry, 'I'm lead to believe that there'll be a gey puckle stirkies in it!'

It was the perfect riposte, pointing indubitably to Tullach, and left Maggie speechless with the blush coming. She turned away, throwing over her shoulder:

'Oh, I don't know!' in as cheerfully a sarcastic tone as she could summon.

As she walked on, anger at herself spirted in her brain for being unable to produce anything beyond that idiotic, 'Oh, I don't know!' Anger, also, at Mrs Hendry. It was too much! She bit her lips. It would be all over the place. Everybody who would look at her would think of her in connection with Tullach. It was bound to have come, of course, but this was the first public acknowledgment to her in person. There was plainly no longer any use in her trying to hide the thing from herself. It had arrived.

She entered the village street with the thing accompanying her like a bodily presence. She returned a greeting here and there, but did not pause until she reached Kirsty's door, somewhat breathlessly glad that she had not met anyone of consequence. She cried through the doorway: 'Here I am, Mrs Sutherland!' and made for the kitchen.

Mrs Sutherland, known as Kirsty or Kirsty Ardbeg, her husband's father having had a croft in the Ardbeg district along the coast, was a bustling woman of ample proportions, with ever the gayest of welcomes, the brightest of talk, and to be found, as a rule, in the process of getting her house redd up.

'Come in, Maggie! Is it yourself! Do you ever find me any way but untidy; and you yourself there looking as fresh and neat – ay, and bonny – no wonder the lads are setting their bonnets at ye! – come off, puss!' She spilled a tortoise-shell cat from a chair, reversed the thin cushion, and made Maggie sit down.

'I'm just coming in on you!' apologised Maggie.

'No, no – I'm just finishing. I'll give a bit scour to my face and – the house will just have to do! There's that many o' them tramping in an' oot that it might be a stable.'

She had a dark smudge across her left cheek; there was a gaping tear in her nondescript apron, a bulging hole below her left armpit, stains everywhere; but her eyes were clean-swept as blue flowers after rain, her face smooth without a wrinkle and singularly comely. A balanced comeliness that held its poise even at moments of affectionate outpouring of her ready spirit.

She drew in a chair beside Maggie and sat down.

'And how's your uncle?'

'Fine. I left him sleeping yonder in his chair. He had been looking after a rabbit or two. That reminds me.' She extended the pail. 'He does the skinning himself, an' I don't stop him!'

'Oh, Maggie, that's by far too much! Really it is!

And you preparing it like that – oh, two o' them!'
Her blue eyes shone with her gratitude.

'Nonsense!' said Maggie. 'It's nothing! We
have more than enough for ourselves. An' skinning
a rabbit is a job I can't abide; so I never interfere!'

'Well, well!' Kirsty considered the pail in her
hand, then looked up suddenly: 'It's the kind heart
you have, lassie!' placed her free hand with a quick
pressure on Maggie's knee, got up, and went
through with the gift to the back-place.

'I'll just give a rub to my face when I'm here,' sang
out her voice. 'You'll excuse me one minute.'

'Don't hurry!'

There was the sound of splashing water. Maggie
listened. That was her pail getting washed out. A
pause. Then a soft, cutting, ripping sound. That
was a codfish being split and cleaned. Maggie's
lips came together in a slightly twisted expression.
She could not help herself. It was foolish of her.
Pride, beyond a doubt. She needed the fish and
Kirsty needed the rabbit. Not that she would have
asked the fish in a thousand years. Yet she had
known she would get it; knew, moreover, that she
had been sent deliberately with the intention of
getting it. Her lips came apart in a smile at herself,
in a small, doubtful smile. Then she looked round
the kitchen, noting odd things here and there, the
boy's stocking that had got caught round a leg of the
dresser, a sodden cap inside the fender, a cheap,
battered doll with a cock-eyed, half-drunken expression, wrapped in a shawl and fixed carefully in
the narrow angle between the green, up-ended meal

barrel and the wall, the stockings which hung from the line that stretched across the fireplace under the mantelshelf, the knee-boots glistening here and there with fish-scales. . . .

Kirsty came in rubbing her face vigorously.

'We're never done in this house!' she said, on the most cheerful note. 'If it's no' one thing it's another!' And passing Maggie to the small mirror which hung to the left of the window, she picked up a comb.

'Indeed, I often wonder how you can manage it all!' considered Maggie.

'It's the bairns, bless them! They'll be in now in no time, and then it's like a circus.'

Maggie's heart warmed to the something in the voice below the surface gaiety, a deep-toned richness of understanding, of blessedness.

'Ay, I'm sure they'll keep you busy enough!'

'If Mary hasn't tore a hole in her pinnyfore you can be sure John'll have tore the bottom oot o' his trooser! Last night Donnie came home wi' a black eye and a cut lip, and could scarcely take his meat – no, not from want of the hunger but from being too filled up wi' pride at having walloped Jeemsie o' Geordie's. I gave him pride!'

Maggie laughed. Kirsty turned round briskly.

'I'm no' much to look at yet – but I'll do, maybe! And now for a cuppie!'

'No, no, really – I'm not going to stay . . .'

'Wheesht! Sit doon! I must get your news surely. And I'm just longing for a drop myself.' She tilted the steaming kettle towards the tea-pot which, she assured Maggie, never had time to get cold, rinsed it out, and in a short time Maggie had a rich cup of tea on her knee.

'And tell me now about yourself,' said Kirsty, settling comfortably.

'And what could there be about myself?' smiled Maggie, but feeling already the uncomfortable throb in her throat.

'Ach, ye needn't tell an ould wife that a bonny lassie like yourself hasn't something looking after her!'

'Oh indeed no!'

'Away wi' ye!' And she threw Maggie a half-quizzical smile. 'And maybe I'm no' so ignorant as all that!'

'All what?' asked Maggie, balancing her cup.

Kirsty's expression stilled somewhat, and she nodded.

'You're quite right. Aye keep something to yersel' ye widna tell to ony! Quite right, Maggie. And why shouldn't ye anyway! Myself, if I was a man, even if I farmed the whole parish, there would hardly be anything in it I'd so soon set my bonnet at! But never ye mind, Maggie; we'll be saying nothing!'

'There's nothing to say whateverway,' said Maggie.

Kirsty sent a glance at the slightly averted face.

'Just havers – and we must aye be saying something!'

This touch of subtle appreciation of Maggie's mood did not, however, help Maggie any. It even embarrassed her the more, so that in spite of herself her face exhibited a faint stiffening of annoyed awkwardness.

Kirsty stooped to the tea-pot.

'Your cup is out!' she cried. 'Come!'

Maggie had not intended having any more, but now she could not refuse.

'No more than a half, please!'

'Bless me, if there isn't Sanny – an' Ivor wi' him! They're that busy wi' the nets th'-day!'

The figures of the men had passed the window, and now Sanny, his black clay against his cheek, entered the kitchen, followed by Ivor.

'Kirsty, where's that – oh, is that yourself, Maggie!'

A medium-sized, wiry man on the right side of fifty, with a quiet, gentle voice, and a quick, attractive smile, Sanny Ardbeg was liked by everybody. Beneath the retiring nature, the ready, courteous sympathies, men knew of a dynamic framework, tough as steel, ready-fisted to the last grain of consciousness; and women sensed it. He now removed his clay.

'Yes – and drinking tea!' cried Maggie, on a sudden gay note.

'What better!' acknowledged Sanny. 'We're trying to be busy getting one or two things together.'

Ivor, having nodded generally, had come to rest against the kitchen table, his back to the window.

Maggie did not look at him, the smiling gaiety centring entirely on Sanny.

'Won't ye sit down, Ivor, an' take a cup?' broke in

105

Kirsty's voice. 'It's not often ye could be so favoured!'

'No thanks,' acknowledged Ivor, shifting against, but not departing from, the table.

'You'll be thinking, yourself an' Sanny, that ye have no time to waste, but maybe ye might both fare farther and waste it worse. What do you say, Maggie?'

Maggie smiled to her cup, then looked up:

'Your husband's saying nothing!'

'He'll be thinking I can do the saying for both of us most likely!'

Sanny, with the expression of a timid schoolboy, put his pipe back in his mouth; then removed it again.

'What have ye lost now, Sanny?' asked his wife.

'That buoy I was working on last night. We're going to test her to see if she's holding in.'

'You'll find it where ye left it,' said Kirsty.

'I was half-thinking that,' said Sanny innocently, going through to the back-place.

'I hope you're no' so throughither as that, Ivor!' challenged Kirsty.

'Well, I don't know,' said Ivor.

'Faigs, you'll back him up! Men are good at that – don't you think, Maggie?'

'Oh, well,' murmured Maggie.

'Wae's ye, lassie, but I'm jalousin' you're untried enough to back them up too. But wait ye till ye get one of your own!'

Maggie coloured a trifle. Ivor whistled a casual note and stopped. The note had sounded empty, ill-mannered – anything but the easy nonchalance aimed at.

'And you, too, Ivor! Maybe you'll be whistling a tune oot the other side o' your mouth some day, an' be sorry for yourself.'

'Do you think so now?' asked Ivor. (What a thing to say! cried his mind, feeling that the something nimble in his brain, which had ever a fairly ready word for Kirsty's quick-witted banter, had got paralysed. Nor could he wipe out the silly smile that he knew was on his face.)

'Think so!' echoed Kirsty, feeling gleefully that she had him at a disadvantage. 'Man, I can see how even being near an unexpected presence puts, as Donul Macaulay says about his skeery horsie, puts the branx on ye!'

'I hope it would take a little more than that to put the branx on me!' (Gode, how awful!)

'Eh?' questioned Kirsty.

Ivor's tongue came between his lips, and he now hung on doggedly to his smile. Maggie regarded the cup on her knee with a quick-witted ease of expression which showed no consciousness of having been personally involved.

'Eh?' waited Kirsty. She had too often to stand male bombardment from a circle of chairs round her hospitable hearth of a night, to let any chance slip of getting her own back.

'I mean,' began Ivor, 'I mean –' But the right words would not come.

'Man, it's fairly tied ye up,' probed Kirsty mercilessly. 'If it needs more than that to put the branx

107

on ye, it's the bonny, the able sight ye'll be when it happens!'

'Ay,' said Ivor, forcing a twist to his lips. He moved against the table. Kirsty caught his expression, a sardonic effort which she read with a sudden touch of the discomfort she had deliberately aimed at arousing in him. Her eyes fell away in a moment, taking Maggie in on their way to the fire. She leant forward and lifted the kettle off the crook. Sanny came through from the back-place, carrying the buoy with him.

'She seems tight enough, boy,' he observed to Ivor.

'That's good,' said Ivor, pressing the blown skin with his fingers and examining the wooden head. He did it carefully, with an unhurried ease. Kirsty thought: 'He's covering up well!' and knew an urge to probe him once more, but forbore – she hardly dared to know why.

'Weel, we'll be off again,' said Sanny, turning to Maggie with his shy smile. 'I hope your uncle's keeping well?'

'Yes, fine, thanks,' said Maggie.

'That's good!' He paused a moment, then backing away in the wake of Ivor: 'We'll maybe no' see ye for a while again.'

'Oh – of course! you're off to-morrow!' Maggie got to her feet, went up to him with outstretched hand. 'I wish ye the best o' luck!'

Sanny shook her hand warmly.

'Thank ye! Thank ye!'

'An' – an' record shots, an' – an' good prices!'

'We'll be hoping, anyway,' said Sanny.

'It might help the luck if you spread your wishes more!' Kirsty could not refrain from crying. 'Are ye there, Ivor?'

But Ivor's footsteps were heard moving off.

'So long!' he cried through the window. Sanny followed him.

Maggie did not sit down again.

'Well, I must be going too. The bairns will be in on ye from the school in a minute, an' there's a good few things to be done up yonder before the night's through.'

'What's all your hurry? And I can't help laughing at the thought that Ivor's not blessing me this minute! He's not often so slow wi' his word.'

'No,' murmured Maggie, not looking at Kirsty. 'Well, I must be off. And thank you for the tea. It was lovely.'

'Oh, your pail!' Kirsty hurried to the back-place, returning in a moment.

'There's the pail, and this is a wee bit fish for your tea. I just don't know how to thank ye for the rabbits. It's a special treat to the bairns, ye may be sure.'

'Oh, but this is far too much –'

'Too much! – I'm almost ashamed offering it to you, it's so little. And heesht ye back again!'

'Oh, I'll be looking in sure!'

'Ye won't be down seeing the boats off in the morning?'

'I'm afraid, hardly,' considered Maggie, '– with one thing or another.'

'Ay, ay,' said Kirsty; 'I can understand.'

Maggie did not look at her as she twisted the pail in the momentary pause of final leave-taking.

'Well, well,' said Kirsty.

'Good-bye,' returned Maggie, and with a quick, warm smile was gone.

CHAPTER EIGHT

KIRSTY stood looking after her a moment, eyes clouding, face smoothing to a reveried comeliness. She saw Maggie throw a look down the street, saw her stride shorten in a half-stumble as she quickly swung round on the uproad homeward. Kirsty glanced down the street also and observed Ivor, bent under a herring net balanced across his shoulders, disappear round the black shed towards the harbour path. 'Poor bairns!' muttered Kirsty, and turned meditatively to her own hearth to deal with the involuntary apostrophe silently and at length.

Meantime Maggie continued on her way at a smart pace, colour high, eyes bright, till she came to the vennel cutting in between two houses to the right. Down the vennel, along the cart-track as far as Hendry's croft, mercifully escaping any further attentions from Mrs Hendry, and so at last to her own path. There her pace slackened. There, indeed, her strength oozed from her, leaving her legs a-tremble with a weakness that would fain have taken advantage of a grassy hummock.

She had been surprised, so gratefully surprised, at the way she felt when Ivor had first appeared at Kirsty's. She had been complete mistress of herself, could have, had need been, chatted with animation; a curious intoxicating gaiety of the head. Then Kirsty had intervened in that talk with Ivor and the iridescence had dulled, died, and in its place – that horrible awkwardness of desperation, interfering with self-command, showing itself in the very struggle to subdue it. Had Kirsty seen? . . .

What could she have seen? What was there to see? There was nothing to see. Nothing. Her fingers gripped spasmodically. Oh, there was nothing!

Her head jerked up and looked swiftly about her as though the great expanse of seaboard could be called to witness – or dared. The expanse lay around her quiescent, veiled – curiously veiled, as though mysteriously alive to its own subtle purposes. The freshness of the year could be felt as a sweet breath, moving over it, quickening. A lark swooped to earth a few paces away in a final tumultuous shaking of notes. . . . Yet the year's dying greyness came through everything, too, like a mist, the pervasive greyness of Northern places that is never utterly consumed let summer and passion riot as they may. It came tealing in on her now, rendered the more poignant by contrast with the earth's mysterious quickening, and in a moment it seemed that even the lark singing had got caught in its sad, imponderable mesh.

But she did not sit down. Evenly she went on, and presently, lifting her head, discerned Geordie and his busy harrows, and Uncle Jeems sowing with one hand. Sowing with his one hand! Symbolic, surely! The note of bitter criticism did not define itself in her mind – but from a little distance how stilted, how mean, that one-hand sweep, instead of the generous, rhythmic right-and-left scattering of the seed! As though he could hardly let the oats through his fingers; or, if let them he must, then with the grasping minimum of necessity!

Normally she could have admitted with a doubtful half-smile that she had allowed her imaging too free scope. There were many crofters, decent men, who could sow satisfactorily only with the one hand. But she allowed no pause for reflection now; had no time for the weariness of excuses. In the final wearied impatience of the mind there is room for ultimate values only. The sowing gesture was mean. The whole croft was mean. Life was mean, mean and bare, with no colour to it, no warmth, nothing but the eternal greyness, that was a poverty, an exhaustion as of animal hunger gnawing at stones for bread.

She turned her head from them lest they beckon to her, and reached the kitchen without interruption, the dumb burden of her quickly created misery heavy upon her.

She did not walk the kitchen with that caged impotence of the man. She went automatically about her endless woman's business. On her knees – too weary even for the strain of stooping – she poked the fire, gathering the clods round a central flame; then with the kettle to the back-place for fresh water; back with the kettle; through again with the milk-pail and the fish; a good-sized blockie (codling) cleaned to a bluish whiteness; slap! on the table; salt on it; into the kitchen . . . pause . . . What had she come into the kitchen for? She could not think. Geordie and his harrows moved across her mind and her uncle with his jerky, one-hand sweep. She went to the window to look at them. There they were!

What figures, what figures of the earth, clinging to it, poking in it, of it! Slow-moving, except for that paralytic jerk of the sowing arm. Geordie stooping forward, though merely walking after the harrows; stooping forward, with now a wallop of the rein against a flank, now a 'Hup, man! . . . whoa, there! . . . hits, ye! . . .' and a running, sucking, clucking sound of the tongue against the right cheek as an audible goad.

What figures! Nosing about the earth like human moles, about that lean, hungry, little patch of stony earth!

And Geordie being there . . . Geordie! . . .

Yes, Geordie was Tullach's man. Geordie, the horse, the harrows, the whole action now going forward – possibly, for all she knew, the seed itself – everything – Tullach! She suddenly had the sensation of Tullach's clothes in her nostrils, a snuffy, human-animal smell. More than that. A smell she could not describe as of vapours of the body caught in unventilated, thick clothing, closing in on her. The abomination of it choked her. She passionately sickened at it. She pushed it from her, till her palms came against the cool window-panes.

Ah, cool, clean! She laughed wildly. The figures nosing about there! Geordie stooping when he had no need to stoop. That jerky sowing hand keeping a sort of grotesque rhythm to the shauchling feet. For ever and ever – that! Oh, Almighty God – that!

She slid into the chair by the table, her head falling forward on her arms. Tears came in a flood;

passionate tears and sobs, drowning everything, all thought, all imaging – except that involuntary dread 'Almighty God.' It was an apostrophe beloved of her Calvinistic minister, and had come from her mind with a deep sense of utter abandon. It got stuck, however, in a tiny angle of her thought, and stared at her now, deliberately. . . . She had been cursing, been taking the name of the Lord God in vain, had dared the Terrible Presence with a loose oath . . . had stained. . . .

Her hands doubled up. She rebelled. With a passionate effort she shut everything out, God and all. She would not think . . . she would not think. . . . Besides, there was a time when one could call on God! . . .

She became subtly appalled. Her body stilled, her tears ceased, but she did not lift her head. To call on God! Was she going foolish? That was – religion! This sort of calling on God – so entirely different a thing from the impersonal ritual of each night's prayer – this personal throwing of oneself at God. . . . Her body recoiled, her soul curled in on itself. Monstrous! What was she thinking on earth to – to call on – That! . . .

She lifted her head slowly, eyes half-veiled and looking carelessly at nothing – as though they feared to surprise Something.

Going slowly through to the back-place, she dipped a towel in water and bathed her eyes. Twice she had cried to-day! Her lips twisted uncertainly. And she could not remember when she had cried last! What was coming over her? What had happened to her? . . . She questioned herself with that indefinite hypnotic questioning which acts as a closing of the door on the mind and breeds a wearied and uncaring forgetfulness; a floating surface-sense of questioning half-surprise fading into an unanswering greyness of existence, like flying wind and sun into a drowning seaboard fog.

Composedly she went about her tasks. As time went on she approached the window to see if they had finished the field. No, they were still busy there, but plainly very nearly finished. The wag-at-th'-wa' struck six. She might put on a bit of fresh fish to boil. Her mind worked over what provisions she had in the house – rabbits, codling, potatoes and herring. Yes, she would put on a bit of the fresh fish for a change. Tea would be earlier to-night, and so she could go for the cow afterwards.

Uncle Jeems came in peching, and, making for his chair, lowered himself into it with a grunt.

'Ay, ay,' he muttered; 'ay, ay,' letting his body settle like a sack – and casting an eye-corner at the table. He had jaloused it would be fish; but no emotion was allowed to touch his face. 'Ay, ay,' he continued to gasp, head nodding vaguely.

Maggie entered with a plate of steaming fish and laid it on the middle of the table. Then she came to the fireplace and lifted the teapot.

'You can sit in,' she said.

He raised himself with an 'Och! och!' and, back bent, as though rheumatically stiffened from his toil, reached the table.

'Weel, weel,' he mumbled; 'ay, ay. . . .'

Maggie set fish, bread, and tea before him. He made no direct reference to the fish, merely asking:

'Had they a good fishing in the morning?'

Maggie paused a moment, suddenly remembering she had forgotten to ask.

'I couldn't say,' she answered.

'Did ye no' ask?'

'No.'

'How no? Surely that was the least ye could have done!'

'Ay.'

'Weel, an' why didno' ye?'

'Maybe I forgot.'

'Oh! Ye forgot!'

His laconic tone stung her.

'An' maybe I didn't,' she returned.

He looked up at her, but she paid no attention, merely going on:

'If ye go to a house wi' a rabbit an' make it your first question to ask how much fish they have . . . well, I don't like to give it away that we are beggars yet.'

'Beggars! Who's beggars?'

She went on with her tea indifferently.

'Is giving away a whole rabbit begging – when it would buy a string o' fish?'

'Who'll buy a rabbit?'

'Look at the price of it in Wick or Glasgow, an' ye'll see.'

'Ay,' she said. 'It's a pity –' She paused.

He understood perfectly, however. It was a pity he did not send his game to Wick or Glasgow seeing no one would ever dream of buying a rabbit in Balriach. His face stiffened, eyes goggling a trifle, but he kept control of his tongue sufficiently to ask:

'What fish did she give ye?'

'A blockie.'

Then he sniffed. 'She took care not to break her hand!'

Now Kirsty was generous in that unreasoning, improvident way which never failed to kindle Maggie's heart, to make of Maggie her instant and jealous defender. Furthermore, she had given two rabbits to Kirsty. For the first time that night her eyes met her uncle's directly, met them and did not waver, while plainly the lash of colour in her face boded words that might be better left unsaid. Her uncle's eyes shifted to his fish, of which he lifted a succulent piece with his fingers, drawing it into his mouth with a noisy suction. From that sound Maggie turned away, and there was silence between them.

Presently her uncle remarked evenly:

'Weel, the corn's doon, an' that's a good thing oot o' the way.'

Maggie said nothing.

'Geordie was telling me that Tullach was thinking o' putting an extra strip under tatties by the east dike yonder.'

She waited. But her uncle committed himself no further.

The meal over, she cleared up.

'The coo'll be getting a good bite yonder,' he said, settling in his chair by the fire and scraping the dottle from his pipe. 'So it's as weel to leave her as long as we can. There's growth in the weather th'-day.'

Maggie lifted the strip of cloth from the table and retired to the back-place to wash the dishes.

Jeems sucked a tooth meditatively, while a thoughtful light gleamed in his eyes. He had said what he had said, and apparently found it good. There was relief in a cunning sense of management. Only, he would have to sell the calf or she would be buying butter. He could see that from the tea. And yet look at the price he'd get in the back-end if only he reared the calf himself! That was complicated again by the milk-selling. And then the calfie might always die or come by an accident. While the question of pasture and rearing. . . . Yet Angus Grant had gotten yon price in the back-end. . . .

The kitchen tidied up for the night and the fire properly banked, Maggie set out to fetch the cow Roy trotting by her side, affectionate but never importunate. A wise brute. The lowing of the cow could be heard a long way off, and when Maggie hove in sight her approach was watched with statuesque attention. She was thinking of her calf. Maggie could tell it from the anxiety with which the head was stretched, the mouth opening every now and then in a smothered mooing, the eyes protruding.

'Well, Nance, what is it?'

The cow whisked round her head after Maggie, watched the stake being drawn, then, horns down, gave a tug at the tether and started for home, pulling Maggie at a sharp pace after her. Nearing the byre,

Nance broke into a run, snatching by main force the rope from Maggie's hands. When Maggie reached the byre door she found Nance, head over the barrier, licking her calf, and the calf dancing and staggering excitedly.

It took some physical persuasion to get Nance into her stall, and then not a little before the chain ask could be clicked round her neck. The task finally accomplished and breathing heavily, hair somewhat dishevelled, blouse pulled out from her skirt at one side, complexion heightened to peach tone and texture, lips moist and pouting in a panting redness, Maggie turned from Nance's head, took a stride down the stall – to find Daun Tullach in the doorway.

She glared frankly for a moment, then, nodding quickly, turned her head away as though to look for something, conscious that her face was burning, that he must have heard how straightforwardly she had been admonishing Nance, but conscious infinitely more of what she had seen gleam in his face.

'Ay, Maggie, you're bedding her,' he said in a voice gone hoarse, taking a step into the byre.

'Yes,' she acknowledged, with swift, cold politeness.

'Ay, ay,' he said, clearing his throat – and remained still, two strides within the byre, blocking the way out. She felt his presence behind her as something ready to swoop, a presence balancing on the verge of losing control and engulfing her, a hungry, dark, passionate gluttony of a presence. Confusion gave way to anger, white anger and cold fear. She picked up the hoe and, turning to the stall, raked the straw down about Nance's hind legs, not hiding her face from him, but exhibiting it in its controlled coldness without actually looking at him.

He wavered. She knew that he wavered; that it was touch and go. Finishing the bedding, she turned her eyes full on him in that level, direct way she had at times, and observed: 'My uncle is in the kitchen.' Her accent, distinctly Englished, bogged him.

But he could not let go in a moment the lust for her blown beauty which trembled in every muscle. So utterly, maddeningly desirable she was, standing there in the first faint dusk of evening.

'Oh, he is, is he?' he acknowledged, a strained surface smile about his unflinching eyes.

Her look passed from him easily, unhastening, and she set the hoe against the wall. Instinctively she knew that if her eye quailed for an instant, flickered the slightest intelligence that she understood what he felt, then he would be upon her, not in words nor in pleading, but physically, with crushing arms, his breath on her face, the smell of him, suffocating. . . .

She looked up at him again naturally, easily, but with a subtlety of stiffening expression something more than passionless in its level regard.

'Yes,' she emphasised, and waited for him to move, with the obvious expectation that he would move. One final, balancing instant, and he turned, throwing a look at the calf, giving his short laugh:

'He's coming on!' An effort at naturalness in his

voice assured Maggie that he was satisfied she had not discovered him. And not being discovered, he could, with countenance, bide his time.

'Geordie finished the corn, did he?' he enquired, going out at the door.

'I think so,' she answered, closing the door behind her and drawing in the clean air to her lungs.

'That's good!' And he moved off to the house, grinding his teeth audibly, beset with a griping consciousness that he had missed something which every blood-beat cried for, that – that he should have, when he had the chance. . . . His fists knotted. But Gode, the next time! His tongue came between his lips, moistening them. His eyes gleamed like a stoat's.

CHAPTER NINE

MAGGIE moved to the hen-house door, which she closed. The stone, however, eluded her uncertain foot, would not turn over up against the door. Even her hands shook. Reaction was now upon her flesh in weak tremblings. She went round the hen-house corner to the barn. She had a wild impulse to fling into the barn and throw herself down. But a sudden terror of the inside of the barn, of being inside any place, gripped her.

She sat down on a small cairn of stones against the wall, her face to the sea beyond the cliff-heads, but seeing nothing, knowing nothing beyond a flooding of dark revelation, an embodied shadowing of unspeakable things, enveloping, smothering gestures. She had not only read Daun Tullach: in a swift moment of awakened instinct she had known what he had felt. Known what he had felt, what had made his voice hoarse; and had escaped from him and it as from a destroying . . .

But she could end no thought, as though every thought must be incomplete, as though knowing everything she knew nothing – except that instinctive, stiffening recoil of the body from the sensation of finality, of a final sinking weakness. . . . No! no!

She could not face it out. She needed something to lay hold on. There was nothing to lay hold on. There was nothing but herself and the grey sea, the croft, the iron land, and now moving through everything – that! She would have to face it, to reckon with it. It would watch her, dog her, wait its chance.

123

With a frightful clairvoyance, she saw herself dodging, wary. . . .

She got up and went to the edge of the barn and peered round. She suddenly caught herself peering. She came back to the stones and sat down. The thing had begun!

Her face stiffened in a grey mask. This was madness, overdoing it like this. She had to keep hold. She had always to manage her feelings. The luxury of giving way was scarcely an emotion natural to the croft. In the byre, she had managed. She had to stick on and not let her imagination run riot.

She tried to hypnotise herself again with words, with wisdom.

But beneath her wisdom a black snaky knowledge whispered that *she knew*.

But she had always known in a way. . . .

Ay, in a way!

She involuntarily choked the debate.

But the black snaky trickle ran now with her blood.

She got up again, and her hand, swinging to her side, brushed the protruding edge of her blouse which had got plucked from her skirt in the struggle with Nance. Colour whipped her face as she hurriedly stuck the edge in again. Her hands went nervously feeling round her waist, her eyes scanning of her dress what they could. Then to her hair where her fingers discovered a loosened plait. He had seen her like that. . . .

Following swift confusion came anger as swift, dispelling it. Tonic anger. She should go in, but she would not. She should go in to prove her perfect unconcern, her undisturbed ignorance of Tullach. But no, not yet – not yet. She would take her own time. She had every right to take her own time. In a surge of dark emotion, she hated Tullach, blotted him out.

Her back to the croft, she started for the cliff-heads at a normal pace, quick-scanning eyes assuring her that there was no one to interrupt. She could be seen from a distance, but equally she could see.

At the cliff-heads she paused, the far-down green floor catching her breath. A curved head-dress of grass covered the precipice immediately beneath her, shutting off the sheerness of the descent; but on either hand where the general line bent seaward for a short distance, the grey-black rock faces, gaunt, weather-naked, immense, seemed to come up against her vision in a dizzying nearness.

She had an instinctive dread of these cliffs, an awful sense of imminent insecurity in their presence. She sat down slowly, holding to the earth with deliberate motions lest a flighty action, a careless movement, precipitate headlong annihilation. She even poked her hands against some grassy tussocks, safely removed from the very verge as they were, to make sure that the whole headpiece wouldn't slip off like a loosened scalp.

Flat on her face, she quickly caught at a sense of perilous security, and as the moments passed and she knew herself anchored, even the under-sense of peril thinned into an indefinite dread, bemused somewhat by the far-down booming and sucking of the sea.

Hypnotic in an awesome way, this eternal mating of cliff and sea. Her eyes followed the line of white foam about the teeth of half-submerged rocks, the suffocating engulfing, the sucking recession, of the tireless green water; wan movement of clinging dark sea-ware; carven heedlessness of perched black cormorants; then boom! boom! as the wave searched out some dark inner labyrinth of cavern. White gulls slid out from high rock-faces, sweeping down, down, to rise on exquisite curves of aerial lightness that hardly called for a wing-beat, every now and then their voices uprising in swift, strident repetition of a single note – a note that for all its piercing shrillness was cavernous, too, and clung about the rock-faces in a way infinitely forlorn.

The green sea, the changeable, the eternally changeless, ever-ready stage of unending drama, itself both stage and player, with man and his ships, for all their self-importance, but little more than supernumerary and stage property. Something of this gripped Maggie, may have gripped her unconsciously in sending her here at all. Her uncle, Tullach, herself – small dots of figures in comparison! To feel as much was to have a sense of taking refuge in this mating of sea and cliff, a sense of being privy to its dark strengths, its perilous eternities.

For a long time she lay very still, caught away from her adventure of the byre into this circle of refuge, of strange freedom; a magic circle of daring and fear, and in some inscrutable way of self-knowledge.

Thus remote, she could look on the byre adven-

126

ture as a thing apart from her and watch clearly herself and Tullach in their parts, acting. . . . He moved . . . he looked . . . his voice. . . .

She suddenly buried her face in the grass. She could not watch. There was that question of revelation, still unresolved, moving darkly in her blood. And she knew, suppress it as she might, that in some mysterious way it had a power, a slow, fascinating power. A dark depth in it, drawing her even to a more privy knowledge of the restlessness, of the strengths and eternities, in this fierce mating of sea and cliff.

Yes, it was there, curling about the secret deeps of her mind all the time; the thing itself – and the actions demanded from her to circumvent it in the struggle with Tullach. For she knew with an absolute certainty, with far more certainty now than if Tullach himself had put a coarse oath on it, that she was his game and he was after her – in that way.

Yet is there a subtle fascination in a certain sort of danger more frightful than the danger itself, more compelling. The awakening heart knows it, burying deep the knowledge. And through that fascination there worms a thin nervous thread that throbs as with a curious inverted sense of elation. . . .

Maggie choked, clinging to the grass. As exhaustion stole upon her, she tried to let all thought, all feeling drain out of her, half-aware that whatever knowledge she may have gained, in composure only could she keep a hold on it. And presently there came upon her a merging sense of oneness with the elements about her. The licking and booming of the sea ascended from unfathomable depths as a crooning monotone, the gull-crying shrilled with a forlornness unreal and dying away into unfathomable distances, the cool evening air moved cleanly in about her body, her hair. She surrendered to a desire to leave go altogether, to slip down the caverns of her mind. . . .

She sat up with a shiver. The dusk was creeping upon the world in a blue dimness. She shivered again. Her clothes felt wet from the grass. Getting quickly to her feet, she looked about her like one who has awakened to forgotten realities. Down along the cliff-heads in the direction of Balriach she saw a figure approaching. She could not be mistaken. It was Ivor.

Without a moment's reflection she turned towards the croft, her footsteps hurrying. 'Why am I hurrying? Oh, why?' But she did not pause; she went on with less hurry, with still less; but on. She could not stop now, anyway. He was yet a long way off. She could not stop – if she would. In a moment that final peace of the cliffs was torn to shreds.

He could not think that she had seen him. There was that, anyway. Without actually turning her head, she tried to catch a glimpse of him. He was still coming on, but sticking to the cliffs. She looked again while yet some yards short of the barn, but saw no sign of him. He might be in the shelter of the whin-bank which ran as an upper boundary to Hendry's croft and finished down by the ditch-side at the foot of her own croft. If he was coming up in the shelter of the whin-bank he might be coming up for the milking. She rounded the barn, making slowly for the back door, trying to still the whirl of her thought to an urgent necessity for something more than composure.

She entered the back-place with an unhurried step, closing the door with an easy slam. She repressed an impulse to hum unconcernedly. The drone of her uncle's voice reached her at once. The other voice was silent.

The silence of the other voice affected her instantly, as though she could see the face only half-listening. She moved about, clattered the milk-pail as she unnecessarily scoured the outside of it. Should she go in?

She would have gone in unquestionably had she not seen Ivor coming along the cliff-heads. To go in now would be to risk complications. Once or twice she had felt certain of a desire in Tullach to carry out the lantern for her. She did not want Tullach near the byre to-night. In truth, it was light so long now that she could be doing without the lantern, perhaps . . . Without the lantern – there! . . .

'Maggie, is that ye?'

That settled it.

She opened the door, entered.

The figures were in the gloom by the fire, and as Tullach turned to her his face reflected a red gleam.

'Where were ye?' proceeded her uncle, with a querulousness that implied the necessity for her presence when visitors were in. A hospitable sop to Tullach.

'Oh, nowhere,' she said, indifferently.

Her uncle spat.

'Weel, maybe ye'd put a peat on the fire at least.'

'I see it's going down,' she observed, turning to the back-place. Going outside to the peat-stack, she gathered two or three whole peats, broke each in halves against a set stone, and tucked them in her apron. The thud of the peat on the stone could have been heard some little distance away, and as she straightened herself she looked carefully down the ditch-side to the whin-bank. Was that a head showing above the whins – or merely a deeper shadow? It moved, coming towards the ditch.

She turned to the house, a throbbing, choking excitation starting from her breast. But why turn to the house – why not wait – to redd up the peat-stack – any excuse? What was she doing? . . . The throbbing reached her throat, but she went on steadily. After all, what could she wait for? To say – what? To behave – how? And presently she would be out to milk, when at least she could behave like one going about her business, could hold on to her business, hands busy . . . and have time. She needed time.

She entered the kitchen with the peats, took the pieces from her apron one by one and stood them expertly on edge round the central flame, until stopped by her uncle:

'That'll do surely.'

She straightened herself without looking at either, but aware of Tullach's eyes so keenly on her that she could only hope the exertion of stooping might account for a warmth in her face. Through to the back-place she went with the unnecessary fuel and dumped it in the empty peat-box, her uncle's voice following her with the suggestion that she 'micht put a bit blink on the lamp in a whilie.'

In a whilie! There was no compelling need for urgency in the using of oil! Yet he spoke in a way that might be considered hospitable to his guest without at the same time unduly forcing Maggie! How she knew him! Living always with that. . . . Could one help being withered in the mind like the grey tufts of grass the very cattle avoided?

But rendered however impatient occasionally, Maggie was rarely aware within herself of the real possibilities of cumulative effect. True, she saw instances of it worked out in the case of many women, single women particularly, going on into the forties and fifties, getting wrinkled, stringy-necked, grasping, in their endless conflict with iron ways and means. But that was too remote from her yet for reasoned reflection and deliberate personal application. Only in the grey moments did vision exhibit the ruthless possibilities, and even then there was a subtle something in the misery of the visioning that was nearer the soft emotion of tears, youth's self-immolating tears, than the stark, dry-eyed, utterly sapless reality.

Even now her deliberate ignoring of that 'in a whilie' held something faintly tonic in its infinitesimal rebellion. She re-entered the kitchen, and, taking a paper spill from the mantelshelf, calmly lit the hanging lamp.

131

Her eyes drooped from the lamp in an even sweep
to meet Tullach's, rested on them a moment without
any showing of embarrassment, moved from them as
they would have from her uncle's. It was perfectly
done, and she knew it. They continued to move
around the kitchen. Yes, everything was in order.
That was good.

Roy emerged from under the table.

'Milking time, is it, Roy?' Her tone held a
pleasant matter-of-factness. Roy followed her into
the back-place, and she pulled shut the communicating door.

As she busied herself with lantern and pail, her
ears were for the sounds in the kitchen. Her uncle
was speaking. Tullach's voice never came at all.

Something in that silence was ominous. The tone
of an interjection, a laugh, would have reassured her.
Her face stiffened a trifle, her eyelids quivered in a
swift calculating. Then with a flick of contempt, too
plainly forced, she dismissed him. It was no good
calculating anything. Why should she?

She hesitated over the lantern. Would she light
it – or not? The lantern, like the dog, was protec-
tion. Against a wild gambling instinct, she lit it, the
very hesitancy bringing a confused light to her eyes.
Had she been sure of Tullach remaining where he
was – would she have lit it?

But she did not allow the half-formed thought for
a moment. And suddenly reinforced by a sense of
right-doing, of conventional right-doing at least, she
opened the back door.

'Come on, Roy!' She went out.

There was no one near the byre door. A flush of relief passed over her. As she lifted the latch, she took a swift look around into the thickening gloom. No one. Following Roy, she shoved the door to behind her.

Nance greeted her with a close-mouthed, questioning low. Maggie paused, looking about her. The calf danced in its crib.

'Well, Nance!' But her mind was acutely occupied with the under thought, 'Will I snib the door or not?' She did not allow the thought, however, to come openly to the surface of her mind, where she would have to face its implications. Hardly even did she pause in her stride as she went to the corner for the creepie – leaving the door unlatched.

Nance was inclined to be a little stubborn, restless. The way they treated her and her calf was plainly a matter that exercised her mind.

'Ye ould fool!' said Maggie. 'Ye an' your calf! Stand over there!'

She got Nance round after a time, then patted her in a way that showed understanding and that, at the same time, was an effort at obtaining Nance's best behaviour. She had a genuine affection for the cow; and to Bess, who had preceded her, she had on occasion told the burden of her mind. Nance, however, possessed an altogether stronger personality than had her predecessor, and Maggie was older.

The elusive tail was at last tied, and the milk in rhythmic patter found the bottom of the pail.

Her cheek against Nance's side, Maggie's eyes became round and steady. Hiss! hiss! went the milk in the quietude of the byre. Occasionally the calf danced, and when the calf danced Nance turned her head, making the chain ask rattle. Then silence again, and her thoughts.

The byre was so quiet that anyone might have been in it and nobody much the wiser. If that had been Ivor – then why? . . . Had the relief, when she had seen no one at the byre door, been a spurious, surface relief – a rush of avoidance – of what? The question was too complicated, and even to admit disappointment now meant . . . She hated to feel herself thinking what it might mean. He could have been here. He might have been here. Though perhaps, after all, he had never intended to leave the cliff-heads, had, in fact, not left them.

And even if he did walk in now – what then? Could she be sure of herself? Did she want to be sure of herself? What had she to say? Could she feel again as she had felt for the first while in Kirsty's – that fine ready gaiety of self-possession?

There came a scratching of fingers on the outside of the byre door. Her heart stood still. There was stealthiness in the quiet rattle of the sneck, the slow inward opening of the door. Then Ivor entered, and, closing the door, stood with his back to it.

The greeting on his face was curiously strained and pale, his lips twisting in a sort of half-defiant smile, his dark eyes glistening in the lantern light. Then his voice, off-hand, casual:

'Hallo, Maggie!'

'Hallo!'

Her hands got busy again, feverishly busy, while her head turned to rest against Nance's side once more. The dog had gone to get his ears fondled. Ivor spoke to him on an undertone, blustering and affectionate. A pause. Then Ivor took a step or two down the byre until Maggie's eyes found his knees within direct focus.

'Well, Maggie!'

'Well yourself!' she returned, but failing to get the necessary touch of banter.

He stooped for the hoe and began handling it this way and that.

'Ah, well, we're about ready for off,' he said.

'Yes, I'm sure,' she acknowledged. Then, as the silence held, 'You'd be hard at it all day.'

'Ay, getting things together.'

'So you're ready for off?'

'At last.'

'I hope you'll get a good morning.'

'Oh, I think so. Though maybe the wind will no' be very favourable for a start.'

'You never know. It might.'

'Sanny says it'll be a good day, the wind going round wi' the sun as it did to-day. But that'll mean it'll back round in the night an' be from the east'ard in the morning.' It sounded a long, trivial speech.

Lord, how trivial the empty, smooth words! Appalling to his ears, with time passing; worse – it was making possible with its wordiness a complete ordinariness that would be the last bitter curse of all to remember.

'You can never be sure, though,' doubted Maggie.

'Oh yes, we can be pretty sure; only, it doesn't much matter.'

The old perversity had touched these last words with a sardonic edge.

The touch thrilled her. She did not answer, twisting on the creepie till she commanded a view of the milk-pail. The froth was mounting. She fixed the pail more securely between her knees, then started in again, forehead against glossy hide.

He watched her, the smile gone utterly, brooding, sombre concentration on his face. As he looked on her there was no room in his mind for anything but what might be said, no conscious desire in his mind for possession of her beauty, nothing but a choking of words, a chaotic choking; as though all that was to be known of her, all that was to be desired of her, was already mixed in the stuff of him, and would be known and would be desired for evermore. His concern meantime – to say something – to hope for some –

Ay, to hope! Ass – dogged by that, driven by that against all reason; up the whin-bank, watching her covertly, seeing her breaking the peats, hanging about until the lantern came, then, knowing her alone, arguing and cursing – yet driven, driven till his fingers found the hanging latch and he stood here – to hope! To hope – for what? That was what screwed in the devil's gimlet! What had he to offer – that he could hope? Mocking laughter had answered him many a time in black shame. Yet driven – fool! And even now trying to resolve this choking chaos into a word, an inkling to her, *an inkling*! . . . And knowing this, and still holding to it! . . .

The silence became intolerable, had to be broken, and suddenly he said:

'Maggie.'

Emotion so instantly gripped her throat that she had difficulty in breathing. Her forehead slipped a little lower on the warm hide.

'Yes?'

He hesitated.

'Are ye nearly done?'

'Yes.'

He waited. She wrung out the last squirts of milk. In a minute she had finished; he could see she had finished. She must get up.

She got up slowly, swift prey to an irrational impulse to temporise, to keep back, to escape. Instinct was strong upon her, urging escape that would be no escape. Tumultuous instinct that trembled, that knew an absolute insecurity, that longed and repudiated, that could not maintain itself, that waited unbearably.

'Well, that's that,' she said, in a voice that astonished her by its evenness. One level look of her eyes now, in that way of which she had the perfect trick. . . . They began to travel upwards, but wavered before they reached his, wavered, broke in a wild look about the byre. . . . Then in an instant her body froze, eyes fixing in a breathless stare.

Clomp! clomp! came footsteps towards the byre door, evenly, surely, clomp! clomp! then a hand fumbling at the door jamb for a latch that hung unfixed. . . .

CHAPTER TEN

UNCLE JEEMS had been in good fettle that night. A fine twenty-four hours lay behind him, a successful twenty-four hours. And he had scored them off this man Tullach, who was so kind to him, so generous. A fine fellow, Tullach, making so much of the land because he had so much of it. Oh, capable at driving a hard bargain, cunning. Surely there was hardly one at all so cunning in driving a bargain. He had the power behind him. He could always say, 'Take it or leave it' – just as one might to the tinkers. Tullach could work a man into the hollow of his hand. No one but could have the utmost respect for him. How fortunate he, Jeems, was! How fortunate! Ay, ay!

He had received Tullach with a deep cordiality, had almost refused his tobacco plug when at last it had been forthcoming; for to begin with, Tullach had been a trifle erratic in his manner, darkly sweeping, heavily enigmatic. But to the great all mannerism is permitted, and Jeems had played plebeian chorus with a proper regard.

'It didno' take Geordie long. He's a good plooman yon!'

Tullach bit off his laugh. His blood still swirled in him.

'I suppose it took him as long as was necessary!' The ould devil had his miserly habit of trying to make a favour look as little as it could. Did he think it was being done for him!

'Oh ay – it did that indeed. I mean I was just

139

thinking ye get good value oot o' a man like Geordie
— he's no' the one for wasting your time.'

'Ay, an' Geordie gets his value oot o' me. He
doesn't work for nothing, ye can be sure!'

'Indeed, that's true! Ay, ay, that's true surely!'
Silence.

'I widno' be surprised,' said Jeems, brightening,
as he scraped at his pipe, 'but we'll have good
weather. The wind's backing wi' the sun an' it'll be
into the east'ard in the morning. I was just thinking
the heaviness was thinning oot the air th'-night.
We might have a speel o' good weather. It would
bring things on in a wheep.'

Tullach grunted, and felt for his pipe. Jeems took
a glance at his face, then blew lustily through his
pipe-stem. The sleep in the afternoon followed by
the sowing in the field, the good fish tea, induced a
physical smoothness that stuck to the chair in solid
ease, leaving the mind free to dodge in and out and
round like an old weasel in a cairn; induced even
more than that, the sense of well-being that was
almost like a faint backwash from old memories of
rum and nights in foreign places.

When the plug was produced:

'No, thankye, man; thankye,' followed by fingers
going through waistcoat pockets with fumbling
haste.

'Oh, here ye are!' and Tullach stuck the plug at
him.

When the plug could thus no longer be ignored,
Jeems muttered and mumbled an expressive gratitude. There was no questioning Tullach's over-

lordship. He had the feeling of the old man cringing at his boots.

Yet all the time Maggie was not coming in. What was keeping her out there? Had she noticed – Gode, his throat had got thick beyond speaking when he clapped eyes on her! Him! What a chance, with her like yon, and the feeling in him that if only he took one step nothing could have stopped him!

That would have brought things to a head at once, and he would have taken no denying. He couldn't. What thing on the earth could have stopped him? She would have struggled. . . . But no, he could not allow himself to feel her struggling. . . . Lord, the ripeness of her, the rich, breathing, red juiciness of her! . . . That look she had, that queer, straight, innocent look. . . . Put the finishing touch to it. . . . Her struggles, natural enough – they would die down. . . .

He was on his feet before he knew what he was doing, then covered himself by chancing on a paper spill on the mantelshelf.

'. . . Early enough, of course. But still, if it lasted. . . .'

What was the ould fool gabbing on about now?

'Eh?'

'Angus Grant last year cut his peats fully as early as this and had them lifted before the weather broke. Ye'll remember that? It bears oot what I'm saying.'

'Does it though?'

'Ay, it does that. If we're in for a speel o' good weather, one might do worse than take the advantage of it. It's aye a gey kittle thing the weather at this time o' the year.'

'No doubt.'

'Of course, I'm just giving my opinion.'

'Surely.'

The ould devil had his land ready, and with that behind him the only other thing that would be an expense, an outstanding expense, would be the peat cutting, drying, and driving. Was he thinking that he, Tullach, was not seeing through that?

'Ye'll be having a whole day's cutting belike,' said Tullach, elaborately.

'Eh? Weel now . . .' and Jeems shifted on his hard chair, eyes shifting, atching the firelight in doubtful gleams. But T llach deliberately did not help him out. He knew that Tullach deliberately did not help him out, that Tullach thought himself superiorly acute in being able to spot every miserly intention that passed in his, Jeems's, mind. It was beyond doubt comforting to Tullach. And one could play to that comfort with proper respect. He covered the halting in his speech by stooping to the fire for a fresh light. Between the noisy draws he stammered out :

'Ay – a day's cutting – ample – ample.'

It undoubtedly got over the impasse and left Tullach in the air, without any retort but the glaringly direct. He had an uncanny knack, this shambling, old, poverty-stricken cringer, of never altogether giving himself away, of reserving a something that might be a pitiable attempt at self-respect, but, again, might be nothing more than the hiding of a slyness, a sort of slyness Tullach could not fathom, considered himself somewhat of a fool in imagining at all, as if the thing could be possible! Yet, at rare moments, positively a sort of mocking slyness! Arrant rubbish to imagine that, to credit him with it! – it was merely that his poky mind and its gleams and its stories exasperated at times, particularly when he got warmed up to the point of forgetting himself on a sort of nudging level of equality.

At the moment, however, Tullach had the measure of the peat-cutting manœuvre, and was in any mood but one of easy compliance. He would let him hang on and fish and dodge as long as he damn well pleased. It was time, in any case, that something definite was coming out of all this. High time! . . . What was keeping her now? What could be keeping her? Had she sensed? And if so, how was it taking her? Where was she at this moment? What was she doing? . . . Gode, the look of her in the stall yonder! . . . His blood spirted in warm flushes through his body. He had been a bluidy fool! As though a look could keep him back! Him! . . . And then the insidious thought: women are queer, unchancy. What did he know but maybe she might have been expecting him to catch her! . . . But no, hardly that. . . . And yet, who knew? Eh? Why not? . . . How many women would jump at the chance! That was the naked truth, as he well enough knew. . . .

Yet through this insidious whispering stared Maggie's look. There was something there that, he felt in his marrow, if he caught at it roughly, brutally, and it rebelled – there would be a wild flare-up, and – an end. That would finish it. Tullach, being Tullach, could not take a spurning, and come whistling back. Not likely! . . . Gode, it was maddening! . . . But he had her handy. It wasn't as if she was running after anyone else. He not only had her handy – the old man as well, the croft. His overlordship was secure, with that proper feeling of being made way for, tacitly acknowledged, as it were bowed unto. He could bide his time. . . .

Jeems had for the moment left the peats and was being reminded of an incident where the 'natives' burnt dung, 'just as we'd burn peats, sure as I'm telling ye. They made it intil cakes, camel-dung, man, an' it smouldered an' burnt wi' a smell like burning coo's sharn. In some o' that places they're hard put til it for any sort o' fire at all. I mind once, a clear, blue night it was, calm an' still, wi' the desert stretching away like the sea. . . . Man, it's no' canny, nights like yon on the land, that far an' queer around ye – anything might come oot o't. Maybe a girl dancing wi' bit veils floating aboot her that are no' much use for hiding anything, or it might be a man's voice oot o' sight, wi' a drone in it like the minister's, calling on Allah. Allah to them is like our Gode to us. An' the camels, they'll stand up against the sky wi' humps on them like far-off mountains, an' a smell that makes some sailors sick; but if ye've been brought up to muck a byre an' move aboot among cattle beasts it's no so bad – though it's different, too. . . .'

Tullach was satisfied that the old man had no intention, sly or otherwise, of showing off his knowledge with the object of making his listener feel small in untravelled ignorance. Yet he could not hide from himself that it had precisely that effect on him. Not so much when he felt in good tune with the world and in a powerful laughing mood that could make a gusty shot at pulling ould Jeems's leg, as when he was disturbed in body and mind by an uncertain sense of his 'authority' being questioned, being slyly, mockingly undermined. He could not express an adequate opinion on camels and dung fires and nude dancing girls. It was as though the ould devil knew he had him there; more than that, as though he, Tullach, was as ignorant of the great world as a home-made kebbuck, while this beggar at his feet possessed the satisfying knowledge – and knew it.

'. . . Howsomever, to get to what happened in that tent place. It was darkish, as I say, an' a heavy scent, thick as smoke nearly, got into yer head an' gave ye queer feelings. I could hear Jeck's breath by me as though he had been running in a race. An' then that fellow in the off corner, wi' his legs folded on the floor like a tailor an' his turban on his head, began playing on a whistle. Soft bubbles o' notes like as though the whistle was made oot o' a fat bit o' wood. Then a flap opened in behind an' a wee dwarf o' a mannie came slipping oot, bowing an' cavorting aboot an' making faces – a wee moniment o' a mannagie – an' up he comes dancing right fornent Jeck an' points his toe at him an' then his tongue. Jeck laughed queerly. There was something aboot the mannie – I don't know what, but his darting tongue – Gode, I don't know. I remember Jeck saying afterwards – long after – that it was like the tempting and unclean spirit o' aal fleshly lusts. Jeck had a great way o' making sentences like oot o' the Bible. He came from doon the Aberdeen coast. His faither was a fish-curer in a pretty big way. I remember hearing aboot him at one time. . . .'

'I think I heard ye mention him before,' cut in Tullach drily, stretching himself. Plainly Maggie must have gone down to the village – or was she still out there waiting? If he went out and then missed her – he could hardly come back. She must be in any moment to get ready for the milking. If he took leave of Jeems when she was at the milking, and there was no one about, he might shove a head into the byre door – as a beginning. As a beginning. The night was not over yet.

'. . . So wi' a last whirl aboot, he sits doon an' puts the bit stickie that he had been twirling in his hand to his mouth. At that he let off a lot o' thin, high-up notes, like a body spinning round. An' there an' then – the flap opened – an' she was oot like a whirlwind. Jeck gasped.'

'I don't suppose ye gasped yersel'!'

Jeems paused and turned his crafty, but half-deprecating glance on Tullach.

'Wheesht! Ye'll know on yersel' what it's like when the blood's warm wi' anyone!'

Something altogether too intimate in this imputation of a common humanity touched Tullach's expression to a perceptible hardening. He would 'know on himsel'.' It was so subtly like a reading aloud of his mind. He looked with deliberate concentration at the grey-whiskered, wrinkled face – but whiskers and wrinkles seemed merely a net in which the old fleshy humours were caught as in a reflected warmth of reminiscence, with the slyness no more than an inverted form of recognition of the properties.

. . . 'She spun once or twice like a totem – an' then she stopped dead an' the fat, bubbly whistle began. She slipped aboot now, coming up to us an' going back, wriggling her body in a way – this way an' that – her belly wriggling an' her chest – an' her body wisno' fat as ye'll see on some o' them – nor yet thin neither – an' it was as alive as a serpent. Twisting an' curling an' up wi' her legs on a skip an' wriggling. . . . As Jeck said afterwards – long after – it would have knocked the Ten Commandments oot o' John Knox an' singed his beard like the King o' the Americas – or words like it. He was a great laad, Jeck. I remember him once . . .'

The back door clicked, and Maggie's footstep was plainly heard. While Jeems interpolated a characteristic reminiscence of Jeck, Tullach listened to the sounds in the back-place, where the rattling of the tin milk-pail held a seduction infinitely more urgent than all the castanets that Jeems's memories ever contrived to rattle.

When in due course she appeared, body and pale face framed in the half-dusk of the doorway, Tullach knew a swift constriction of the heart, breath sticking in his throat. His eyes followed her while she stooped to the fire and raked its embers; followed the dark disturbing whirl of her body as she withdrew for the peats; had a wild involuntary imaging of her as that dancing, half-naked woman in the dusk, swaying, flashing, with the heavy scents, the beating blood. His Presbyterian conscience suddenly choked on the picture, gorged. . . . No need for that foreigner's nonsense – the body itself –

The light from the lamp fell on her upturned face, and when she finally fixed the glass her eyes drooped to his own face, quiet, unmoved, untouched in their virginal regard; paused a moment and passed from him, absolutely untroubled.

Damn him, the thing was beyond him! Yet not exasperatingly. By no means. To be his own – to change that unconcern – to smother it up. The untouched innocence – a lure of the true delight. No leavings for him. And the coolness – all girls were good at that sort of thing in any case. She would look differently – look differently when. . . . Gode, she would look differently then!

The jumble of his surface thought kept him from hearing Jeems's words for a time. A subtle, cruel elation wormed about his under thought. A sensation of imminent contest warmed his body till he became conscious of its surface heat, and involuntarily pushed his chair back from the fire.

Jeems's tale gathered momentum for a conclusion in an affair of knives – at least, of a knife. It was to be gathered that Jeck forgot himself. 'Had he gone aboot it quately as a matter o' business – it would have been all right. But he clean forgot himsel' an' went barging his way. He had drink in him an' money on him – an' when he was like that he always wanted to do the high an' mighty; an' now hardly anything would have stopped him but wild horses – except one thing – an' that was a man's hand in his pocket. It was in a jerk to himsel' that he felt it. He reared like a stallion. "Ye bluidy monkey!" he shouts, drawing back to let at him – when the fellow drew a knife. Before ye could wink Jeck had his wrist, an' there they staggered. But Jeck's muscles were all gristle – an' the knife went back – back – till all at once the fellow crumpled up an' was a heap on the floor. I had gotten a grip on Jeck by this time. "Come on, for Gode's sake!" I cries in his ear. "Ye've done for him!" He stood sort o' dazed, looking at the thing at his feet. I pulled him by main force. They were on us. We fought backing oot – then we passed the word between us an' on the instant took to our heels. . . .

'It was a night till we won clear! . . . Oh ay . . . ay . . . yon was the night! . . . och, the night it was!' . . .

Jeems's talk dribbled out into a memoried silence wherein his eyes glimmered, Tullach apparently forgotten for the moment.

Tullach watched him, his thought arrested in a satiric effort at clairvoyance. That battered hulk there, that wrinkled, grey-haired, done cratur – him an' his women! And not women as he, Tullach, knew them, but these dusky, full-bosomed women whom it was difficult to look upon without thinking what they were made for. His eyes went to the tea-caddies on the mantelpiece. One often saw them on tea-caddies. Then his eyes dropped again – from no more, as it happened, than vivid green parrots – to the old man before him.

It was as though the colour of the green parrots, however, remained an intangible film on the mental retina. An exotic, Eastern, lust lure. This ould done cratur, with his scents and his dancing girls – and his unspeakable, naked bodies like naked serpents – Gode, what use could he have made of them! And that he, Tullach, a man of possessions, playing Dives to this Lazarus, should have been denied – when this thing here before him should have been given all that, over and over again, without any fear of neighbours or of being found out – perfect freedom to wallow . . . a thing like that, and he, Tullach, with his bodily urgencies, his – his . . . Gode! . . .

'. . . . It ended' – Jeems's voice was at it again – 'in one o' the most terrible fights I have ever seen, a fight that came aboot in the cutest, easiest way that ever ye could think o'. Ye see, Jeck never could be sure if he had killed the fellow or no'. For days he went aboot sort o' queer, speaking aboot it now an' then, terrible doon in the mouth, but no able to keep off it. "D'ye think I killed him?" he would ask, quate an' sober-like. "No fears!" I would say to him. "They're slippery as eels, yon chiels! He just pretended!" He would start walking up an' doon again, muttering to himsel', "Gode, I don't know."

'I took it very seriously mysel' for a time. We got in the way o' whispering aboot it at his back. Ye

could hardly help looking at him as he kept apart, an'
wondering in yer own mind if he had actually killed
a man. In a way, if ye'll understand me, it was sort
o' awful to think it. An' he would be catching us
looking at him. But when he'd get ye alone an'
speak to ye – then ye'd be cheery an' naetral to him
an' sort o' laugh it off. But there it was – an' him
being cut adrift more an' more, an' us showing more
an' more respect for him.

'Now one of the crew was a fellow we called "Tom-
the-Baltic." Whenever he got the chance he would
always get, as he would say himsel', "as fill as the
Baltic." He had a sort o' jealous nature and a nasty,
sharp tongue when he could get away wi' it. Weel,
this Tom-the-Baltic began to laugh at Jeck's back.
"Canna ye see he likes it!" he would say, meaning
that Jeck, if ye follow, was in a kind o' way enjoying
himsel'! Lord, it had never struck me like that, an'
I told Tom that he needn't think everyone had his
own nature. Howsomever, the idea got a hold on me,
an' I did find, one night that I laid mysel' oot to cure
Jeck for good an' all, that Jeck wouldn't take curing.
"Gode, I don't know," he would mutter. "I think I
knifed him. I feel sure o't."

' "Rubbish, man!" I told him. "He saw that ye
were stronger nor himsel', an' so he just crumpled
doon at yer feet. I've seen many a wrestler do the
same trick. If ye had followed him doon he would
most likely have got a hold o' ye by the back o' the
neck." "That's very kind o' ye," says Jeck, "to put
it like that. But you don't understand how the knife
– the knife – it went in . . ." "Devil the fear o't,"

says I; "just into his clothes." "I wish I could believe ye," says he, getting a little stubborn. "I only wish that." An' so we argued aboot – till I saw I had to stop.

'A night or two after that – I forget how it came aboot – but I can see it yet as though it was happening before my eyes at this very minute. Tom-the-Baltic had one or two inside him, an' Jeck was there wi' two or three o' us. Jeck said something – I forget what now, but Tom-the-Baltic's mouth opened back in a laugh. We all stiffened, waiting. An' slow an' deliberate, Tom-the-Baltic says:

' "Jeck the Giant Killer!" '

Jeems paused and peered at Tullach as though to assure himself he understood. But plainly Tullach's understanding was not appreciatively deep, and Jeems turned and spat in the fire, continuing:

'Oh, yes, Jeck would have killed him, would have killed him sure. Maybe he didn't actually kill the native, but he surely would have killed Tom-the-Baltic. It took three o' us to drag him off and hold him doon while we shouted to Tom to make for his life. An' when we were holding him doon the foam was coming through his teeth.'

'Ye seem to have been kept busy at it one way or another,' pronounced Tullach.

'Ah, ye've no idea, man,' nodded Jeems; 'no idea.'

'I suppose not,' said Tullach.

A pause.

'I mean – things oot yonder – it's no' like at home here. It's no' the same. Someway ye don't feel just the same.'

152

'Really,' said Tullach.

Jeems regarded the fire reminiscently, his brows puckered as in a slight ravel of thought.

'It's queer – yon,' he mumbled.

'Ye had yer fill o't anyway,' said Tullach.

'Ay – oh ay – in a way. It was dreich enough whiles.'

'Wi' the dancing girls an' them kicking their jingles.'

'Och, the dancing girls – it was just like going to a concert here or a traivelling circus.'

'So long as it was no more,' said Tullach.

'Ay ay,' observed Jeems, nodding thoughtfully to the fire.

Tullach watched him. The ould devil was backing out a bit now, as though he feared he might get the thing brought home to him.

'It's queer how things will remind ye,' nodded Jeems. 'It was speaking aboot the peats that minded me o' the camel dung.'

The reminiscent cast of his features never altered by a shade. Yet – the peats!

But the sudden metallic striking of the wag-at-th'-wa' arrested Tullach's satiric amaze, and brought home to him with a curious sense of expectant shock that Maggie's milking must be nearing an end. Yet here he was – still undecided! Here he was, listening to this old fool babbling of dancing girls and worse, while he, Tullach, sat frightened to give his own wild blood a chance. His simmering blood answered the mockery. Out there in the byre – alone; and him here, listening to the mad exploits and pluck of a

153

dotard! The visioning of that dark loneliness in the byre, the figure he had already seen blushing in red ripeness, whelmed him, and for a moment the old man wavered indistinctly through the rushing of blood to his eyes. He got to his feet.

'Well, we'll see about the peats.'

'Ye're no' off? Surely ye're no' off! Maggie'll be in in a minute.'

'Good night!' And with a short bark, Tullach turned to the door.

CHAPTER ELEVEN

HE strode to the byre. Damn, he would take Maggie in his arms, come what would! In the pulse of his deep recklessness he knew a satisfaction that exulted blindly. Where was the latch? Ay, hanging, of course. He put his hand against the door and it swung open before him. Silence and the lantern light and the animal smells of the byre, pervasive, lusty, animal smells; then a stride – and a convulsive stiffening.

The two figures were there, scarce a yard between their shoulders, looking at him, something in their eyes of tense expectancy passing into staring realisation, into acknowledgment, then into a slow hardening of intangible defiance in the case of Ivor, into a falling away of Maggie's eyes preparatory to some instinctive body movement that would snap with whatever naturalness could be assumed the impossible tension.

But Tullach gaped. Having had no warning, his mental processes were necessarily slower; realisation took longer in coming. Not until Maggie had actually stooped and picked up the creepie, did his face break.

'Ha! ha! ha!' very rapidly, an instinctive barking. 'Eh! Ye've company, Maggie!' The blood could be seen darkening his face, as it creased in a frightful mirthlessness.

'Yes,' replied Maggie, stooping and depositing the creepie in the corner.

Tullach's eyes gathered gleaming light, concen-

155

tration. Round this light the facial creases now wavered and grinned. From following Maggie, his eyes shot up to Ivor's.

'Eh?' he said, grinning most treacherously.

'A fine night,' said Ivor, with an effort at coolness too thickly obvious. His whole body had gathered taut and supple as a whiplash.

'Oh, a grand night for the race!' replied Tullach, and laughed again, the sharp, harsh echoes an incredible offence. For when the words had been shot out they gathered in their wake a consciousness of the current schoolboy jibe with its 'What race?' and the scoring answer, 'The human race!'

Ivor knew a slow gathering of murderous forces. Of their own accord his fists clenched. He swayed a trifle, what had been meant for a tentative answering grin, fading utterly.

'Eh?' said Tullach, the grinning word prodding like a goad.

But Maggie saved Ivor the necessity for any sort of answer. Turning from the creepie, she picked up the lantern and sent vast shadows swinging round the byre. With milk-pail in one hand and lantern in the other she took a step towards Tullach and the door.

Tullach hesitated, wavered, then half-stumbled sideways – to let Maggie pass.

'There's the calf to feed,' she said.

'Oh, the calf,' said Tullach, getting out of her way again.

'The coggie –' she began, setting down the milk-pail and throwing the lantern light into the darkness

156

by the door. Tullach brought the coggie. Her back to Ivor, her face to Tullach, she stooped and poured the calf's portion. Then righting the milk-pail, she carefully placed it to one side, so that Tullach, at whose feet was the calf's dish, had time to lift it and set it down inside the barrier. Raising the lantern, she balanced it on the wooden edge between Tullach and herself, leaving Tullach to guard the coggie against the antics of the calf, while she shed the necessary light. Behind them stood Ivor.

Stood watching, out of it. As second followed second, defiance, antagonism, got caught in the old web of personal futility, which now kept spinning itself out of his stiff awkwardness. Substanceless, of no account, out of it. . . .

'The calf is coming on,' said Tullach. 'Steady there, ye brute!'

Maggie's eyes never left the calf.

'He's about fit for the sale,' proceeded Tullach. 'Eh?'

'I suppose he is,' said Maggie.

The calf suddenly butting the coggie with un- expected force and spilling some of the milk, Tullach grunted and hit it heavily across the face. 'That's what ye need to keep ye in yer place!'

Appalling futility! Standing thus stiffly, ignored, behind them, became unbearable. Ivor had a vision of himself suddenly striding from the byre without a word, out into the night, striding. It was with a strong effort of will he kept himself from moving, some dogged sense of defiance, some perverse pride, holding him to his ground. That swift slap on the calf's face, too, touched the brute primitive in him like a whip-lash. It had been an exaggerated slap, plainly a momentary outlet of the brute primitive in Tullach. One could deal with things in that way. The thought hardened. There could be that, futile or not. His eyes, as they searched Tullach's back, narrowed and glittered. He remained without moving, until at last Tullach straightened himself, bringing the coggie with him.

'Well, that's that!' said Tullach, looking at Maggie but failing to catch her expression, and continuing the straightening and turning movement of his body until his glance took in Ivor. His glance paused on Ivor.

Tullach felt himself in the baffling, maddening position of not knowing how most effectively to behave. There had penetrated a sneaking, twisting barb of a thought poisoning him with the idea that he was an intruder, a mean dog of an interferer, who instead of clearing off stuck on against every sense of dignity or decency – and, particularly, that they thought so. His only weapon against this poisonous idea was one of behaviour, to behave in a way as nearly natural as possible so that he might not appear to be conscious of intruding. Such considerations swirled about the major instincts with an ineffectiveness which got steadied for the first time when his questing eyes now got fixed by Ivor's, and instinct met instinct nakedly. But a moment, and Maggie had the shadows swinging drunkenly, blotting out all stark outline in a grotesque dance.

She stood waiting for Tullach to make way by going on before her.

There seemed no reason for Tullach's throaty laugh as he turned to the door in a sudden heavy lurch. He swung it open, and Maggie waited for him to pass out. He passed out. Maggie followed with lantern and milk-pail, the dog at her heels. As Ivor emerged, she laid down the milk-pail as with the usual intention of snecking the door. Ivor snecked the door. She saw his face.

Tullach was given the opportunity of lifting the milk-pail – but no, he was having no more of that now! To snatch at the polite chance of cleverly having the final good night at the back door, without being directly asked by Maggie – by no means! Of such doubtful clevernesses Tullach shared the seaboard's instinctive derision. His gorge rose now at tricks, rose at everything that might interfere with the almost brutal urgency for vindicating his dignity. The possible relations between Ivor and Maggie he faced not at all, after the first blind moments. They existed as an undeterminate knot of feeling, which could be unravelled in direct contact with this young fisher fool who had not two pennies to rattle against each other.

They all three stood at the door. The dark, unmoving moment seemed without end, when Maggie broke it, half-turning to Ivor:

'Well, good-bye, Ivor,' she said quietly. Then, infusing a slight, timid warmth of gaiety: 'I hope you have a good fishing – a very good fishing to you.'

He started, swayed on his feet.

'Thanks – thanks,' he said. 'Well, I'll be off.' And instantly he strode from them, level stride upon stride, his body glooming indistinctly until it faded completely by the ditch-side. Hand-shaking was not a facile custom on the seaboard.

She picked up the milk-pail.

'Well, I must be in.' Her voice was immeasurably cool, self-possessed.

Tullach could not find a word to say; emotion itself was stifled. What did force itself upon his mind was so cast in the nature of perverted jocular reference to the meeting in the byre, with a satiric prompting to 'draw' her brutally, that the very coarseness in its grain, fronting her calm self-possession, denied him words.

Yet before she actually took the first step, he said involuntarily:

'I went in – without knowing.'

The enigmatic indefiniteness pulled Maggie up, but, as it seemed, only long enough to make her pause to say:

'Oh, that.'

'Ay, I had no idea.' His enigmatic tone firmed just perceptibly.

'No, you wouldn't have, I'm sure,' she agreed, conversationally.

But he felt his thought gradually gathering to an outlet, and this mental directioning drew in its wake the whole pack of instincts and desires.

'No. Had I known it was like that. . . .'

She should have let it go at that, but the tortuous challenge in his voice was rather much.

'Like what?' And she moved a step towards the door, not abruptly, yet with a polite sense of withdrawal.

He followed her, his purpose growing clearer, with a feeling that at any moment he would corner her in such a way. . . .

'Eh! Like what!'

From his advance Maggie turned wholly, and –

'Is that you, Jeannie?' she enquired of the shadows by the door.

'Yes,' came Jeannie's timid voice.

'And you, Tibby?'

'Yes.'

She turned to Tullach.

'Good night,' she said evenly, nodded, and, speaking to the little girls, ushered them in at the back door.

Until the door had actually closed, Tullach remained rooted at the spot where he had first become aware of the presence of the little girls. And she had known all the time! . . .

Done! Fooled! . . . Exclamations of the sort laughed in his brain as he turned from the house, echoed uproariously, and between each echo his jaws ground together and curses choked.

He walked from the croft directly towards the brae-heads, but half-way there he abruptly stopped, looked back to the croft, began walking to and fro, prey, now that he was alone, to every sort of vain imagining. For in addition to the evening's subtle undermining of his dignity, of his self-assurance, of his power, there came a first breath of the positive emotion of jealousy.

That he would own Maggie in due course had
been as accomplished a fact for his mind as his working of the croft. It had even been so certain that at
times he had felt he was doing too much on the croft,
but had continued to do it with a warming sense of
magnanimity.

And now – what if he never got Maggie at all?
Never got her at all, eh! He strode up and down,
his mind almost numbed in its first sheer amaze.
The working of the croft – for nothing! Everything – for nothing! The joke seemed altogether
too vast for possible perpetration. Yet . . . eh?

Blindly he strode. These two – how far had it
gone? How long had it been going on? Every
night? In the byre yonder, together . . . kissing
each other, their arms round each other, straining.
. . . Gode!

He cleared his throat raucously and spat on the
night. That going on! Had it? Eh? Had it? . . .
The question tortured him, while his mind rushed
on imaginary intimacies. The imaginary intimacies
obsessed him till he could hardly tear free from their
twining octopus arms. A twisting akin to physical
strangling gripped his whole body, became insupportable. Gode, he would smash the fellow –
pulp him!

He started instantly for the ditch-side where not
so long since Ivor had disappeared. Possibly he was
lingering about the ditch-side yet – with intentions.
Ah, possibly lingering about the ditch-side yet –
. . . with intentions. With intentions, eh? A
throaty, chortling sound issued between his teeth.

With intentions! Tullach's sinewy fists shut and unshut, while his face grinned in horrible contortions. His approach became more wary, his quick eyes darting. . . .

But Ivor had strode steadily down the ditch-side, down the whin-bank above Hendry's croft, to the cliffs, evenly, pretty much as he had foreseen he would but now actually with much less passion, with hardly any passion at all. She had dismissed him – and Tullach had remained.

Well, there it was; that was that. Everything had its end; everything. He walked, head erect, eyes questing the far grey strip of the horizon. So this was an end. He had the wearied sense of the tide of the body having ebbed. That murderous black wave which had surged up and over him in the last moments in the byre had spent itself on nothing. Only dark eddies here and there, of self-contempt, of realisation of his nothingness; satiric black eddies with phosphorescent gleams, gleams of cold, mocking light, showing now and then in a twist of the features, the gripping of a fist.

But underlying all this surface acknowledgment of the facts, this mockery of self-chastening, lay depth upon depth of bitterness, dammed up by the utter futility of its recognition.

He sat down in a grassy dip near the cliff-head, eyes to the sea. It was plain that he no longer had any quarrel with Tullach. That was a pity, a vast pity. Had his dismissal not taken place so obviously, he could have had a quarrel with Tullach. At this minute he might be waiting for Tullach. They would meet – thrash at it – welt upon welt. Sweet. He could smash Tullach in the end. He knew it in every swift-flexing muscle of his body. Smash! smash! – fist in his face; jumping back and in – smash! smash! His knuckles tingled.

It would not only be smashing Tullach, but also in some way smashing at all Tullach owned. It would not only be a victory but also a vindication of inalienable manhood, which should be more, as his bitterness felt, than any chance business of possessions. But that was where the utter folly of his bitterness had to be dammed.

One lived and married on possessions. Without them – the grey poverty, nothing.

There was no good either in his bitterness having a fling at Maggie. Perhaps, for all he knew, she wanted the man himself. . . . But no, Gode, he could not accept that yet! Not that! Not that! His mind griped in a convulsion and time passed over him.

Raising his head again presently, things appeared to him in a wearier, finer clarity.

Tullach and his possessions represented a good match for any girl, a fine match. Tullach himself – there was nothing against him. Maggie–it was not only certain she would accept – it was inevitable. Every girl would do the same, and every man and woman in the district would account her lucky. That was merely the law of things. Measured against Tullach, what had he to offer? Mockery of mockeries! . . . The thing was settled. . . . And for all he knew, she wanted the man himself.

He faced it this time, bleak-eyed. For all he knew. Could he think otherwise? Had he any right to think otherwise? . . . He did not propound these questions in so many words to himself, but on the heels of an intuitive sense of them came the deduction that, therefore, he had no quarrel against Tullach. He might want to smash the man's face for the satisfaction of his own bitterness, but that, in the circumstances, could be no satisfaction to Maggie! No, hardly any satisfaction to Maggie, in the circumstances! There had been Tullach, working the croft for them, helping, going in and out, for years. He and Maggie . . . it was inevitable. And now here he was himself, talking at large about smashing Tullach! Fool! Gode – what a fool! What a bluidy, empty fool! . . .

A thudding on the grass near at hand; footsteps. A figure bulked suddenly. Tullach!

Ivor's body, doubled up like a boulder, stiffened immovably, every muscle tense, breath held, while crawling over his brain went a thin cold shiver of hate. The thing was upon him here at the cliff-heads – the cliff-heads, with that headlong emptiness down over them. The shiver became an exulting madness. Nearer, nearer – now, now . . . he could grip an ankle with his fist . . . the stertorous peching of the swine was thick above him . . . now . . . thud! thud! – Tullach was passing, thud! thud! . . . gone past him.

Tullach had missed that boulder-like figure in the slight hollow between the indiscernible path and the brow of the cliff, and that figure still crouched as

165

though the body had got cramped in a prisoning nightmare of inaction.

The nightmare snapped and the body was on all fours like an animal, by the path-edge, peering after the disappearing form, silhouetting it against the grey night-sky, panting thickly, torn in a frenzy of whirling indecision.

Why shouldn't he? Why? Oh, why? cried a voice within him, whipped the voice. How could Tullach have missed him, anyway? How could he? If Tullach hadn't missed him, if Tullach had by chance kicked him, given any excuse, anything. . . .

After all, that was it: he needed an excuse to attack Tullach, something as slight as that tripping kick; anything would serve; but he could not deliberately trap the fellow, smash him without any excuse, could not – with Maggie at the fellow's back. It was Maggie who had prisoned him in that momentary inaction.

Yet he could not let it go at that. Some unthinkable chance might arise. . . . He got warily to his feet. Where was Tullach going, anyway? Where had he been? Plainly he had been to the village. As plainly he was going home. Yet he might not be going home. And if he wasn't going home – then where?

Even as he followed, he was aware that he was following because he could not help it; because he could not screw himself up yet to an acceptance of Tullach, of his own eternal emptiness. Could not leave Tullach alone. And his dislike for doing what he was doing curdled an extra venom. He would follow him up. Something can always happen. . . .

Presently, at a certain point, he went flat on his stomach, eyes questing away in front where a short, pronounced slope in the gentle rise should throw part of a figure against the sky-line. Something suddenly moved against the grey, a bobbing head – inward; going inward – most indubitably Tullach going back to the croft!

Ivor watched the bobbing head as though he could not credit his sight.

'Great Gode!' he gasped.

This was beyond everything! Rage swamped utterly all consciousness of irrationality, and instantly he was following Tullach with a remorseless wariness.

He lost all chance of a silhouetted glimpse once he got Tullach between him and the croft buildings, and, crouching low to the ground, he cut leftwards for the ditch, so that the house front should open up just sufficiently for the front door to be commanded, and the back door and outbuildings to be under peering observation.

Flat on his stomach along the ditch bank less than a stone's throw from the square of yellow light in the kitchen window, he watched, teeth grinding on a withered grass stalk that they bit from the soil. He would see now what Tullach was up to. Finally and definitely, he should know.

Nothing moved by the front door, nothing at the back. As minute followed minute his jaws ceased from their grinding, his body grew rigid in expectancy, in insupportable suspense. Where could

Tullach have gone? Where could he have gone? Was he, like himself, watching the house, waiting for someone to come out? Or – his fists clenched on the grass – was she out already? Round at the back of the barn there? Even – in the barn?

No, not in the barn! Hardly in the barn! He thrust his face into the cool grass and gripped at the old earth, held on. No, hardly in the barn!

Why not in the barn, eh?

But no; argument was impossible because it was unbearable. He choked the inner logical devil instantly, and with eyes on the buildings, watched, waited, forcing his mind to a blank of expectancy.

But nothing happened; no move, no sound. Except for that yellow patch the buildings huddled utterly lifeless, inert. No cry, no whisper. Yet Tullach was there somewhere, crouching, waiting, or – or some unthinkable thing else.

Minute followed minute. He suddenly found himself drawing his body up the ditch-side inch by inch, and finally desisted only when he saw he might lose sight of the window light.

And just as he desisted, a shadow moved across the window blind, ould Jeems's shadow. A second or two and candle-light flickered in the ben window. The old man was going to bed. A second shadow crossed the kitchen blind. Maggie's shadow. A moment and there was the distinct clicking of the front door lock. Locking up for the night.

It was early to lock up for the night. Surely it was early, unusually early. Why so early? Why was she locking up so early, locking up – *the front door?*

The acuteness of his mind in suspicious speculation became ungovernably, shamefully intense. He crawled nearer, inch by inch, sight straining on the back door, until he could crawl no farther without leaving the cover of the ditch. If anything went in – or came out – by the back door there could be no hiding it from him now.

Once he thought he heard footsteps dying away in the field beyond the house in the direction of Tullach, but got the sound so mixed up with an instant thudding of his heart that he could not be sure. And the longer he listened the more certain it seemed that there could have been no footsteps.

The point came where the tension had to be broken in a deliberate reasoning effort. He lay close. After all, all he had to do was to lie close. He could become dogged at the job for that matter. He could last anybody out. All he was there for – was to make sure.

A long time passed. He found himself getting cautiously to his feet, crossing on tiptoe to the barn, going all round and into the barn, round the byre, round all the premises until he came to the ditch-side again. The kitchen light was now out. Maggie must have gone to bed.

He sat down, lips twisting, brain sardonically questioning. Had he in some extraordinary way been fooled? Yet how? He could get no grip on the business. A malevolent sense of insecurity beset him. It was certain that Tullach had gone as far as the steading; equally certain that Maggie had never come out of the house and that Tullach had made no effort to get in touch.

He got up, walked uncertainly away, looking back now and then at the dark croft house. Finally his face twisted up in a slow, bitter smile, and he spat the blade of grass from his mouth.

CHAPTER TWELVE

IN the harbour the following morning there was an unusual stir of life. Three boats, the last of their race in Balriach, rode the slight swell which came in round the corner of the quay, bows dipping in slow, easy acknowledgment of the old pulse of the sea. They knew the pulse of the sea in all its fevers, from the languor of its exhaustion to the smashing of its delirium. They nodded to it now, ready; a grace in their lines, exhaling a pleasant tang of fresh tar, of new paint; a trim, compact readiness for any encounter.

The first of them, her forefoot cutting the water at the very quay-point, rode *The Dawn*, skippered by Davie Mackay, with Sanny Ardberg second in command. There was a saying in Balriach that *The Dawn* had come after many a wild night, the sort of joke that had had its pale exultation of hope in the long night hours when the smashing seas seemed to be pounding the beaches of eternity. Perhaps Davie Mackay, with his wiry darkness and ready tongue, held something in his temperament that knew the thrills of chance and conquest, and instinctively reacted to them. Certain it was, anyway, that with his hand on the tiller *The Dawn* became a lady of uncanny spirit, leaping on the destructive forces with a heart that never faltered. And in these dark moments Davie had been known to shout to her above the screaming of the demon legions, 'Well done, my lassie!' And her whole body would shiver like a wild thing caressed.

171

Not that the inhabitants of Balriach were given much to hyperbole. Yet old Peter Sinclair, leaning on his stick at the corner of the braeheads, legs and back gripped in rheumatism, and altogether unable to make the quay, could not keep an excited laughter out of his eyes, a chuckling out of his throat.

'. . . my last fishing – but I'll never forget yon time. We had come oot o' Castlebay, making for the Lews, an' the farther we left Castlebay behind the worse it grew. Then rounding the Point yonder we ran into it thorough. Oh, thorough, boy! Clean from the Atlantic, smashing over her in white smok'. We were fully expecting everything to go clean by the board, waiting for it every second. Lashed there to the tillie was Davie. Boy! boy! the sicht o' him keeping her at it, an' no more thocht o' giving in than – than that coo there would have o' stopping eating the grass. Then in a heap, one byordinar lump struck her. She heeled. I knew she was off wi' it. But no, by Gode! An' then through that weather rose Davie's voice, crying at her: "You have cast one mast before, my bonny lassie: you can cast a second – and welcome!" '

Peter took a step or two, momentarily forgetting his rheumatism, stumbled, and clapped a hand to the small of his back.

The young schoolmaster, who had paused to speak to him before going down to throw a parting word of luck to the adventurers, did not laugh aloud, but Peter was satisfied with the way his eyes narrowed and lit up in a small measuring smile as though they were following the action in some inner visioning of excitement. Then the eyes turned on Peter and deliberately searched.

'That's as true as I'm standing here!' asserted Peter, flattered by that searching look. ' "You have cast one mast before, my bonnie lassie: you can cast a second – *and welcome*!" ' putting the English on it! 'Och! och!' Peter jerked his head, his reddish-grey whiskers jutting out of a flying, reminiscent humour. 'Ay ay!' His eyes fell away to *The Dawn*. 'Man, she was my leddy!'

The schoolmaster's eyes followed Peter's to the three boats against the concrete quay wall, with the line of folk knotted into a group opposite each. School children, not due at school for an hour yet, were dodging in and out, their shrill voices mixing with the clamour of circling and plunging gulls. Such of them as were fortunate would later exhibit by stealth to their fellows a Barra biscuit trophy while the master's back was to the class and his face to the blackboard. . . . His face to the blackboard, grouping chalk figures with plus and minus! A game, that! He saw Davie, the pleasantest and gentlest of men normally, with an eye ready to glint, a tongue equal to any challenge – saw him aft there, the warmth of a Castlebay dram still in his flesh, his brain flinging out a supreme challenge, eyes snapping – ready to sail his mistress down under, if that was her humour, to any Valhalla or Gehenna there be.

'Ay, he was the great laad, Davie,' came Peter's voice. 'Give him a dram an' things trying to be against him, an' ye wouldn't see him for smok'. But I'm speaking now o' the ould times. Things are no' what they were. It's changed days.' He paused, reflectively. 'Look at the cooperage yonder, wi' its roof falling in an' its windows broken an' boarded up. I'll sometimes be thinking the boarded windows are dead eyes. The thought came on me one night in the darkening an' them gaping there.'

The image, indeed, had arisen in the schoolmaster's own mind. Peter's idea that the times were not what they had been was literally true and not a token of the usual beliefs and regrets of age. Even the stir in the harbour this morning seemed to accentuate a subtle, pervasive sense of decay, the three boats themselves little more than a forlorn gesture against encroaching doom. The small concrete lighthouse structure for the harbour lamp at the quay-end tilted over above the water, a black gaping crack cleaving through the quay-wall some half dozen yards behind, so that the whole quay-end, lighthouse and all, was ready to block the harbour entrance whenever the sea had made up its mind to the desperate work. Farther in, the great stone wall that bounded one side of the basin sagged and bulged perilously, while the basin itself was slowly silting up with the ruthless inevitability of all natural processes. On the off shore, hauled boats lay rotting at their moorings with that indescribable stillness of decay about them which had once made the schoolmaster think of rotting dreams.

Times weren't what they had been. A hundred – two hundred – boats in the fishing season, gutters, fishcurers' stations, a teaming hive of life. What industry, carried on at what speed, with gaiety like

174

blown spindrift on the crest of it! Vanished – as a race vanishes! Why?

The schoolmaster stirred.

'I hear the Fishery Board won't do anything,' he said.

'Just that!' said Peter. And then after a moment, 'Nor the proprietor nor the County Council nor any council o't!'

'I suppose it's had its day and is dying,' said the schoolmaster.

'I suppose just that,' said Peter; then old visions suddenly stirring in his eyes, 'Man, ye see the refreshment hoose there wi' its rotten black roof that the gulls are painting all white – many's the queer time I've seen there! I mind once –'

The schoolmaster listened to Peter's story, told in circumstantial detail, careful of the racy minutiæ, lingering over realities that could still warm the old flesh, but he listened to it with an ear that caught at echoes of legend rather than at a recital of events scarcely a generation old.

Out of that old swarming of life, emotions and gaiety and work, a communal life self-contained, self-supporting, self-centred, could have been woven any web of vision, with a coloured thread of any motif twisting its thematic arabesques. But out of it as an echo of legend – the Fiona Macleods! Was that it? . . .

Peter was laughing, and the schoolmaster's smile showed an inner appreciation of the finished tale. Then he nodded to Peter.

'Well, I'll go down and see them off.' He pulled

out his watch. 'There is time for me yet.' And he started down the steep zigzag.

Folk nodded to him on the quay, their friendly greetings floating on an air of subtle courtesy. The boys duly dodged him in a game of exhilarating excitement. There was, in truth, a general excitement pervading the whole quay-wall. The adventurers themselves moved with a sort of relaxed deliberation, lolling back against a mast or winch with ready laughter or chaff or talk, and the next moment laying on a rope or catching something thrown from above with a restrained play of muscle that suggested inexhaustible reserves.

Altogether a fine body of men, blue-jerseyed, easy-swaying, sun-tanned, with open faces, and eyes that had an unconscious trick at odd silent moments of staring past one into invisible infinitudes. And perhaps in that stare was something more than a trick, for there was gravity in it, and the longer one considered it the more that gravity seemed of the essence of their unconscious attitude to life, like a steadfastness of fine integrity.

Everything was ready. Some hand-shaking, greater laughter, more chaff. 'See ye fill her to the gun'les! . . . Good shots to ye, Davie! . . . Keep the skimmer busy, boys! . . .' Mooring ropes were slipped from the bollards, dropped on board with a thud. With oar-purchase on the quay-wall, the crew of *The Dawn* soon had their lady sniffing the sea. Then krk! krk! krk! went the rhythmic song of the halliards as the great brown mainsail swung its lifting peak.

The pulse of the sea caught them, rocked them. Ivor felt it under his feet, a gliding heave and roll, a sinuous continuous passing underneath of an insecurity that no land knew, a living insecurity taking them to itself, cutting them off with a profound sense of finality.

Dipping and rising, already a different smell in the air he breathed, the sea smell, a broad salt-water tang from all the oceans of the earth.

Cheers came from the white strip of quay. *The Dawn* was perceptibly gathering way. Cheers of youth. Hurray! The eyes of one or two women brightened, filled. No answering cheers from the crew: merely smiles at youth's exuberance, a wave of the hand, a nodding, pleasantly-flung 'So long!' Most casual of all adieus!

Gathering way; Davie at the tiller, issuing his occasional word quietly, but with expert eye to the sail and to windward. The two other boats were putting out. They would never pass *The Dawn*. There would be no show of racing, of course; hardly a word amongst the crews themselves – but nothing would pass *The Dawn* though every canvas stitch and every human sinew were stretched to bursting point in the endeavour. It is better to start behind and play with the leeway than start first and be surely passed. Philosophy of the sort saves heart-burning – and gave *The Dawn*, by the same token, the quay-point berth.

She was perceptibly lying over to it now, alive in every plank. The quay was slipping behind, its back wall shutting out the line of folk, except for such as climbed precariously on to that back wall or peered round from the very quay-point.

Soon they opened out the cliff-tops and the long straggling village of Balriach. The land was already curiously diminished in bulk, the houses like squatting pigmy houses with sunk claws holding them to the earth in a dour immobility. Securely fixed there, earthed in the one eternal spot. The sea-board now swept for miles on either hand, curving just perceptibly from headland to headland in a marginal line of sheer rock-face. A grey strip, backed by far inward moorland crest sweeping eastward, and to westward by broken-backed mountains culminating in a peak that was the fisherman's loadstar, the first far glimpse of approaching homeland. How tiny the croft patches, how insignificant those midden scratchings of the earth! To think that men could live on them, squeeze out of them children and gaiety and rancour and Calvinism and a jealous God! How numerous, too, unexpectedly numerous on a broad survey, the croft houses and scratchings! To think that so many could exist on so little! Pigmy figures, grey molehills of houses, moving specks of cattle beast or horse.

Ivor's eyes, not in suspicious fixity that might draw attention but in a negligent roving, took in with precision the whole of Jeems's croft. Nothing moved on it. Nothing. The grey flick of thatch, the black blot of byre and barn, the dark-ploughed plot. A toy croft, lifeless as a toy. A sudden yearning came to a lump in his throat. The flesh on his cheeks stiffened as his teeth closed behind his closed lips –

and the eyes roved easily, only an involuntary lowering flicker of the eyelids indicating any secret inner stress. . . . Then the flicker steadied in a faint indefinable irony, an imperceptible hardening of bitterness. Tullach farm-house and steading made an altogether bigger blot, dug its claws into the earth with an aggressive immobility, a latent power, a squatting self-sufficiency.

Ivor turned slowly to look behind him. The *Sea Swallow* and the *Endeavour*, brown sails gleaming in a burst of sun, were in their wake. They heeled to it gamely, crowding every ounce of wind they could properly steal on every inch of sail.

But Davie sat quietly, casting no look behind. Ivor caught his eye flicker from sail to sheet. He might ease off a shade or haul closer. There were innumerable factors, from the wind that might die down if the sun decided to come out for the day, that would shift point by point possibly in any case, to the north-about course with its tidal currents and landfalls.

'I think we might ease an inch,' suggested Davie to Sanny.

'Ay,' said Sanny.

The slope of *The Dawn's* deck became just perceptibly steeper. Big Jock Swanson, fair-haired, full-faced, stretched himself in a careless easing of cracking joints, and in the process succeeded in taking in the two boats behind. As in an unthinking indolence, he kept looking at them, saw them take off a shade, too; then with a sly smile forcing its way through his elaborate unconcern, he turned back

179

again, and on the way met Jimmy's eye. Jimmy
Mackay was nephew of the skipper, the youngest
of the crew, cabin boy, skimmer, twenty years of age,
and every inch the man, but with all of youth's
gayest irresponsibility in his well-knit eel of a body.
His left eyelid now went the length of a half-wink to
Jock Swanson, who half-acknowledged it before
turning away.

The smile started involuntarily to Ivor's face as
he followed the by-play, and a zest for the game
caught him in a momentary thrill. This was living,
anyway: no stodginess here. A man's game. A
cutting-adrift. Continuous vigilance, uncertainty,
chance. There was this anyway, with the unknow-
able ahead.

He shifted to take in the croft again, and instantly
his eyes were riveted on a spot of white that waved
to and fro, three times while he watched, on the very
cliff-head down from the croft, then vanished utterly.

For a moment astonishment so gripped him that
he glared in all openness, body rigid. Then remembering himself, he stole a casual half-glance about
him. No one else had noticed. Settling himself
comfortably, he set his eyes to lie dreamily on the
rocks – with a vision that missed nothing. His
heart-beats had suddenly thudded, so that it took a
few seconds before speculation could question.

And speculation was inclined to more than questioning, to more than satire, once it got going. As
though Maggie had come down there to wave to
him! Instinctively he shifted round to shield his
expression.

No more preposterous waving; no more indication of anything; as though the white speck had been an illusion. Perhaps a gull gone mad! Perhaps – But it was no good sneering heavily like that. It had been someone.

Anyway, even if it had been Maggie waving, even if she had been waving to him, which was the mad thought his spirit had first leapt to, what then? What did that signify? Anything more than a friendliness which was worse than any mockery? . . . Mockery! Mocking him! There he went again! What the devil was his mind jumping about like that for!

Feelings were swift and wordless and ran the gamut of speculation with a jeering impatience in which there was something centrally hard and fierce. . . . His lips curled in a grin. Taking the thing seriously! Actually taking the thing seriously – as though something had been meant! Thought he had done with all that last night! Oh! . . . Whistling softly a note or two, he turned and bespoke Jimmy:

'I bet ye've forgotten to take the cards wi' ye!'

'What d'ye bet?' asked Jimmy readily.

But that night he did not go below early. 'Don't feel like it yet. I'll have another smoke,' he said to Jimmy, alongside whom he slept in the forward bunk up against the bulkhead. The sun had gone down in a flame of blood red, paling through rose overhead to a final ethereal green. A haze crept over the land giving it a curiously detached mysteriousness to the watcher from the sea. He took out his pipe and, lighting it, sat very still, eyes on the land.

The ravelled perversity of his feelings, the self-jeering bitterness that is manhood's dark safeguard, smoothed out into a condition of being as detached from him in a way as the land, as mysterious, as impersonal. The preceding nights of wild thought, of mental struggles rendered the more exhausting in that there had been nothing on which to lay hold but bodiless futility, had had a whole day of toil and sea and wind to help to induce at last the quiescent state.

And now this enwrapped mysteriousness of the land drew his detached spirit, not beckoningly, but with a sudden strange poignancy, self-induced. He regarded it wide-eyed, its indifference to all human longings, its queer beauty, its fathomless brooding wonder, for itself, of itself, complete.

He had never seen it quite like this before, never felt it so near the pulse of indefinable desire. Something in it strange, unreal, like . . . the schoolmaster's poetry! The schoolmaster, then, had his queer longings – and the poets who wrote the lines were men, with the longings, too! And so all that stuff about the cabin and the bean-rows was a sort of longing thrown out towards that land there.

Ay, it was foolish that, but not worth the while jeering at now. For that land there was a land of crofts and mean, hard soil and mean, hard men, mean and hard because poverty-stricken. That's what the mysteriousness covered. Obvious enough the bitter truth underneath it all.

Yet now – there it lay, so remote, indifferent, beautiful. On a night like this surely one might live in it, sit at a croft door, and watch the darkness come on the blue hills to the west as he had seen it come many a time. And with him – or moving behind him there in their house, their cabin for that matter – Maggie. He could hear the sound of her feet there moving behind him. The sound of her feet moving behind him. The sound of her feet moving about became a music too sweet to bear, and on the pipe which he had taken from his mouth a fist knotted.

CHAPTER THIRTEEN

To Maggie, feeding the hens in the grey morning, the night that was gone was a memory of one acutely persistent thought. It had attacked her in all ways, boring in unerringly, creating a network of logic within which her flushed flesh had turned and tossed unavailingly. But only in fitful sleep had the full power of the thought been exercised. For only in her sleep could she do what she had not done when saying good-bye to Ivor by the byre door, while retaining Tullach, could she shake his hand. In her sleep her fingers closed round his – and spoke to him.

Exquisite, idiotic torture that of the missed hand-clasp. If only she had had the wit at the moment she could have let him feel through her finger-tips the pressure of her heart's pulse. And in some way which she could not explain she knew that pulse would have been met by pulse, and a memory created which would have lingered persistently, drawing him back. Felt so certain of it that not even the thought, 'I'm just thinking that because I didn't do it,' could banish it.

Fool that she had been! after having carried through the impossible situation so well, after having kept them apart. She had said good night to Ivor, had sent him away – so that Tullach might remain with her alone! That was not only the way it must appear, it was actually what she had intended should happen. Yet if only she had stretched out her hand . . .

And now the grey morning with a strange empti-

184

ness in its feel and vision as though an eternal farewell had drawn the living virtue out of it and left a spent ghostliness of unreality. It required an effort of will almost to break the way her eyes had of growing round and gazing fixedly, to refrain from sitting down and folding her hands in her lap and staring before her for ever.

She went about her tasks automatically, the memory of her night thoughts and desires clear to her mind, but altogether drained of their poignancy. Once during the night she had longed for Ivor in a swift, whelming cry-out of longing; had caught him, hung on to him blindly, not caring what he thought. She remembered it now. Wanted to sit down and gaze the memory into an unending vagueness of something eternally lost.

The flush of the night was still in her skin. She felt it there as a curious surface warmth, a spent warmth that would shiver at a breath. Empty unreality of life, of grey morning; immaterial husks drained of all pulse-beats through mornings to come to the end of time. If only she could sit down and gaze and gaze, so that she needn't think, but slip down, and down. . . .

She scraped the hens' dish carefully and returned to the back-place. Her thought was too vague, lacking in passionate urgency, to compel action of its own accord. The fatalism bred of the grey coast, woven into the stones and soil of it, came out in its fruits. Maggie could have her longings and desires, but the law was to endure and to accept.

And in the strength of the longings overcome

might the measure of acceptance be gauged. As eight o'clock drew near, her vision began to flit about the harbour. She had seen the setting out many a time, had played in and out the string of folk on the quay. She wondered if Kirsty was there. As a rule, the married women did not go. Some of them might be seen in the distance, watching. As a lassie it had seemed to her natural enough that they should not go. All married women were old, and that mothers of them should go and laugh and chatter about a quay would have been unthinkable. But she understood better now! She could not have gone herself. But she could see herself stealing quietly up to a group of women, standing by Kirsty's side, smiling and looking and waiting. She could see it, could feel it, smiling there and talking away, and the heart heavy. . . .

A quarter to eight. She wavered, poised on a thought, then suddenly set about getting breakfast, swiftly, silently, so that no clatter of haste might indicate any unusual purpose.

Her uncle's querulous glance from the clock, she met calmly. He had been a bittie tired, forfochin, last night when he had taken his candle, and had thought that maybe he mightn't have his breakfast quite so early as usual. His tiredness had seemed a sort of comfort in which he had stretched himself with show of some complacency. He had glimpsed Maggie's face when she had come in from the milking. Possibly he had found there evidence of an unconcern a trifle overdone.

'Was that Tullach's voice I heard?' he had asked

with the most casual air. She had hesitated a second, then:

'Ay.'

'I thought he might meet ye on the way,' in a voice that 'passed it off.'

Now Tullach could not have met her on the way, could not have met her without deliberately waiting for her outside or joining her inside the byre. The thought of Tullach standing waiting outside the byre door for however short a time was the sort of impossible humour that could not spontaneously occur to either mind. So the old man knew that Tullach must have been in the byre, and, by way of it, never let on!

A sudden twist of anger bored through Maggie's brain, sending it blindly searching for a word that would be a sting. And it did not help her to know that she actually refrained from saying anything at all out of a sense of instinctive cunning that left her uncle's thoughts to take what colour they liked. Her uncle was too cute to force matters, but it would keep him from interfering, from that horrible 'Has he said a word?' if he thought that things were duly moving to their appointed ends. Mean, exasperating acknowledgment of cunning! And he had stretched his ould body, thought he would do himself the luxury of a few extra minutes in bed.

And now here he was, looking from the clock in grunting, querulous enquiry. Maggie paid no attention.

'Ye're gey sharp on it th'-day!'

She threw a computing look at the clock.

'Not much earlier than usual.'

'Oh, ye're no', are ye?'

She did not answer him; laid his bowl of milk by his steaming porridge. He muttered, mixing the porridge noisily with his spoon.

'It looks most desperate hot!' He slapped it this way and that. 'Terrible hot. Foo-o-o!' He blew on it. 'Oh, it's hot! How can anyone take porridge as hot as that?' Then he tried its heat, and instantly opening his mouth wide, breathed rapidly in and out to cool the drop on his twisting tongue. In a little he managed to swallow it. Then he slapped the spoon, which he had been waving to and fro, into the porridge and wiped his eyes.

'That's terrible porridge. What ye can be thinking o', dishing porridge like that, beats me. Foo-o-o! Every morning it's the same – though ye know I just can't stand it. Foo-o-o!' He was very mad, and his exaggeration in that 'every morning' was the measure of it, for though he had found it hot two mornings out of the last three, normally, and often for months on end, it exhibited the lukewarm placidity of his liking.

Maggie's unconcern was tinged with a faint derisive annoyance she cared not to hide.

Her uncle proceeded to an elaborate spreading out of the porridge on the wings of his plate. The wag-at-th'-wa' struck eight.

He took a long time over his porridge, scraping a little from the plate-edge on to his spoon, allowing it to lie in the milk for an appreciable time, sucking it into his mouth with ostentatious care, then pushing out some more matter from the central body to cover the vacant spot on the edge. Maggie was up and already busy in the back-place before he had finished. As he pushed his plate from him, Maggie, entering, immediately cleared it. The immediacy of the action was not missed.

'Oh ay, I'm finished,' he observed.

'I wonder what weather's on her th'-day!' he mumbled, stretching for his cutty to the mantel-shelf. 'Something, ye may be sure!' He dealt faithfully with his cutty and at some length, a disgruntled pech of satire relieving the general mental situation from time to time. Then puffing voluminously, he turned to the window. His eyes caught the newly-sown corn-patch, and the sucking smacks gathered a fine easy-going fullness, an unction. The bit ground looked fresh. Ay, just that. Uhm! Looked fine and fresh. He made for the front door and considered the ground anew. Oh ay. It was all right. He stood on the doorstep many contemplative seconds, then turned away to the outhouses, where Maggie would be pottering about, busy most like at something or other.

There was so sign of Maggie, however. Instantly an indefinite grievance moved in him. He had nothing particular to say to her, yet he had seen all along that there had been some sort o' weather on her. Her and her hot porridge! What she could be on to now beat him. He cleared his throat and spat fully. 'Get oot the way, ye brutes!' he admonished the hens, with a hardening eye on a great gawky cock. 'Ah, ye!' and he half-lunged at him. The cock

189

took one or two dancing strides, head and twinkling eyes so high that his feet struck the ground audibly. 'Kok! kok! kok!' he said, in inane astonishment. 'I'll kok-kok ye!' replied Jeems pithily.

Without, however, following up his threat, he shambled round the barn corner. She was not about the place at all. In an instinctive gesture, he lifted his eyes to the sky and let them fall along its expanse to the sea. 'It'll hold,' he muttered of the weather. He gazed at the sea in a long look, the seaman's look, and the trivialities of his humour slowly faded into a steady gravity. Presently the tail of his eye caught a sail and he remembered that this was the morning of the boats' departure for the West fishing. 'That's *The Dawn*,' he muttered, satisfied as to the cut of her mainsail even at that distance. A light came into his eyes and in their open regard they never wavered. Once or twice he nodded and shifted his stance. When the three sails had been before him for some little time, he began walking up and down, up and down, and in his nostrils was the old smell of the sea, and in his blood an indefinable disturbance, in which any memory of Maggie's existence had no part.

And Maggie, in the grassy fold by the cliff-head, had forgotten the croft's existence, as though not only her body but her thought hovered on a precipice's brink. The under sense of being eyried was indeed so real that a beating and fluttering in her breast asked for relief in some wild headlong outspreading of wing. A dangerous excitation that, however, she had to make no conscious effort to curb.

For above the fluttering her eyes remained steady on *The Dawn*, her mind debating with itself in a wordless hesitancy, in a turmoil of intuitions and fears and hopes. Her intention seemed a monstrously foolish thing now that she was here, a futile intention past any chance of carrying out. Yet her mind lived on it hungrily, greedily. She had not thought of *The Dawn's* looking so small, standing so far out, a consideration that at once helped her conspiracy of secrecy and defeated its object.

It was not, however, until she had crawled round the edge of the grassy depression to ensure that she would be unobserved from the land, and thereupon in a wild thumping of her heart had waved a bunched white apron back and fore, back and fore, to the brown wings of *The Dawn*, that she realised what great folly she had been indulging. The blind impulse impelling to action once satisfied, her mind cleared appallingly.

Supposing they had seen the action from *The Dawn*! All of them! Had she been thinking that he alone would see and understand? Each boat carried its spyglass. Supposing at this moment . . . She slipped to the bottom of the grassy declivity and lay still, her face plunged in the grass.

Presently, deep down, there stirred a rebellious feeling whispering that nothing mattered if only he had seen, if only somehow he could have got an inkling. . . . What did she care for the rest of the crew, for anyone else anywhere, if only he had seen the waving as a – sort of hand-shake. . . . Besides, she might have been waving to Sanny, to the boat generally. Even if they had seen the waving they might not have thought of her at all. And certainly they wouldn't have had time to get the glass. . . .

Foolish, tortuous argument. She was just beaten. She lay a long time, too spent to care. . . . As she returned by the whin-bank, instead of straight on the barn, she knew that she was avoiding – as she had avoided going out – being observed from Tullach. Why?

She found her uncle mucking the byre. He looked up at the sound of her footsteps, peered at her face as she passed, then stooped again to his task, the sound of his hoe as it scraped the causey following her into the house.

The day lay before her, and then days on days, every one the same; resignation the keynote, if it is possible to conceive such resignation being keyed to anything; an even greyness, a living in it. Out of it occasionally the spirit might flare in tortuous spasms of desire or longing, as it had flared – to sink back again like a guttering candle. The momentary rebellions or blind spasms meant nothing, could mean nothing, because they could lead nowhere. Therein lay the beginning and the end of resignation.

She went through the same performance with Nance in the darkening as she had done the previous evening. Only she did not struggle with her. She levered her away from the calf and into her stall with the hoe. A cold indifference had come on her spirit, an unfeeling that could rap Nance smartly without rousing any note of over-ready pity. 'Stand

192

up, there!' She got the chain ask round her neck and turned indifferently to the door, yet not without an involuntary eye-flash at the opening and to her own clothes. But the opening was empty and her fingers found her hair all smoothly secure. Picking her steps with deliberate care, she passed out, closing the door behind her.

In the kitchen her uncle sat in a heap by the fire, his eyes staring vacantly into the heart of it. He had been sitting like that when she went out, thinking what endless thoughts? But, actually, she felt he wasn't thinking at all: he was merely staring, his mind a sort of vacant haze. Often Nance stared like that when she hadn't any calf to occupy her mind and her belly was full. She herself could stare like that, too. Things could combine to make one stare like that. And much more easily when the things were no-things. It was silly staring like that, vacant, empty. It could be irritating.

She took up her knitting, and as the needles clicked in and out she stared at them, but not with vacant eyes; not at all with vacant eyes. Every now and then they would snap and lift. They snapped and lifted in a dull anger that she could not explain, that had somehow come on her, and that would pass. Her uncle stirred.

'He's no' coming th'-night, surely.'

Her needles went on clicking.

'I was thinking he might be in th'-night; it's good weather.' He levered himself to his feet and took a spill from the mantelshelf; then, reseating himself, removed the lid from his pipe, pressed down the dottle, and set a flame to the half-consumed contents.

'It's good – smack! smack! – good drying weather.' Then he relapsed again, but more thoughtfully.

She threw a glance at him, but said nothing.

'Ye haven't heard if Angus has been at the hill yet? Murdo Campbell was saying that the banks are drying wonderful.'

So that was it – the peats! The peats – and Tullach. That was the next thing!

'I didn't hear,' she answered.

'I don't suppose you would,' he reckoned, with a simplicity that mightn't have been dryness to anyone but Maggie.

'No,' balanced Maggie.

The subject was left there.

In a little while he craned round at the clock, but made no comment.

Presently Maggie got up and the unobtrusive Roy accompanied her to the byre. But she did not speak to the dog to-night. Not that Roy minded, for life to him largely meant being taken for granted. Most of the day he lay curled up in a corner by the back door, sleeping or silently observant, and now and then nosing around with a speculative eye on the behaviour of his master.

Entering the byre, Maggie snibbed the door on the inside. If anyone should chance a hand on the outside latch, she would call: 'I'm just coming!' What if anyone did? Well, let them!

But as the milk went rhythmically hiss! hiss! into the pail, her mood waned, the edge on it dissolving altogether. Her forehead leant more heavily against Nance's hide. A faint weakness stole insidiously over her body, a weariness. 'I don't care,' she thought; 'I don't care,' making no effort to define her thought, yet not caring with a final lassitude in which there lingered a trace of bitterness like a prompting to tears. Hiss! hiss! went the milk, to be smothered in a frothy choking.

She felt her power ebbing, that cool guardian power. It was as well the door was barred. She might be smothered and choked like the milk, without the strength to hit out, without the strength to care.

But Tullach – he would not come that night. Surely he would not come. She divined the humour he might be in – a dark, sneering humour, a violent humour, the sort of humour that could hardly see itself competing with young fisher fools to lick the hands of ould Jeems's belongings. Not likely! Perhaps he would be saying to himself that the damn paupers could be getting someone else to do their croft for them and their peats. He would be black mad.

But she felt also that such a humour would not last. It might hang about him for weeks – but maybe only for a few hours, to end in a sudden decision to put everything to the test. So that he could come in on them any moment, tramping in, charged with a heavy, enveloping power.

Click! went the sound of a foot against a stone. Her hands stiffened, her heart leapt. Uncertain, light, wandering footsteps. Silence. She could hardly finish the milking, could hardly wring the last of the milk from the generous udder. All strength had left her fingers. She lay against Nance for a little. Nance shifted uneasily, lowed through her nostrils. Maggie got up.

The feeding of the calf took time. If it had been Tullach – he must now be in the kitchen. He would not hang about out there. And if in the kitchen – what was he waiting for, saying what?

She slipped the wooden bolt and went out, her questing eyes immediately discerning little Jeannie, who, it might have occurred to her, was invariably in good time. Had it only been Jeannie?

'Well, Jeannie!'

'Well.'

Maggie paused, wondering how she might put the question on her tongue.

'Was it you who came in by a moment or two ago? I thought I heard footsteps?' she asked lightly.

'Ay, it was me,' said Jeannie, in her quick timid way.

'I thought it was a big grown-up person's steps!' reckoned Maggie, in whimsical fun.

'No,' smiled Jeannie.

'Come in, then.'

From the back-place, Maggie could hear no sound. She must make sure, while she had yet an excuse to return to the milk pail, and, entering the kitchen, she observed her uncle still hunched up in his chair by the fire. He was alone, had obviously not stirred, did not stir now. Taking an unnecessary spoon from the drawer of the kitchen table,

Maggie went out, closing the communicating door behind her.

She spoke in a light pleasant voice to Jeannie, asking her whether she had seen the boats leaving in the morning and whether she would miss her daddy. Jeannie's replies were informative and polite. Patting her head, Maggie accompanied her beyond the back door.

'Are you sure you'll manage the four pails yourself? Where's Tibby th'-night?'

'Her mother asked her to go a message to Mistress Sinclair's at the braeheads.'

'I see. And how is Mistress Sinclair keeping?'

'I think she's keeping well, thank you. Tibby's mother was sending her a bit fish.'

'Oh, yes. Good night, Jeannie.'

'Good night.'

Maggie watched the little figure dwindle down the ditch-side and fade in the glimmering night. She stood a long time looking upon the silence and gathering mystery before her. In the silence was an ineffable loneliness bringing a lump to her throat. Something floated there so remote, withdrawn from her, it was like eternity.

She suddenly could not go in. On an impulse she flitted past the byre and hen-house, round the barn corner to the cairn of stones. There she paused – on a swift fear that a figure might come looming at her out of the night. She stood stiffly, looking on the grey sea-floor beyond the cliff-heads, but with senses strained, alert. She could not sit down. A sense of over-strain became unbearable. Not only that figure, but also the sea, the night, eternity itself, pressed in on her, with their power, their dark stifling power, choking her longings, her desires, before they could be born to her own thought, with a heedlessness, an utter heedlessness. . . . Swallowing the hot tears in her throat, she returned to the house to go about the last of the day's tasks.

CHAPTER FOURTEEN

The peat-bank was a very tiny cutting in the expanse of the moor and the figures that worked on it but so many moving specks to Tullach as he approached the scene from afar. But a sense of the immensities did not weigh on him, nor did his imagination conceive of himself as a correspondingly crawling speck on that sun-drowsed, immemorial waste. As the wheels of his trap crunched the gravelled moor-road peewits swung up on either hand, their wings and two-winged cry beating the air with a passionate vehemence. Pee-wit! pee-wit! the cry every now and then deepening midway to a sibilance of anxiety – pee-z-wit! – that swooped at him on drumming wing-beats of taut silk.

Tullach flicked his horse, the peewits but a manifestation of life that could be seen on a smaller scale in the persistent buzzing of bluebottles. The happy chance of the comparison, however, did not occur to him at the moment, for his mind was so steadily set on the peat-bank that its uncertain and indefinite workings were sufficient to engage his attention to the point of a brooding exclusion of all else.

The moor was very literally a waste, a dead place of peat-hags, and the gradual dip and then slow swell of it to the far mountain-sides on the west lay barren and utterly motionless under the clear sky. A day of summer, with spring's incredible youth in its sunlight: and the peat-bog lay under it with a still austerity that had an air about it of changeless-

199

ness and the eternities. A remoteness, a withdrawn, timeless silence, that might be a hushed waiting on the passing of the footsteps of God, or no more than the infinite unawakening of sodden death. In any case, a mover of the heart, austerity and immobility holding the flutter of its wings midge-like in space and time; nay, further, austerity and immobility drawing the heart to a communion known of it through all space and time.

Tullach flicked at a daring peewit with his whip, his face twisted in a sudden vindictive challenge. Not that a mere wanton cruelty moved him, but that out of the uncertainty of his mind irritability came edged. Moreover, he was drawing nearer every moment. However, he knew now what he would do — certainly up to a point. He would first of all pass the peat-bank on which the squad was working and go on to the greater bank – the Tullach bank – on which the squad had been at work the last three days. Not having been up yesterday, he must now inspect the completed Tullach cutting. The squad at the moment was working about a hundred and fifty yards back from the road on ould Jeems's bank. He would merely acknowledge them with his whip in the passing, and go on.

But after he had inspected his own banks and assured himself that their bellies were properly finished off for drainage purposes, he would return to ould Jeems's bank, stake Princie by the roadside, and go in over the heather to talk with Willie, who was on the tuskar and in charge of the operations. So far, everything would go smoothly.

At this point Tullach's thought balked. Maggie would be there. He would treat her, of course, as he would the others; that is, ignore her in a general nod. It is what the others would expect. But if he did it to Maggie – would he not – what then – His thought dodged the issue. It would be a sort of gesture of finality, driving Maggie – He had so little to go on, even her own real desires in the matter were so obscure. Driving Maggie – how? where?

He had not spoken to Maggie in a fortnight, not since the night he had caught them, that Cormack fellow and herself, in the byre. That night – how it had stuck in his gorge! Gode, how it had stuck! To think how he had been fooled! The torture of stringing night on night that the two of them must have been having together! How it had pursued him for black hours, for days; pursued him yet; with such an intimacy in the visioning of it! That night – how he had hunted the fellow, with a gluttony in his fists that would not have stopped short of killing him! The tortured, endless night thereafter. The lascerating of pride, of passion, of every atom of thought, of feeling, a rage, a madness, lashing itself into a cursing, rampaging lust of madness. What he would do! Ha! ha! ha! what he would do! Their bluidy croft an' their poverty, the bitch! That was her game! Great Gode, an' him ploughing the land for them and carrying on with the innocence of a babe unborn! . . .

All through the following day his madness accompanied him, but the hours had succeeded in hammering the red heat to a deadly edge. And sometimes the steel-chill of it touched his mind in a satisfying shiver.

But when night had come again and the darkness covered him, he stopped short of the croft, of the byre. His vision recoiled on him, fought him, and for all his cunning and blasphemous dodging, it fought him to a standstill. It was hard to endure, this vision of Maggie, not as a woman he would damn well deal with now thus and thus, but as a pale, challenging figure with eyes on him in that way. No one had dealt with that figure thus and thus. . . . He flung his arms at the thought, jeering, blasphemous. Hadn't they! Night on night! . . . But he could make no headway against those eyes, that figure. Without a flicker they barred his way to a standstill.

And it was, too, as though some traitorous thing in the depth of him helped her, as though this vision of her stood for a something, an inscrutable power, which dared him like a naked thought about innocence or God. And then secretly, beyond that traitorous thing, the wild leap of his mind – to possess for himself that fresh figure with its pale power and its innocence!

Balked, balked horribly; blasphemous derision instantly besmattering innocence or God; yet balked, there on the field by the very croft.

The days brought a more rational cunning to salve the wounds to pride and overlordship. He met Jeems on the main road to Balriach, drew up Princie and spoke to him.

'Ay, Jeems, d'ye think it's going to drought?'

Jeems took a slow survey of the heavens.

'Ay; oh ay; I think it will.'

'We could do wi' a spell o' drought now for the peats.'

'That's so,' acknowledged Jeems, nodding thoughtfully, 'that's so indeed.'

'The rain we had yesterday wouldn't go far in.'

'Wouldn't go in at all. No' an inch.' And he again regarded the heavens. Tullach reined in the restive Princie.

'I was thinking,' said Tullach, '– steady there, ye fool! – I was thinking of making a start on Monday.'

'It would be as well indeed,' agreed Jeems. 'It's as well to take the advantage now if the weather's the thing.' And still his eyes did not meet Tullach's.

Tullach's lips twisted. He had a good mind to say 'Ay, that's true,' and drive on. But actually his tone was more off-hand than ever as he added:

'I was thinking Monday, Tuesday, and Wednesday for my own bank; an' then, seeing the squad would be in the run o' the work in any case, they might give ye Thursday.'

Jeems's eyes blinked in quick embarrassment, looked this way and that.

'It would be too much,' he mumbled, 'too much.'

'They would be thereabouts, anyway,' said Tullach.

'Thank ye, Mr Tait. I – I – thank ye. Maggie would take up their food, an' – an' do what she could. My own ould legs –' He laughed brokenly.

203

'Oh, the food's all right. They'll get that where they usually do.'

'I mean – I mean it's the least we might do –'

'It's nothing,' said Tullach, straightening himself and preparing to give Princie his head.

'Weel – it's poor thanks –'

'We'll leave the thanks just now. So long. If I don't see ye before then mysel', Geordie will.'

And he had driven off with a confidence in his own beneficent powers marred the least trifle by the thought that again he had failed somehow to make the ould devil beg. He had solaced himself with an 'Ah, well,' a ruminant flick at Princie, while a pervasive consciousness remained that he was still himself. They would find that he was not so obvious in his feelings as to drop Jeems all at once – just because he had happened on a scene in a byre. They wouldn't have that satisfaction. He would do with Jeems what he might – but not all at once. The two things must not abruptly join issue. There must not be talk about that sort of thing; not about anything. The thought that folk might say that Jeems's lassie threw him over, though he had worked the croft for years by way of a bargain for her . . . any mortal thing on earth but that! It was so annihilating a thought that he could not admit its existence. That was the last thing of any.

And here was the Thursday of the peat-cutting and the specks growing larger, rapidly becoming discernible human beings, with Maggie there on the outside at the spreading.

These specks, however, had spotted Tullach a long way off.

'That's himsel', sure enough.'

And as he had drawn nearer there had been casual comment, but comment of a sly, searching humour that Maggie soon discovered was conditioned in its reticence by the fact of her own presence.

'Ay, he just didn't manage to make the length o' us yesterday, someway,' said Donul.

'No man; the needle o' his compass, as ye might say, hadn't the airt,' replied another. This allusion was felt to be obscure enough for a short, appreciative laugh.

'Ye're a lot o' blethers!' said Donul's wife, who was throwing to Maggie. 'Tullach's a better man nor most this side o' John o' Groats.'

'There was never anyone denying that,' ventured her husband.

'I should think not!' replied his wife.

This calmed matters for a little. But the satyr imp of suggestiveness could not be kept down indefinitely with such a succulent subject as courtship on hand, and presently it reared its arrowy head.

'He has wonderful success wi' his beasts – a grand breeder,' said Hendry o' John's, a trifle heavily, his big-boned face beaded with sweat, his eye roving.

'Oh, capable at the breeding.'

'Reliable, most reliable.'

'In fact, as ye might say, he –'

'Donul!' admonished his wife sharply.

Donul looked at her, eyes rounding in mock anxiety.

'Gosh! I thocht something had come by ye!' he said, heaving a sigh of relief at seeing her quite herself.

'Your wife knows when to stop ye, Donul,' observed Willie, twinkling, as he heaved the innermost peat from his tuskar and turned to the outer edge again.

'Oh ay,' acknowledged Donul, 'she'll ken how one thing does breed another.'

'I ken one thing, anyway,' clinched his wife, 'an' that is that ye've no breeding in ye at all.'

Donul paused, aghast.

'Think shame on ye, Bets, maligning me like that, when ye've five o' them at the school an' two oot o't.'

Bets gave him her back.

'We won't be listening to that trash, Maggie,' and she smiled companionably. There was a slight flush on Maggie's face as she smiled back but said nothing. She knew that Donul and Bets were about the most happily married couple on the seaboard, and Bets's efforts to keep Donul's doubtful humour in check were as well known as they were ineffectual, for there is a certain way in which a man can always put a decent woman to route.

But the conversation made her feel extraordinarily uncomfortable. There was something about it that only began at that point where it coupled Tullach and herself together. To have incidentally coupled Tullach and herself in a passing thought would have been enough. But this talk that went beyond, that was meant good-naturedly, but that probed so horribly – how it tortured her with a sense of unclean shame, how passionately she hated them for doing it!

The wave of Tullach's whip diverted the talk, and in a little while:

'Here he comes,' said Donul.

Tullach advanced at his leisure, eyes to the bank's formation, towards Willie, who paused with foot on the tuskar's step as Tullach said:

'Well, Willie, you're getting on.'

'Oh ay, no' so bad,' replied Willie, his voice full of a quiet manliness.

'Ye've finished off the banks yonder, I see.'

'Oh, yes.'

'Ye had three good days.'

'Ay, fine days; oh, yes, fully better than last year.'

'Ye did?'

'Yes. The upper bankie we ran oot an extra ten yards. It's good all the way. I tried it, too, here an' there farther in still. Fully as good peat, I should say, if no' better.'

'So ye mean we might follow on another year?'

'Well, the stuff is there, whateverway.'

'That's good.'

A pause.

'You're doing fine here, I see.'

'Pretty fair.'

Tullach examined the body of the bank with critical glance, nodded once or twice. It would be the simplest matter in the world to ignore Maggie along with the others. Yet to ignore her, seeing that it was her uncle's, her own, peats his squad was cutting would, he now perceived, be an over-studied, over-elaborate act, certain to draw comment. He must acknowledge her – must – and not merely for the comment's sake. Yet he knew now that he wouldn't, that he couldn't. He must let it appear, standing thus with his back to the rest while addressing Willie, that he was perfectly at his ease to the point of absentmindedness. His eyes came back to Willie. There was nothing like praise for showing the ease in a man's mind.

'Well, Willie, I'm glad everything is going all right. You're all making a fine job.'

'Ay, the peat's coming away fine.' Willie was recognised as an expert at the tuskar.

'Yes, fine stuff.' He bent down and fingered the black, moist slabs. Then he straightened himself.

'Ah, well, I thought I'd take a turn up to see ye were all right.' He nodded again. Why in the name o' Gode had he come at all? What had drawn, tempted him? What had he hoped for? – setting out making himself believe it was his duty!

He took a slow step or two away, examining the tail-end of the bank apparently. Willie raised his voice.

'It's dry enough. Would ye like a cup o' tea? We're no more nor finished.'

'Oh, no, thanks.' Tullach smiled.

'Weel, perhaps,' said Willie, 'Maggie still has something –' He turned to Maggie. Out of months of surreptitious scraping Maggie, to keep shame from the occasion, had managed to procure a half-bottle of whisky, in which, as the men knew, there was still a taste.

'Go ye, Maggie,' said Bets instantly, nodding her head in the direction of the picnic bundle and the still smouldering fire.

On the way, she heard Tullach's voice upraised, protesting. 'No, no, Willie!' Should she pause? How could she? To appear to hesitate would break the law which was still as inviolable as it was spontaneous, the law of hospitality. Plainly she couldn't stop now, no matter what Tullach might do, or how far away he might be before she came back. She rummaged through the tea things, got the flask, the glass, and, turning, saw Tullach there still.

She came up to them with a faint flush, a faint smile covering the thudding of her heart, yet with an apparent ease that was anything but pronounced embarrassment. 'Gode, she's canny at it!' said the discreet twinkle in Donul's eye. She came right up to where Tullach, with his back to her, was still making remarks to Willie. With a half-imploring smile she made to hand flask and glass to Willie.

'No, no,' said Willie; 'it's no' mine.' Not his the honour of hospitality.

Tullach turned, the tan of his face gone a dusky red.

'Eh! what's this?' He laughed shortly. 'Goodness gracious, eh!'

Maggie had the cork out of the bottle, was pouring its amber fluid into the whisky glass. Her hand shook a little, the spirit gushed at the final tilt and overflowed. There was a groan from the belly of the bank which Donul adroitly finished off into a polite cough.

'Hits!' said Willie, with the slow humour which does not presume; 'skailing the mercies!'

As Maggie held forward the glass, Tullach's hand came to meet hers. Fingers touched, and Tullach instantly had the sensation of that touch all over his body. His hand momentarily shook, too, and the liquid spilled perceptibly all round the rim.

'Gosh!' said Tullach. 'Eh!' He smiled in a way that was meant to imply, 'Well, am I not in luck's way!' He steadied the glass before putting it to his lips, raised his head – and suddenly beheld every eye on him. In that instant's look, before heads could be dropped or hurriedly disposed of, Tullach, by an involuntary acute intuition, read every mind about him, saw the figures of himself and Maggie staged before them. His smile never wavered as he pronounced the expected:

'Well, here's luck! Slainte!'

He drained the neat spirit at a draught, handed back the glass to Maggie, his eyes now on her face. Its fresh bloom above her knit, lithe body, its expression of proper timidity, restrained in some subtle aloofness, was a vision of final desire.

'Thank ye, Maggie.'

She took the glass from him, smiled, and turned away. He had the sensation of a flame turning from his body.

'Ha-a!' he cleared his throat, and half-faced Willie.

'As the saying goes,' suggested Willie: 'it's better nor a bad word!'

Tullach laughed abruptly.

'Ay, it's that!'

Willie spat on his hands and took a preparatory grip on the tuskar.

'Well, you'll make a good day of it.'

'We should,' agreed Willie.

Tullach nodded to the bank generally and moved off.

Down through the heather he went, untied Princie, mounted, flicked the whip, and set off at a spanking trot. His thoughts at the moment were beyond any rational control. The reality of Maggie there on the moor had had a quality about it not merely unexpected but in some way incredible. He saw yet that faint-flushed texture of the face, the eyes with their inscrutable restraint, the clean curves of the bosom in that tight-fitting jersey affair, the upstanding, easy poise. The faint-flushed texture lingered. 'Gode, she's ripe!' ripped the words out of him.

He unthinkingly struck Princie, and then had to break the instant gallop back into a trot. The short struggle on the reins exhilarated, and for a few moments he let his mind have its fling. Not that he imaged his thoughts with any precision, or foresaw clearly possibilities of a wild delight. Yet the foretaste of image and delight was like a subtle scent in his nostrils.

Sobriety came quickly and with cunning, yet no longer with dark, brooding cunning; the whisky in him, the vision, the power of his flesh, of Tullach, of his possessions, combined to a gaiety of cunning. He could bide his time, but by Gode! . . . He let his thought run out in a thick, throaty laugh. The peewits swung up on either hand. The moor lay still, austere, under the wide sky, lost in its immemorial dream of awaiting the passing of the footsteps of God. The wheels of Tullach's trap crunched over it in excellent style.

CHAPTER FIFTEEN

MAGGIE heard the clash of the front door on her way from the byre, and involuntarily quickened her pace to a half-run, entering the back-place noiselessly and slipping out of sight behind the open door. All ears she listened, breath held, blood pulsing audibly.

Momentarily raised voices at the front door, then footsteps thudding their way round the gable-end – Tullach's footsteps. Her uncle's clip-clop shauchled over the kitchen floor back to the fireplace.

There was no window behind the door, but her inner vision followed Tullach clearly enough as he crossed from the gable-corner to the byre door. There the footsteps paused. He was in the byre. She had milked early, immediately after taking the cow home and without coming into the kitchen as a lantern was no longer needed. To anyone in the kitchen it could thus not have been quite certain when she had started milking. Tullach's calculation must have been a trifle out; or possibly had not made allowances for unusual haste.

His footsteps came out of the byre, paused, went off towards the barn. 'He's gone!' thought Maggie. But the thrill of relief was checked on hearing the footsteps return. They hesitated opposite the back door, shuffled uncertainly; there was a mutter, and the footsteps moved off. Presently the front door rattled. Maggie's eyelids flickered calculatingly, ears straining for what might be said.

He was patently making some excuse or other for

213

coming back. No matches – light his pipe – was it? In the kitchen again. His short laugh. Agreeable voices. Carrying it off all right, but actually wanting to know where she was. To-night, the last night before the boats came home, God willing. Seeking her out. For a whole week she had avoided him successfully. She must avoid him to-night at all hazards. Timid footsteps were suddenly at the back door. Jeannie.

Maggie came immediately and greeted Jeannie in quiet, normal tones. To any listening ears she had doubtless been doing something in the back-place all the time.

'So you're expecting your daddy home to-morrow?'

'Yes,' said Jeannie.

'You'll be glad of that!'

'Yes,' said Jeannie.

'It's –' she began, and checked herself, finishing, 'it's going to keep up. I think they'll have good weather.'

'Yes,' said Jeannie. 'They'll be home not long after dinner, they're thinking.'

Maggie had been about to remark that the failure of the fishing as far as the Balriach boats were concerned was bad news and that everyone was sad about it; but it had suddenly seemed a wanton thing to say to Jeannie. She filled the four pails and, still talking to Jeannie, got out of her apron and tidied her hair.

'I'll carry two an' you'll carry two,' said Maggie, with a friendly smile. 'I'm going to the village.'

She closed the door quietly behind them, and did not speak again until they were by the ditch-side.

'Yes, I'm sure you'll be glad to see your daddy again.'

'Yes,' said Jeannie.

'Has it seemed a long, long time since he went away?'

'Yes.'

'How long?'

'Ever so long,' said Jeannie.

'Yes, it's a long time,' agreed Maggie, and they walked on in silence for a little.

'And what are ye expecting?' began Maggie, unthinkingly, awaking from her own thought.

'Nothing,' said Jeannie, as Maggie paused.

She had not meant to have asked the question; now she could not let it pass.

'Nothing at all!'

'No. I heard mother say he'll come back with nothing but – but –'

Maggie waited impotently.

' – debt,' completed Jeannie, the word plainly holding a dark significance for her.

'Surely it won't be as bad as all that! – an' he'll have a kiss for ye, an' surely that's something!'

'Yes,' said Jeannie.

Debt! Poverty is bleak and sapless and bad enough. In its moods it can be as gaunt and slow as a living skeleton, or it can be as grey-cold as a sea-fog creeping in on the land; but in the ultimate there is something about it that is passive, with the passivity of staring eyes and folded hands. Debt is poverty's black pall. Thought worming its underground ways has an oppressive knowledge of it as of something imminent, closing in, annihilating. Thought avoids it if it can. Eyes avoid it, shifting this way and that; so that it is being constantly avoided by the mind and obliquely seen by the eyes. A black mood grows out of this, a heavy shiftiness, which sucks vampire-like at the free movement of manhood.

The fishing had been a failure. The wise men were being justified. The days of the sailing-boat in the fishing fleet were numbered.

Maggie's eyes were on the far black headland that brooded over the darkling sea. It was several weeks since the peat-cutting. She could now read the mind of Tullach with a terrible clarity. After the peat-cutting he had still kept his distance, and then gradually had begun to come back. All done very nicely, in proper self-respecting stages! But every night this last week she had avoided him, hiding from him, dodging him, all sense of shame gone. She must avoid him till the boats came back. Beyond that point she did not think. Any dodge, any shift – she did not care – until the boats came back. If she could reach that point, then –

But her mind would not go beyond that point. Sometimes, it is true, it found itself swimming vaguely beyond in a sea of half-explanations, Ivor swimming there, too; a gleam of the eyes, a fragment of a mood, a broken gesture – straws which she clutched at, which they clutched at together, turning towards each other – until, with a quickened pulse, she dismissed the gleaming figment and saw only the date of the boats' return. She knew nothing of Ivor, nothing of herself, nothing of life, beyond that point. But she would dodge everything till that point was reached, even the contemplation of poverty, of black debt. That point would be reached to-morrow.

She turned to Jeannie and asked her about the school, what standard she would be on after the holidays, and whether she liked going to school.

'Is that yoursel', Maggie? – an' is this little Jeannie wi' ye? Well, well!' Mrs Hendry came round the dung-heap, her voice laughing.

'Yes. It's a fine night,' greeted Maggie pleasantly.

'An' wi' yer pails o' milk an' all! Ay, a bonny night an' a good wind for the boats, they're saying.'

'Yes.'

'So ye'll see yer faither to-morrow, Jeannie! Won't ye be the happy one then?'

'Yes,' said Jeannie.

Mrs Hendry regarded her with smiling beneficence for a reflective moment. Then:

'Ow, poor thing,' she said, the laughing note fading. 'Ow, but it's sad aboot the fishing; sad, sad!' She smoothed Jeannie's hair with a motherly hand. 'It's sad to think what it's all coming to.'

'That's true,' agreed Maggie.

'The ould man was saying that they'll have been hard put to it, an' maybe they'll have had to sell some o' their nets – not that that would clear them; but to get provisions an' things like that ye need the ready money. But it's no' for me to know. No. . . .' She paused, the 'murning' of her gloom touching Maggie instantly to uttermost misery. 'Yeth,' she resumed, sucking in her doleful wind as from far-off reflections, 'it's a terrible state o' things.'

'Ay,' said Maggie.

'An' it wouldn't be so bad if they could be sort o' sure, as in the ould days, that a good fishing might follow a bad one. But how can they be sure o' that now?'

One might have an involuntary aversion to this personification of murning gloom, a derisive hatred of it as a wanton, thowless slayer of gaiety and courage; yet there it was – the truth, the unavoidable truth, truest of all in its suffocating atmosphere. A passive acceptance, a murning, that in a last analysis seemed positively to have a moist unction about it. Yet, God help it, there it was – with a bitterness of truth for the sensitive soul that overwhelmed.

Maggie did not answer, and as her eyes lifted to the grey line of the horizon their attempt at deliberate inexpression could not cover a perceptible gathering and glistening of emotion, of hurt.

'Yeth,' pursued Mrs Hendry, vaguely gratified by this silent sympathy and understanding. She sighed. 'Yeth.'

Then with an apparent inward effort, she brightened, her face smiling again. She shook her head slowly. 'Well, well, we are all in the hands of' – head-shake – 'of Higher Powers, my dear. It may all be for the best. Though it's difficult whiles to see His ways.' Her smile brightened more pronouncedly. To force cheerfulness through inevitable gloom is an act of courage which an understanding

218

of the young demands. 'But perhaps better times will come, my dears! We mustn't always be looking on the dark side!'

Maggie smiled uncertainly in response. Jeannie, close by her side, was regarding Mrs Hendry with round eyes, a choking sensation of tears in her throat.

As they walked to the vennel which gave on the village, neither of them spoke. At last Maggie looked down on Jeannie and smiled companionably.

'Mrs Hendry is good at the murning,' she said, with a whimsical twist.

Jeannie's eyes immediately lifted to hers, hesitated, melted in a bright, shy smile of half-clairvoyant understanding.

'But she doesn't know everything,' said Maggie.

Jeannie's courage returned completely.

'She's no' as bad as cripple Mairag,' she ventured timidly.

Maggie laughed spontaneously. Mairag was altogether taken up with religion and the ways of the Lord, and would groan audibly in a very uplift of murning. During the time of the Sacraments her art reached a high level of excellence, attaining finally a bodily rocking of perfection. In temporal affairs no instance was known of her ever having been imposed upon.

At parting, Maggie said:

'Now, you'll give your daddy a great welcome, won't ye, Jeannie?'

'Yes,' said Jeannie, with a quick intonation of courage.

As Maggie proceeded on her way to Kirsty's that

final 'yes' lingered with her. The wee thing understood – already. Her father would be needing the warm welcome. . . . Maggie went on evenly, sudden absurd tears behind her eyelids.

She called to Kirsty from the doorway cheerfully 'It's too late to come in!'

'Come away! come away!' shouted Kirsty's voice above a perfect babel of sound. Then as Maggie appeared: 'This house is not fit to be seen by any living being!' Kirsty was beaming from the midst of indescribable disorder. 'They've taken the clean upper hand o' me th'-night. They're that excited aboot the boats an' their faither coming home tomorrow! They've just gone beyond themselves an' me!'

Maggie's entry had caused a lull; but already tweaks, suppressed exclamations and giggles, surreptitious chair-scrapings, a worming activity, were manifesting themselves afresh. Before she had had half a dozen sentences with Kirsty pandemonium reigned, so that they had to shout to each other. Donald, aged ten, having backed inadvertently too near his mother's chair, got a sudden wallop from her that sent him sitting on the floor. The humour of his position completely overwhelmed the others.

'Take ye that!' said Kirsty. 'An' if the whole o' ye are no' in your beds in two minutes, I'll skelp each one o' ye before Maggie. Now!'

This vast and grotesque threat (with just enough of possibility in its absurdity) moved them to cunning derision, a derision of emphasis. This derision centred on Donald, who plainly could not make up

220

his mind whether to cry or laugh at the whirlwind onslaught on his dignity by his mother.

Stumpy Sanny, aged six, asked, with slow articulation:

'Was that sore, Donnie? Did ye fall on yer dock?'

Convulsions of laughter at the vulgarism. Flattered, Sanny proceeded to indicate how the affected part might be rubbed.

'My lad,' interposed his mother, 'you're running on it!' Then to Maggie: 'I tried to put them to bed. It was no use. I just don't know what to do wi' them. But sleep will overtake them in a whilie.' She snuggled her hands in her lap. 'Ach weel, the bairns!' she said.

'Ay, the young things!' agreed Maggie.

'Maybe they'll grow oot o't, an' we manage someway!'

'Indeed yes.'

'An' what's seeing ye doon aboot the village at this time o' night? Just having a stravaig?'

'Just that same.'

Kirsty smiled shrewdly at her.

'You'll be a little tired o' your company whiles, is that it?'

'Well, one's own company can get dreich enough.'

'Ay – an' other folks' forby! Whatever, it's a real pleasure seeing you. They'll be home to-morrow.'

'So I hear.'

'Ay.' Kirsty turned her eyes on the fire and for a moment gloom troubled them. Then she lifted them directly to Maggie, candidly.

'They finished as they began – nothing! One

keeps hoping for a last shot. But no. They had no luck.'

Maggie nodded.

'So I heard,' she said quietly.

They were silent for a little. A sudden, fierce yelling uprose. Sanny was reaping Donnie's vengeance.

Kirsty got up, and for a time there was martial law. The youngest she began very forcibly to undress. Sleepiness' had bred peevishness, a cross-grained rebelliousness. It took half an hour to clear the floor. At last Kirsty sat down. Rumblings, odd skirls, dying sobs, from all airts. . . .

'They'll fall off in a whilie,' said Kirsty.

'But I mustn't be staying. He'll be wondering where on earth I've gone –'

'Ach, let him!' said Kirsty good-naturedly. 'Don't get up now. It's a sort o' throughither night this, an' I'm glad to see ye.'

'You'll be waiting on for to-morrow.'

'Just that. They'll be welcome, fishing or no fishing.'

'Surely.'

'Though it's beginning to look – for the young fellows, anyway – that there's nothing left in the fishing for them.'

'No; that's true.'

'Ay, it's true, Maggie.'

In this sudden use of her name Maggie caught a nearness of meaning, but she strove not to show it, nodding solemnly.

'There's nothing for a young fellow here,' went on

Kirsty. 'The fishings are dead. It's no job for a young fellow, anyway, going to the sea.'

'I suppose not.'

'I don't think mysel' there'll ever be a living in it again – not in these little places. They'll have to turn to something else. And as there's nothing here, they'll just have to go abroad or somewhere.'

Maggie nodded, eyes on the fire.

'It's a pity, too, in a way,' considered Kirsty. 'I can remember in my young days there was a great life of it – plenty of fun an' carryings-on; good times. . . . Yes, an' bad times, too, but some way it was a life that was going on. It's no' the same now.'

'No,' said Maggie.

'I'm tired o' the sea,' said Kirsty, after a little. 'Many's the time – many a night – I've hated it. You'll hear the wind moaning round the house, shaking it, an' them at the sea. I've hated it so much that I've seen me cry to mysel'. It's weak, maybe, I know – but ye just can't help it. An' on a wild, stormy night it's terrible how the crying an' the moaning o' the wind will get at ye.'

Kirsty spoke simply, reminiscently, her comely face strangely attractive to Maggie.

'It will have to do us our time now,' continued Kirsty, 'so we'll just have to make the best o't. Though when ye think o' the men working as they do, their lives always in their hands, hard, cold, coorse work, week in, week oot, day an' night, an' after all that – nothing! It's enough to break any-one's spirit.'

'Ay, it is that.'

They both stared at the fire, and its licking flames danced in the sombre film of their eyes. Then Kirsty gave herself a shake, and turned a searching, smiling glance on Maggie.

'Ach, anyway, Maggie – that won't be bothering ye!'

Maggie did not meet her look, the colour on her face deepening.

'No,' she replied.

'That's right,' said Kirsty, aware that Maggie's 'no' had been the closing of the door on her secret heart. Each instantly knew it, intuitively aware of the other's knowledge. The moment of awareness became acute. Maggie got up.

'I really must be going.' Her smile was rich-toned, evasive, and ineffably friendly. It was like her troubled heart speaking.

'Weel, if ye must go, ye must,' said Kirsty. 'But I feel the better for your visit, Maggie.'

'I feel the better myself.'

They moved towards the door. There was sudden inadequacy in words, a knowledge of them as hard, surface little sounds.

'Anyway, you'll be doon to-morrow evening – early, now!'

Maggie was silent, head already turned in departure.

'Well – I don't know –' She hesitated.

'Surely you'll come doon to get the news an' give them a word?'

'You'll be that busy –'

'Busy nonsense!'

Maggie laughed.

'Maybe I will – but I'll no' promise.'

'Mind, we'll be looking for ye!' called Kirsty. A 'Good night' came back to her on a fragment of a laugh.

Returning to her kitchen, Kirsty mechanically tidied up stray bits of clothing, then sat down, hands on her knees, face to the fire.

She brooded there for a long time. There was something queerly companionable, near the heart, in Maggie and her attitude to life at the moment. Why hadn't she told Maggie outright that poverty and the sea were terrible things to face – when there was the chance of not facing them, the fine chance? She should have impressed that on Maggie in some way.

Into Kirsty's brooding came a fathomless misery. Her mind swam in it for a long time, finding nothing. Then Sanny's face formed itself on this sea, then his whole active body, and the boat tossing and coming on. The cold, watery sea, heartless, ready to drown without caring, without a sign. She saw the men and their quiet faces, coming back – with nothing. Carrying the brand of failure on their faces, although their faces were men-faces and showed nothing at all.

A terrible thing, life, lived as they lived it. But far, far more than the problem of Sanny and herself was the problem of the children. Her hands gathered from her knees to her lap, her body rocked perceptibly. The thought of her boys being delivered to the sea was agony.

Maggie's face came curiously to comfort her. Here was the lassie, through the secret troubles of her own heart, wanting to come into all this, to face it and to endure. She might not know what she was doing; but Kirsty felt her heart open to her to that last innermost place where all the women of the sea are known of one another. A warmth gathered in her breast, slow tears filled her eyes. Poor lassie, God be kind to her! . . . Life was a dumb fathom-less sea with a sound in it like a knell. . . .

Kirsty awoke from her reverie and went and locked the door. Before getting into bed, she paused to listen for the wind.

CHAPTER SIXTEEN

MAGGIE's footsteps hastened at first as though they were bent on catching up a hastening of her mind. There was at once the relief of freedom from company and the lingering warmth which company had bestowed. As she had avowed, she felt the better for the interval with Kirsty and the bairns.

Not until she had reached the vennel and passed through its deep shadow did she overtake her mind. She saw in a moment that she had not wanted to overtake her mind. If only one could always live in a hastening excitement which was an awaiting on some event! . . .

There sloped the rise to the croft. The night lay on it, an imponderable gloom, dimly irradiated by a pallor of reverie. Flower and shrub scents were sifted by a small wind. The smell of the earth itself was subtly pervasive and touched primal instincts to a dark disturbance.

Kirsty had understood Maggie's recoil from the intimacy of another's understanding: yet that Kirsty had understood was curiously companionable. Only, it was companionable so long as one did not think beyond to-morrow.

What Kirsty had said about the sea had not been so much a pointed warning as a simple truth. That took away from its effectiveness – and increased the companionableness. Kirsty had been merely telling the general truth. It had not been allowed to touch Maggie personally, like a direct injunction. Besides, it was all vague and beyond to-morrow. She was not to be done out of to-morrow.

She passed Hendry's croft, and, rounding the whins, came on the ditch-side. There was a light in the kitchen window. Uncle Jeems was not yet in bed. There was only one deduction: he must still have company.

Maggie paused, head erect, eyes on the window, its yellow light steady and unwinking. . . . A poverty-tinged, jaundiced yellow, known of body and soul with the all-pervasive intimacy of a smell. She felt her emotions wither in its light.

He should have been in bed. What in the world was keeping him up to this time of night? Could they possibly be waiting to ask her something?

The thought was surely preposterous. They could hardly go that far! Her footsteps started on again, slowed, ceased. Hardly as far as that! She regarded the yellow light with a sudden overpowering mistrust.

She turned from it – and met again the wistful gloom of the night. A dim, listening loveliness weighted down by reveries. It gathered around her, in about her heart, then stole out again to infinite spaces. Her nostrils quivered to the elusive scents. Such a sad loveliness was this earth asleep. Only, it was not asleep: it was dreaming its still, sad dreams, like freighted memories of forgotten poetry.

He was there in the house now. What was she to do? There was only one thing to do and that was to go right in. Yet why should this happen – before to-morrow? Oh, why should it? Why? . . . The

228

earth dreamed and the young corn hushed itself in a soft sighing. It was cruel all this. It was wrong. It wasn't fair. They had no right. Life could be a thing like the night here, its sadness no more than a crying of the fey heart. There could be the crying of desire, of the soul's longings – even in this grey land of hunger and lean soil. Even the land itself could dream its own inexpressible dreams, once it was free of the day's slavery and the dealings of men.

She started again. There was no good in being afraid. Anyway, she couldn't hide about until Tullach left. . . . *Couldn't she?* She went on. She could easily hang about for a little time. Sit in the ditch. No one would come along the ditch-side now. She could lie on the other side of it, just over the hump. She went on steadily. But before leaving its shelter, she paused, her mind now insistently troubled by the immediate practical issues. She could hide about – but no, she wouldn't. She couldn't. Not, anyway, until she had made sure.

She left the ditch-side, walking with a deliberation dignified and irreproachable – yet with a lightness of footfall that was quite noiseless. She reached the gable-end – and involuntarily stopped dead, full figure drawn up, breath held with difficulty, ears catching nothing but the quickened beating of her heart. A slow glance about her, three or four sudden stealthy steps on tiptoe, and she was by the window, listening with strained intensity. Nothing. Not a sound. Not a move. She tiptoed quietly back to the gable-end, got down on her heels, and tramped deliberately to the back door.

The bolt had not been shot. She entered. Walked over the stone-flagged floor with, if anything, more marked slowness and unconcern in the tapping of her feet; presently sat down and took off her shoes. There came no sound from the kitchen. It was either empty or the old man had fallen asleep.

The old man turned in his chair as the door from the back-place rattled and closed behind Maggie. His face was puckered in querulousness, his eyes grown small with sleep and ill-temper.

'What time o' night is this to be coming home at?'

Maggie paused, regarded the eyes which had not risen to the level of her face, then went on to hang up her coat at the bed-head, offering no word of explanation.

'Stravaiging all over the place at this time o' night! That's a fine carry-on – oot on the roads till all hours like any common – any common –' The word that persisted in coming to his mind he could not utter, but its absence was emphatic enough.

'I wasn't out on the roads,' said Maggie evenly.

'Oh, ye weren't, were ye?'

'No, I wasn't.'

'Oh, indeed!'

'You could have gone to your bed,' said Maggie.

'Oh, I could, could I?' Impotent wrath seized him in a spasm. 'I could? Ye'll remember that while ye're in my hoose ye'll no' go strumping aboot like any randy. Ye'll remember that! This is a decent hoose: no' a – a –'

'Ay,' said Maggie.

230

'I'll ay ye, ye limmer! Ye've no spark o' shame in ye! But I won't stand it, no –'

'Ye needn't,' said Maggie.

'Oh, I needn't! That's the next o't! Though I've brought ye up till now, though I've done everything that mortal could for ye, ye'll turn round now wi' a tongue an' a brazen face –' His old gnarled fists closed rigidly on the chair arms, his eyes were leaping at her face, but his words got choked as though his irritability, his wrath, could not be given whole-hearted utterance because of something that lurked restrainingly behind. Already he had gone too far, whispered this lurking cunning. 'But I won't stand it. No, I won't stand it.' He turned to the fire, spat explosively into the heart of it, muttered, mumbled.

Maggie went about preparing things for the morning. There had been something tonic in the outburst. She felt extraordinarily cool, self-possessed. She could have gone further. After all, there was no need for anyone to put up with her. By no means. There was a wild, tingling pulse in her self-possession which told her she could go as far as she liked. She could tell him that, too, if he liked. What was he sitting on there for? It was past his bedtime. Long past it. Though it wasn't that late – and he knew it. Just as he knew that most likely she hadn't been on the roads at all. He had something on his mind. What? Had Tullach, then, at last . . . But no, that was their concern – whatever they cared to talk about. There was no need for her to think about what Tullach and he might have been saying and planning. None. She moved about.

The old man got up, threw a look at the clock.

'A fine time o' night!'

She paid no heed. He mumbled and muttered; stretched for a spill to light his candle. Then finally the true grumble became articulate.

'Leaving the hoose all night – when ye knew there was folk in!'

A legitimate grumble, and Maggie felt the hospitable force of it. But the words randy and limmer had stung, even though they might be no more than the outcome of ill-temper over her desertion. She was silent.

'What took ye off? Where were ye?'

'I can go out for a walk if I like.'

'So ye were on the roads?'

'No.'

He glared at her.

'I went down to see Kirsty – who gives us the fish.'

The last five words were a subtle thrust.

'Fish! Huh! Ye've been good at the fish!'

'They've been away,' said Maggie evenly. She always hated herself afterwards for losing her temper with the old man. It left behind a sordid taste in the mouth, made life wretched and mean. It could be wretched and mean enough without that.

'Ay, they've been away! Fish! Ye take a fine interest in the fish! Ay, a great interest! Oh, very great!' And he turned and lit his candle elaborately.

Maggie stood rigid, a swirl of incredible belief swiftly flowing outwards, all over her, till she knew that its colour was in her face.

'Oh ay,' repeated the old man to himself, knocking the flame off the spill, 'a most terrible interest!'

Maggie gave him her back and began picking up certain odds and ends from the bedcover. Tullach could not have told him about Ivor; surely he could not have mentioned the meeting in the byre! Tullach might do anything – but surely not that, were it only out of pride! She felt the old man surreptitiously watching her, felt him calculating whether he might say something now that would be very definitely to the point. In a moment she turned from the bed, her face charged with a calm that was a subtle, cold hauteur, that dared him with an unconcern which had apparently heard nothing, nor would hear. Without looking at him at all, she turned efficiently away, carrying the odds and ends to the back-place.

He hesitated. There followed her a guttural rumbling that was like a lengthy curse, but no sound of his footsteps moving off. He could not go without saying something. His nature wouldn't let him, she knew. But what he had to say was a momentous and final thing. Its bigness, in face of her threat to look after herself, was maybe frightening him a bit. His cunning would be telling him to go canny, and so, at the same time, would be maddening him. At last he spoke in a thick half-shout of command:

'Weel, maybe ye'll be in another night when folks call!'

She made no answer. Still he did not go.

'An' to-morrow night –' He stopped, significantly. More guttural rumblings. Then clip-clop went his slippered feet ben the house.

233

She came into the kitchen, moved about setting things to right, locked the doors, satisfied herself her uncle was ben for good. Then she sat down by the dying fire.

The anger, the defiance, of her spirit had for the time being given her thought an edge. She could reconstruct a possible conversation between the two of them there in the kitchen, with a sense of the cunning workings of their brains intuitively and clearly grasped. Tullach would not mention Ivor and the byre incident off-hand. Not likely! But he would come at it in a roundabout way that plainly did not affect him, but that yet, with satiric hint and nod . . . so that what wasn't said would be searching in its implication. He would do it with a flicking whip, baiting the old man. That time when he had gone round and in again at the front door, after finding she wasn't in the byre, he would have been pretty mad, most darkly, agreeably mad, would have cruelly flicked the old man – and then when she had cleared out with Jeannie – to what lengths might he not have gone! He would have said nothing directly against her, of course – not directly! But the byre and what might be seen in it, the peats, the croft – everything would have been worked in without exactly a direct mention! All in the same heavy, baiting way, with an air of satiric friendliness! She could hear his final laugh.

Or, perhaps, they had come to direct words. Perhaps there *was* some understanding between them, and Tullach had brought it forcibly to the light. Always that possibility of money business, a hold on

234

the old man, a stranglehold. And Tullach's mood would then have been thick, a heavy bludgeoning.

Or was she now merely becoming fanciful? Her uncle's mood no more than a bloodshot perversity, seeing she had not been there to welcome Tullach, to make much of him, to keep in with him? So much depended on Tullach. Everything depended on Tullach. Her disappearance, her apparent independence, would be exasperating to her uncle, maddening. It was a wanton flying in the face of Providence. Was that it?

She smoored the fire, began to undress. Perhaps there was no more in it than that. Yet her uncle had meant something when he had spoken of the fish, had been getting at her. Pity she hadn't said something and drawn him. Why hadn't she? She ought to have made sure. . . . But she couldn't have made quite sure. Not without asking too plainly, without giving herself away and having the whole case stated.

In bed she thought: And why shouldn't I have had the whole case stated?

But to ask the question was to let her mind slip out on the sea of grey misery. Twist or turn it as she might, its twistings were like desperate efforts at keeping afloat where the underneath was fathomless and of no buoyancy.

Moreover, she now hadn't that intimacy of faint hostility between her uncle and herself which always filled the sails of her thought with a surface tautness and directioning. Curious the feeling that was between them, the abrupt monosyllable, smileless enquiry and answer, the living from day to day like that. She had no words for it. There was something satisfying in it that could not be explained, as though flesh spoke to flesh crudely, in some way jealously. That either should meet the other on the same plain of understanding, emotion appreciating emotion, openly, face to face, word to word, was a condition of existence almost unthinkable, certainly not to be thought of. They could go on living as they lived; existence became possible as a dour test of endurance, body and soul jealously self-contained, each reacting on the other with a tonic individualism, and possibly in this way creating a tonic atmosphere of hostility in which blood kinship could breathe and in which an ultimate jealous affection need not wither.

But where to find a haven in this grey outlook of the years? The fishing had been a failure. Let her look at it – as she must. For the young fellows, as Kirsty had said, there was nothing. The days of the sailing-boat were passing, were already past; the days of the small fishing creek, like Balriach, were surely dead. The cracked grey quay, the sagging curing sheds, the silting harbour-basin, the rotting away in final dissolution, in death . . . There was nothing for the young fellows; not, anyway, for the young fellows of any spirit. That was what Kirsty felt about her own bairns. It came out of her sometimes. The sense of struggle, of heroic fighting, of great days – gone for ever (if, indeed, to the women of the sea they had ever been).

With the fishing no more – what then? There were no crofts. And what was that but a relief and a secret blessing! The women of the sea might have their haunting fears, their sorrows; but for the women of the crofts was reserved the misery that knows no end, the profitless, warping drudgery that knows no rest but that of the kirkyard.

No fishing, no croft. There remained the slums of Glasgow, or the remote world of Canada. And to Canada they all went. If you had a trade at your finger-ends you might do well; otherwise you took your chance, with a hand ever ready to turn to anything. The young fisher fellows would be the worst off of all. For years they would go on living as they could, and working a terrible long day as hard as they could be driven. None of those who had gone out in the last six years had yet managed back to see the old folk. That was Canada.

That was – Ivor! She felt her body flush warmly at the subterranean way she had thus worked him into the web of her thought. As though he were thinking about her, had ever thought about her, in that way at all! She knew that he liked her, that in some way his spirit had spoken to her. But, after all, what was that but maybe a thing of the moment! Would that bring him back? Bring him back, for example, after six years in Canada? How foolish the thought! She was merely hanging on to some such vague notion in order to gain time for her mind in the near encounter with Tullach.

It was near enough now, as near as to-morrow night. She had staved it off shamelessly, because she had wanted to see Ivor once more. She felt that if only she saw Ivor she would understand finally, and her way would be made plain.

That, too, was foolish, maybe. But never mind – she could surely allow herself so much now.

Then – Tullach. Could she? She had faced it before, all round it – the farm, the comfort, the work, her uncle secure, everything secure. It was good. Tullach himself? She suddenly saw him there in the byre – and her body stiffened, while she watched his eyes. . . . Could she? It was cruel to have to answer that. She could not, she would not . . . not yet! But the sensation of his bodily presence remained, till an unreasoning, subtle warmth caught at her own healthy body. She had a sudden choking sensation, and convulsively pushed the bedclothes from her as though they were alive.

She had a feeling of exaggerating the convulsion, knew herself siting up in bed with an over-forced distaste, while a subtle something penetrated her soul as though it had been soiled. She threw off the bedclothes. How close the night! The stone floor met her feet in an exquisite recoil. Through to the back-place noiselessly, where she filled a bowl from the water pail. How cool and clean, how pure, the well water!

In the kitchen again, she went to the window, and pulling the blind a little to one side, peered out on the night. The still, pale night, more hung about with reverie than before, more deeply lost in swooning ecstasy, as though it could not move under its freight of dreams. Strange the world out there under the great sky where the stars were. She looked at the pale stars. Infinite! Down to the earth again. The earth was near, near her body and soul.

She got into bed, cooled, stilled, but no sooner had she drawn the bedclothes up over her body than the thought which she had banished so convulsively came back insinuatingly, took on the guise of life and stooped to her ear. . . . 'Anything can take place . . . even that.' She turned over and buried her face in the pillow, and the tears came in a drowning flood.

CHAPTER SEVENTEEN

THE morning was the morning of the day, breaking to a subtle difference from all other mornings that had been. The wind had freshened since the absolute calm of the dawn to a steady breeze from a little south of east, so that the sea was heard in the cliffs, while out beyond the cliff-heads it ran white-flecked. The clouds were high and mackerel-backed, long combed-out 'horses' tails' here and there as wind symbols. The boats would come racing up the firth to-day. In her mind's eye, she saw them coming.

Returning from the barn-end, she dished the porridge. It would be cool enough this morning, anyway. The day would be got through without a hitch. She would keep her distance of last night, a cool danger-distance. He needed that, it would serve him right; it would also serve her purpose.

He came through without a word, shuffled into his chair, peched loudly as he got into his boots. The peching showed a contumacious mind, exhibited the master on his own hearth-stone. He might not care to communicate his mind. That was his privilege, his indifference to the sort of she-material about him.

Maggie cleared the plates and went about her business, now and then conscious of a twinge of the heart. Plainly the old man had not slept well. The veins in his eyes were red. Could he have had a bad night? A touch of exhaustion, of gasping weakness? Twice in the last fortnight she had seen him enter the kitchen and crawl into his chair to breathe heavily, stertorously while he gaped at the fire. The first time she had asked him if he was feeling all right, and had been snapped at for her pains, had, in fact, left the kitchen, conscious of her presence as an irritation to him.

She now made no overture, and presently he came stamping through the back-place and out to the barn-end to look upon weather and sea. In a little while the sound of his hoe on the causey stones of the byre rose in a harsh clacking and scraping as though his hand were heavy upon it and deliberate. The morning wore on to the midday meal of potatoes and herring.

Throughout the meal he had looked more subdued, more reflective. Maggie could see that for minutes on end she was forgotten rather than deliberately ignored. These lapsed periods gave his face a curious dignity, a dignity of preoccupied age, in which there was no craftiness. But what was going on in his mind she could not guess.

An hour or two later, in a trip to the barn-end look-out, she came on him squatting on the cairn of stones. Before she could command herself she had started self-consciously. He turned and looked at her; then focussed his long sight on the sea again.

'That's *The Dawn*,' he said.

She followed his look, and there, the fore-and-aft dip and rise perceptible even at that distance, was a toy brown sailing-boat making its way through the white caps. The sight affected her in an instant excitation of all the flesh on her body. The apparition was suddenly incredible, the nearness of it:

racing up the firth there for the harbour 'down over' at Balriach.

She turned away without a word. Wandered hither and thither aimlessly, unseeingly, till she came to rest in the kitchen. The kitchen had been washed out from door to door, the grate black-leaded, the house prepared for any visitors; the usual daily routine, awaiting completion in her personal ablutions.

She set about washing and dressing herself with a thoroughness that was punctuated by prolonged, still pauses. But when she came to her face in the looking-glass, the reflectiveness gathered life, a glimmering, appraising consciousness. Her face was red from the towel-rubbing, too red. But it would settle back to its faintly browned pallor. And – it wasn't a bad face. She bared her lips from her teeth. They were white teeth. And the touch of brown wasn't so much brown as a pale sun-duskiness, making her eyes the darker, her hair the duskier. A smooth face. And the eyes could look so – and so – and so – and then with that quiet, level look – so. She suddenly flushed. But she didn't care. Her eyes gleamed. Say what one liked – it wasn't a bad face. And the neck – and down – Life tingled – and got mixed in a sudden resurgence of the excitation she had experienced at the barn-end. A sense of the surging fullness of life caught at her breath. She had to sit down – but took the mirror with her, and, propping it against the wall, proceeded with her hair-brushing.

The sense of being at a loose end drove her outside, and between the hen-house and the barn-end she met her uncle.

'I'll go doon an' see them coming in,' he said, without looking at her.

She had no intention of going down to the harbour herself; yet she watched him trudge off with an intentness that was curiously wistful.

At the harbour, juvenile excitement, just freed from school, ran high, the more daring spirits clinging in a cluster on the back wall of the quay-point.

'Here she is! . . . Boy, she's putting it off her! . . . Did ye see yon! . . . Ach, go away, man – yer faither's boat will no' be in the Pentland yet! The *Sea Swallow*! – more liker it the Sea Crab! . . . Ay, or the Sea Partan! . . . Oh, is that so? If ye'll no' watch I'll give ye a sea partan on the ither side o' yer mouth! . . .' Partisan feeling ran high, brute force prepared to deal with the unanswerable in the best international fashion.

Jeems got talking to Peter Sinclair, who had had an early view of *The Dawn*, and had hirpled to the harbour with much effort. The conversation was of a gloomy cast, the atmosphere of failure seeming to pervade even the Portland cement. Things were not what they had been. Things could never be. The fishing grounds were going farther and farther away. Ay, and even if the grounds were just out off Balriach at least motor power would be necessary to get the catch to the nearest direct rail-head. So how could the fishings come back? . . .

A cheer from the quay-head drew their eyes to the

harbour opening. *The Dawn* came with a thin wafer of foam at her forefoot.

'Man, ye could tell she has it in her!' came involuntarily from Peter Sinclair on a note of enthusiasm. 'She's proud!' And there was a pride, a subtle, unvanquishable pride, in the lift of her bows. As she neared the quay a sudden hush fell on those waiting, as though for a moment the pride and the failure touched each soul to an inexpressible quickening of emotion. The first shout of greeting broke the spell, and *The Dawn* had arrived.

Peter Sinclair had gauged the berthing-place to a nicety, and now Jeems and himself looked down upon the upturned, smiling faces of the crew. No note there of solemnity or gloom. No hazard is played with such stoicism as the hazard of the sea. Greetings were given and taken. 'Ye've got back! . . . Is that yoursel'! . . . Ay, a good passage . . . Yes, we left just before them – they shouldn't be long. . . . Well, well, an' how are things wi' ye? . . .'

Young Jessie Cormack, Ivor's sister, was standing beside Jeems. She could not spot her brother anywhere and did not like to shout. She plucked nervously at the girl beside her. 'Where's Ivor? Can ye see Ivor?' . . .

Davie, the skipper, caught her face.

'Is that you, Jessie? You'll be looking for Ivor, but he wouldn't come back wi' us. I'll go up by an' see your mother th'-night.'

'But where – where –' stammered Jessie. A listening silence fell on the quay-wall.

Davie looked at her with a half-whimsical humour.

'He's off to Glasgow on the boats, Jessie, to make his fortune!'

No further question was asked either by Jessie or anyone else on the wall; for it was instantly felt that Davie had thus quietly laid his finger on the failure of the home-coming. Jessie edged out of the clustering group and, after walking a little way with proper decorum, quickened her pace and at last broke into a run. She had a deep affection for her brother, and the news was so overwhelming that her heart was bursting with it. Not until she got inside the front door of her home and gasped it out would she find time to realise it, to look at it. Meantime, all she could see was her mother's face, that wise face with the smooth dark hair combed Madonna-wise.

Davie climbed the iron ladder to the quay. They had their nod for him again, the odd word of welcome, their eyes not lingering over-long on his face. He stood with Peter Sinclair and Jeems.

'She could do wi' a puff o' steam in her, able as she is,' said Peter.

'That's what it amounts to,' agreed Davie.

'Ay,' said Peter.

'Yes,' said Davie.

On his way home Jeems was overtaken by the schoolmaster. They acknowledged the fishing failure.

'So there's Ivor Cormack gone,' said the schoolmaster. 'That's the meaning of it.'

'He must do something for his living,' considered Jeems.

'Yes,' acknowledged the schoolmaster meditatively. 'I was talking to him a night or two before they left.'

Jeems threw him a look, but the schoolmaster was plainly preoccupied.

'What'll he do now?' he asked suddenly. 'What exactly did Davie mean by the Glasgow boats?'

'It's likely he meant,' said Jeems, 'that he was managing a passage to Glasgow. Maybe he signed on on one o' the West Coast cargo and passenger boats, small boaties. But it'd take him to Glasgow. He could get a berth on one o' the big boats there.'

'Going away abroad, you mean?'

'Ay.'

'That is, he would be, as you say, before the mast?'

Jeems looked at him again.

'Just that,' he agreed.

The schoolmaster appeared to consider this, then remarked thoughtfully:

'That wouldn't take him far.'

Jeems's expression flickered dryly.

'It would just take him all over the world,' he said.

The schoolmaster plainly had not been thinking of physical distances. He now did think of them.

'It would,' he admitted. 'That's so. He would at least see the earth. What I meant, however, was that there wouldn't be much chance of his getting out of the bit.'

'Weel, as to getting oot the bit . . .'

Catching the tone, Moffat looked at the old man quickly, then smiled.

'We're all in the bit. Is that it? Ay, I suppose we are.'

246

'It's what I did mysel',' said Jeems.

Moffat's smile got fixed in a small access of thoughtful astonishment. He gazed at the old face, the grizzled beard.

'Of course. So you did,' he said at last. 'You have been all over the world?'

'I might say many times,' affirmed Jeems.

'Really!' He regarded the old face, the grizzled beard, more closely still.

'Ay, many times.' Jeems paused a moment to get his breath. 'My wind is no' what it was,' he admitted wryly.

'Going up here would take the wind from anyone,' said the schoolmaster with quick sympathy.

'I've seen the day!'

'I've no doubt.'

They went on again.

'All over the world – in all the Eastern ports, too?' pursued Moffat.

'All the world over in many a strange place I've seen many a strange thing. So will he.'

'I suppose he will.'

'Ay. Staying on here ye canno' understand it,' said Jeems with subtle impersonality.

'No,' said Moffat, with apparent thoughtfulness. He stole a look at the old man.

'He'll see life, anyway, whether he gets on or no',' considered Jeems.

'He must,' agreed Moffat. Then after a moment, tentatively, 'Couldn't he study for his certificates?'

'He might,' believed Jeems. 'He might do that – or, again, he might not. There's no saying.'

'Ah, just so,' nodded Moffat. They went on in silence. At the vennel they parted. 'I wonder if he was somehow getting at me?' thought Moffat to himself as he pursued his way up the village street. 'Or was it just the natural utterance of the old chap?' The faint bafflement held something elusively belittling in it. Then, after a while: 'True enough! What was I talking about getting on for, anyway! Getting on! The old chap was quite right if he was trying to have one at me. I wonder if he was! Dammit, I wouldn't like him to think I had been. . . .' Sensitiveness squirmed a moment.

But Jeems had forgotten everything, except the flavour of his own words in the conversation. It remained satisfyingly on his tongue for a little, then got absorbed in the general wary attitude of his mind.

Maggie was in the back-place as he entered. He took in her appearance in a glance, but lingered a moment on the vivid life in her face, vivid for all its expressionlessness.

'*The Dawn* is in,' he mumbled.

Her eyelids flickered, but she concentrated the more closely on the small white thing she was washing in the basin.

'She's in, is she?'

'Ay,' he said, and went on to his chair in the kitchen.

He settled himself comfortably, letting his legs stick out at their pleasure before him, his head fall forward a little. He glinted from under his eyebrows in puckered thoughtfulness at the white square of the window.

248

After tea, which he noticed, without remark, was earlier than usual, he got out his cutty, observing casually:

'We'll maybe be able to get a bit fresh fish soon.'

Maggie took a moment. Her back was to him.

'We might,' came her voice levelly.

'It would be a change,' he considered. He watched her going through to the back-place, then settled himself to his smoke. He puffed contemplatively, spitting every now and then with deliberate precision into the fire. Presently his pipe went out and he stuck it in his waistcoat pocket. The dish clatter had ceased. His head drooped an inch or two, his eyelids closed.

But he did not fall off at once. The sound of Maggie's footsteps went tap-tapping through his mind. They came into the kitchen, and suddenly ceased. He did not open his eyes. On tiptoe, noiselessly, across the kitchen, and swiftly back; the communicating door closed in the faintest of clicks. He opened his eyes, turned them on the communicating door, stared at it with a concentration that gradually twisted into satiric understanding. He listened a few seconds, then got to his feet and moved quietly to the window. There she was, setting off! He nodded, lips closing and sending his breathing heavily through his nostrils. 'She wouldn't want to waken me likely!' he jaloused. 'It was thoughtful of her surely!' In his eyes was a derisive light that his head nodded to. He could not take his eyes off her. He watched her till she was out of sight. Then turning from the window to the chair,

249

he muttered aloud: 'An' anyway, by Gode, if I'd been her I think I'd have waited!' He drew out his cutty and, lighting it again, pondered this last remark.

A similar notion was troubling Maggie's mind. Was she being forward? Had she all along been deliberately shutting her thought to the possibility of there being no first-night meeting with Ivor? How had she been so sure of a meeting? Was she merely going to Kirsty's to make sure? Or, in other words, wasn't she going to Kirsty's knowing that Kirsty, who understood much, would somehow . . . Her thought balked at adding the words 'arrange things.' She did not want things arranged. She was merely going to Kirsty's because she had promised to go. She shrank from the idea of anyone arranging a meeting between herself and Ivor. That her mind could think such a thing at all! . . . She would not go to Kirsty's. She would go into Mairag's for a penny candle. The candle was needed, anyway, and she had a penny in her pocket. That would be excuse enough for appearing in the village. Then she would go home again. She went into Mairag's and bought the candle.

Coming out, she hesitated on the doorstep; then all at once her footsteps began of their own accord to go down the street towards Kirsty's.

She let them go. It was foolish being sensitive over nothing. She would see Kirsty and the bairns and talk to Sanny. She liked Sanny; something lovable about his quiet, shy ways, the quick responsiveness of his expression, the teeming kindliness, and underneath it all something profoundly virile.

Whereupon, the decision taken and justified far enough, a lightness came to her thought, an airiness of tingling expectation, that was not lessened because opposite it hung the cloud of Sanny's failure, of the failure of all of them. The failure was a failure in the game of the sea for which there was no one to blame. . . . What if she happened to run into someone on the street? He might come round the corner of a house any second and be there before her. Her footsteps, involuntarily quickening, took her to Kirsty's door in safety. Though that was probably only taking her the more surely – She knocked at once and opened the door.

'Come away, Maggie!' called Kirsty's voice.

She had a consciousness of several people in the kitchen as Sanny stood before her.

'How are ye, Maggie?' His quiet voice, his smile, his outstretched hand. She caught it with a quickening of the heart.

'Ye've got back!' she said shyly.

'Yes. Go' bliss me, you're surely looking bonnier every time I see ye!'

Some old voice laughed; it was the Pilot's.

'Did he say as much to yoursel' now, Kirsty? Eh!'

Maggie went over to a chair beside Kirsty, and without looking at anyone in the room knew that Ivor was not amongst them. An indescribable relief suspired from her spirit. How impossible it would all have been here! To have talked words, to have broken the meeting with words, here, without looking at each other . . .

251

'An' how's your uncle keeping?' asked Sanny.

'Oh, fine!' responded Maggie. 'Fine!'

'He's no' troubled wi' his back like some o' us ould codgers?' enquired the Pilot facetiously, as he fluffed his white beard.

'Well –' began Maggie.

'Do ye believe he thinks himsel' ould?' asked Kirsty, nodding sideways towards the Pilot.

'Surely not!' said Maggie.

Slow, fat Hugh-the-butcher laughed:

'If you're no' careful, Maggie,' he wheezed, 'he'll be having an eye to yoursel'!'

'Weel, I might no' go just altogether the length o' that, Hugh. That would be more in the line o' swack young fellows like yoursel', now!' The Pilot winked, then laughed abruptly. Hugh's bald head took on a touch of colour.

'What in the world would the lassie be doing wi' ould fellows like us whateverway! What do ye say, Maggie?' put in Sanny.

'Ah, weel, ye see,' pursued the Pilot, who had a disposition for poking fun, 'after all, the young fellows are nowadays getting scarce. Perhaps the ould fellows will be having their turn over again. What wi' Canada, an' now that young swanky fellow o' yours going to the Glasgow boats – eh? What do ye say, Hugh?'

'Indeed, I believe ye might stand a chance,' said Hugh. 'Ye have the grand tongue for it!'

'That's one for ye, Hugh!' and Kirsty laughed. The Pilot joined in the laugh; then fluffed his beard and looked at Maggie.

'Don't ye think we should have more sense, Maggie?'

Maggie's smile sparkled with a touch of embarrassment.

'Though indeed it's true enough,' commented Hugh, 'how the young fellows are leaving the place. What'll he be looking for on the Glasgow boats?'

'Oh, just a berth on board one o' the trading boats. What more?' said Sanny.

The Pilot nodded.

'Ay, it's a whole-life job wi' nothing in it – even if they do say ye have a girl in every port!'

'Ay, a long job,' nodded Sanny. 'I canno' say how vexed I was to lose him. We all were. I prigged wi' him mysel', at least to come home an' think over it. But no, he was determined on it. I don't know why.'

Kirsty was not looking at Maggie, whose mind was caught in an intangible puzzlement. A faint smile in them, her eyes were set with a subtly controlled expectancy on the men's faces.

'His mother will take it pretty bad, I know,' said Hugh.

'Ay, that's true,' agreed Sanny. 'Davie was going up to see her th'-night. There was just this aboot it: there was nothing here at home for him. Such of us as are committed to it, we'll have to make the best o't. But wi' a young fellow – he might only waste himsel'. It's his brother, Dave, has the croft, anyway; there's a few o' them an' the croft is small.'

'The only thing she'll feel,' said Kirsty, face turned completely from Maggie, 'is him going to the sea. Especially going to the sea in that way. She'll have the sort o' feeling that she's seen the last o' him. An' then – all his life going in that way. Oh, I ken! Poor woman!'

There was silence for a little.

'I suppose there's that in it,' said Hugh.

'Ay, he'll never come at much that way,' reflected the Pilot. 'Of course, if he's a steady chap he'll keep himsel' well enough.'

'He was always steady enough,' said Sanny; then paused, brows wrinkling in thought, 'an' some way he likes the sea. He's always taken to it. An' there's no young fellow alive I'd rather be wi' in a tight corner. He's strong – an' he's quick forby – an' – an' something more, too. I prigged wi' him – though for that matter, what could I say?' He paused again. 'I hope he'll do all right.' Sanny's spirit was queerly troubled, and his discomfort touched the rest.

Kirsty sighed, and in drooping her eyes to the hands in her lap she saw Maggie's body beside her sitting stiff as a stone.

'If we had had any luck,' pursued Sanny, 'it might have been different. But as it was, ye see . . . Weel, once ye begin to go away foreign . . . I don't know. It was like saying good-bye to him for altogether. I didn't like it. I prigged wi' him. . . .'

'Weel, ye could do no more. If he was set on it, he was set on it,' said the Pilot.

'Oh, yes,' nodded Sanny, 'that's right enough.' But his eyes were on Ivor. He had seen him that last night. Ivor had had some whisky. There had been something obscure and brutal in him that laughed.

That was early on in the evening. 'What the devil's the use o' my going back, Sanny?' His eyes had not been dour, gloomy, disappointed: they had glowed with a sort of brutal darkness in them. A reasonable brutality of the spirit that had laughed. It had taken the wind from Sanny, as though he could not realise, could not get a grip on, this enigmatic transformation. On the instant, from being the lad he had watched grow up, he changed into the man, complete, self-reliant, challenging, on almost more than an equality with Sanny himself. He had been the last to see him of all on *The Dawn*. Had gone out of his way to see him. There were a last few shillings from the sale of his nets, and he had said: 'Come on now, Sanny – have one wi' me – the last!' As though it had been some secretive occasion or other – with that enigmatic air about it that troubled Sanny – rather than a farewell.

The conversation, given a realist touch from Sanny's manifest perturbation over Ivor's defection, went on to consider 'what it was all coming to.' Kirsty, with her bairns pulling at her heart, was absorbed to that point which is a mixture of anxiety and dumb fatalism; while at the same time she was aware of Maggie beside her, never moving. Once or twice she was on the point of turning round to Maggie with a smile, but somehow found herself unequal to it. Her man's home-coming had had its moments of the bitter-sweet, when she had been almost shocked at the sudden strength of an irrational desire in her to shed tears; a blind desire to give way and seek the comfort that would be a shelter, a relief from the immediate past, from the penniless struggle of the immediate future, from the dark shadows.

Maggie was on her feet.

'I'll have to be going,' she said.

'What, Maggie! No' already, surely!' and Kirsty was round on her.

'I've to take the coo in – an' milk.' Her tone was an apology for interrupting them. Kirsty stared at her a moment.

'Are ye sure, now?'

'Oh, yes; I must. It's getting on. I thought I'd just run down an' see you all again. Good night everybody!' She was making for the door, smiling timidly. They all had something to say. The stir of her going banished the conversation's gloom. The Pilot called to her to be 'watching hersel', in case . . .'

At the doorway Kirsty was saying with delicate poise:

'Everything's just no' turned oot for the best, maybe.' But Maggie was plainly not lingering.

'No, it's hard to have gone through all the fishing for nothing. I – I can imagine what it must feel like. . . .' She gave Kirsty her eyes a moment. They glowed with understanding, sympathy. She was gone. Kirsty knew a subtle uncertainty as she watched the retreating figure, and returned to the kitchen carrying that uncertainty with her.

CHAPTER EIGHTEEN

HE heard the back door opening, her footsteps in the back-place, and turned somewhat in his chair so that he could see her as she entered without appearing to look. She was taking her time. Perhaps she wouldn't come in; was making ready to go for the cow. It was late enough. The communicating door swung open and she entered.

In a moment he saw that her face was as expressionless as before, but now the vivid flame of life behind it had got blown out. The expressionlessness was clayey. Involuntarily he rubbed his eyes as though a blur had come on them distorting clear vision. A watery blur often troubled his sight, altering in a freaky way what was before them. His eyeballs glucked noisily in their watery sockets. When he looked again she was hanging her coat at the bed-head. As she turned, he felt the necessity for saying something.

'Ye haven't the coo in yet?' he grunted.

'No.'

'If ye started to take her in a bit earlier ye might feed her up the low ditch. The grass is wasting there.'

She made no comment, and as his mumbling followed her she thought: 'He might try it himsel'.' But the thought knew little ironic energy, hardly any at all, and faded almost instantly.

She heard footsteps behind her as she left the gable-end and headed for Matthew's Woodie, but did not turn round to look. They might be Tullach's footsteps. They mightn't.

257

Tullach eyed her as she walked. There was something about the poise of her body as nearly expressionless as perfect poise can be. It walked so smoothly, faultlessly, head a trifle high if anything as though eyes were on the far moor, walked almost somnambulistically, the curves of it, the ease, the unfaltering, steady progression. . . . Gode, even the look o' the back o' her head got him now! . . . That body, that form, with its ravaging, cool grace, how it affected him with an instant desire to stop it, to put his arms about it and draw it up to him, so that its life, its warmth, would wriggle against him! He felt a surge in his chest as he opened the front door.

'Is that yourself, Mr. Tait? Come away! Come away!'

Jeems got up and surrendered his seat.

'Ay, man,' said Tullach, accepting it, 'been a drying day.' He stretched himself pronouncedly. 'Och ay!'

'Ye've been busy?' said Jeems, appearing to appreciate the indications of relaxed tiredness.

'Oh, nothing oot the way; nothing byordinar'.'

'There's always a good lot doing aboot a place like yours,' jaloused the crofter, subtly bowing to magnitude.

'A thing or two. Ay, one thing or another.' Tullach yawned, and in the yawn, half-affected, was a faint tremulousness of a receding passion-surge. Maggie could affect him now in this way! But already he was beyond exclaiming at it, and the ould devil couldn't fossick it oot, not the feelings, cute as

258

he might be. Tullach's yawn finished in a twisted half-smile.

'Though for them like us it's a slack time enough,' nodded Jeems. 'The crops are getting a sort o' good enough beginning, too.'

'Yes, no' bad. We could be doing wi' a spell o' dry weather. Though perhaps it's not exactly original on this coast to say that!' The critical estimate of unoriginality touched Tullach to a dry laugh. A mouthful of English had its curiously superior uses. A subtle sense of well-being went trickling through him, of power. He could, as a rule, more than hold his own when it came to talking. Not many had tried to take him off with any success . . . except, begod, when he came to think on it, this ould devil here! Not that it need be admitted that even he had ever done it – a mere thinness of skin on his, Tullach's, part, an over-sensitive fancy, having created the feeling now and then. . . . However, he was not likely to do it again. No, not likely!

Jeems laughed, 'He! he! he!' at the 'original' joke, a discreet, appreciative laugh. Tullach felt for his golden-bar plug.

'What aboot a smoke, Jeems?'

'Weel, now – weel –'

'Here ye are! I know ye like it.'

Jeems smiled again, deprecatingly, and took the plug. Tullach would have his joke! . . .

Tullach laughed, the short barking echoes penetratingly harsh. An unctuous fullness moved in his body generating a heady froth of teasing derision.

'Maggie says it's got a nice smell aboot the hoose,' said Jeems.

An inspiration; for Maggie had merely once commented on the fragrance with laconic irony that had penetrated the husk of miserliness and had 'taken off' Tullach. To turn that irony now into simple commendation was a delicate revenge to Jeems. It also 'took in' Tullach, who felt himself impelled to stretch his feet to their last inch. After a few moments of subtle deliberation, Tullach acknowledged with an innocently searching:

'Well, there's no reason why she should have to go without it, uh?'

Tullach was aware of the quick look that was chrown him. But the ould devil was taking no risks by way of jumping to rash conclusions! Tullach pulled forth his own pipe, looked openly at Jeems, with such a sly yet apparently meaningful openness that the old man nearly cut his thumb through the blade of the knife slipping off the plug-end.

'For,' concluded Tullach, 'ye can surely afford a plug now an' then yoursel'.'

The silence became so audible that Jeems heard the chuckle that was Tullach's dark smile. He had fortunately, however, given nothing away; and after a moment:

'Ah, weel, for that part o't the bogie roll does me fine. Not,' he added, 'that I don't enjoy a change.'

'Changes are lightsome,' noted Tullach.

'Ay, oh ay, they're that indeed.'

Tullach looked away towards the fire, his mind plainly full of provocative delicacies, when Jeems literally spat through the web of them by remarking:

'The boats are home th'-day.'

Tullach removed his pipe; blew a thin smoke-stream slowly.

'Ay, so I heard.'

'Not that it was much o' a home-coming. They were hard dealt by.'

'So I believe. I heard they made nothing at all.'

'Nothing,' nodded Jeems. 'I don't know what it's all coming to It's poor enough on them an' theirs. Nothing but debt.'

'Not much o' an outlook for the shops.'

Jeems's face puckered just perceptibly.

'There's that in it, too,' he said.

'But ye weren't thinking so much o' them?' remarked Tullach.

'It didn't just hit me at once,' admitted Jeems. 'It's a different way o' making a living forby the struggle o' the sea. It's hard work at the nets an' no' always safe, not exactly.'

'Everyone can't make their living the same way.'

'No, that's true,' agreed Jeems, then left the silence to Tullach.

Tullach spat.

'They're always talking aboot it being hard work an' no' safe an' putting a poor mouth on it. The shopkeepers can't help that. They don't get their stuff for nothing.'

'That's certain,' acknowledged Jeems. 'It's hard on everyone the same. Did ye hear aboot Davie in that storm the other week?'

'No, I didn't.'

'Ay, he was caught in it, an' far enough away to make their chances look gey hopeless; so he shot all his nets, tied her up to the last one, an' rode it oot three days an' three nights, wi' everything battened doon. They came through.'

'Indeed!'

'Ay.'

'Uhm! An' weren't the others caught in it?'

'No; they managed seemingly not to be there.'

'Had Davie been risking it, then?'

'It would look as though he had been taking chances.'

'Well, of course. . . .'

'Ay. But Davie's no' a great one for being safe, like the shopkeepers!' And Jeems smiled what was apparently meant for a joky smile. But Tullach was not deceived.

'So the other boats were safe, too?' he argued, pointedly.

'Ah weel, maybe it's a good thing to be safe,' considered Jeems, broadly.

Tullach's mind quickened in a sharp anger-spasm. This sort of puckish evasion in the ould devil he would pin down and smother. Just then the back door was heard to open, and Maggie's footsteps went tap-tapping. There was no rattling of the milk-pail, but doubtless she had come in for it. Presently the door closed again and there was silence. Altogether the intrusion had somehow been curiously discreet, and now the silence that she left behind held no invitation.

Or did it? Wouldn't she be out there with the

milk going hiss-hiss into the pail, wouldn't she be out there as he had seen her – yon time, with her clothes pulled out, her face and mouth . . . He shifted on his chair, and a sudden worm-sack of venom seemed to secrete itself in his brain with the intention of spiriting its deadly juice at the old fellow opposite. Damn him, the sly in-and-out weasel! He had had enough of him, with his 'safe' and his stories o' the world. What the devil was he trying to get at now, as though he, Tullach, couldn't see through his crawling, misery-ridden mind! Why he, Tullach, should suffer himself to get tied about somehow, to be made – to be made –

'I see that that lad Ivor Cormach hasn't come home,' broke in Jeems, conversationally.

Tullach choked.

'They say he's gone off to the Glasgow boats. That's likely the last we'll hear o' him for many's the day,' and Jeems nodded to himself. 'Ay, the last.'

'Perhaps he'll be safe,' managed Tullach.

Jeems, glancing at him, saw the storm working up. He laughed deprecatingly.

'That most likely was his idea.'

'Eh?' persisted Tullach.

'There was nothing else for him,' said Jeems. 'He had that much sense anyway.'

Tullach glared steadily.

'Oh, he had, had he?'

'Just that,' said Jeems. 'Ay, just that, just that!'

'Oh!'

'Yes, man. Ay ay!' Jeems moved uneasily, yet his expression was not uneasy, the innocence of its pro-

263

found craftiness was almost expressionless. Tullach swallowed, then rammed himself back in his chair till the wood protested and ground the stone floor. Not yet – not yet – not causelessly. No, hardly yet, by Gode! He produced a measured, derisive snort.

'Ye're handy wi' yer tongue!'

'Me, is it? Och, och! But maybe that comes from being away so much.' Shyness at being complimented seemed to touch his expression. 'I mind once – at Valparaiso it was – big Lachie that ye've heard me tell o' –'

'But there are times ye could be less handy.'

Jeems scratched his whiskers contemplatively, apparently trying to catch Tullach's drift. Then he smiled as though to cover his own obtuseness.

'Ay, maybe I told ye aboot it. My memory is no' what it was.'

Tullach watched him. The old face was glimmering in a mild reflectiveness. Tullach's eyes narrowed. The old face was following its memories. Or was it? Was it?

'Ye can understand in a way,' said Jeems, out of his reflectiveness, 'what made me think o' yon lad. After all, it was no more nor what I did mysel'.' Continuing to muse, he did not lift his head. 'Davie said to that Jessie one o' them that he was off to make his fortune!' The musing smile broke on a rich 'He! he! he!' of satire.

'He'd be following your example,' said Tullach.

'Ay – especially aboot the fortune!'

'Particularly aboot that,' agreed Tullach, still watching.

And apparently Jeems could not go on musing indefinitely. He braced himself with a dismissive sigh. 'Och, och – weel, that's him oot – that's him away!'

'Away? What d'ye mean – away?'

'I'm saying that's him gone away.'

'I see,' said Tullach.

Jeems shifted on his seat.

'Weel, he's better oot the way, isn't he?' he considered, thoughtfully. 'An' after all, to give him his due, it needs a little spunk to – to go away like that. I mean, it's no' much he can be expecting from the Glasgow boats an' then off foreign. You're seeing me here – after over fifty years o't.'

'Ay, I'm seeing ye,' said Tullach. 'So ye think it needs spunk, eh?'

'Weel, I mean anyone can stay aboot on the land – on a croft. But when there's women left behind to do that . . .' He paused. 'There's a few o' them on the croft,' he concluded.

'I see. The land should be left to the ould women, eh?'

Tullach's tone could now no longer be ignored.

'Good gosh, man, I never thought to mean anything that way! I was just thinking o' him.'

'Ay, ye seem to be thinking o' him the devil o' a lot, eh? The hell o' a lot, what?'

'No, no! I was just saying –'

'Ay, ay, ye were saying! . . . I'm no' a fool, Jeems, an' I can let much pass – not on your account. No, not on your account!' He got to his feet.

'Hits! Mr Tait –' twisted Jeems anxiously.

265

'Hits! be damned! I'm sick o' your – your –'
His mouth snapped shut. 'But I'm settling the
thing now – this night. Ay, I'm settling it!' He
stood, square chin uptilted, eyes glooming imperi-
ously on the darkling window, stood stiffly, with a
rigidity that at any moment might become galvanic.
Jeems said nothing, under a crumbling weakness.

Tullach stood immovable for the few seconds his
mind needed to cover the grounds of provocation
to the thought, 'Gode, it's for it now!' It was
maddening to have the sense of being rushed,
especially by an old twisted rag of humanity like this
thing on the chair. With his spunk and his women
and yon lad being out the way! Out the way of
what? Out the way so that he, Tullach, might have
a clear field and no rival! To be measured like that!
He, Tullach!

Yes, he'd pay for it – but not at the moment.
That could wait – until this other . . . And at least
this maddening knowledge that he was for it now
would give the other thing inevitability, would
sustain him. The strength of his rage was upon him.
She was out there in the byre, in the dim gloaming of
the byre. He would face her. He would say –

His glooming immobility snapped and he strode
to the door without a word, banging it after him,
shutting the old man in like a dog. Not only say, but
do. Why not? Why not tear through – everything?
Eh, begod!

He met Maggie just within the byre door. She
was coming out, milk-pail in hand, and her face
quested his sudden appearance with a look that was

open-eyed, incuriously cold. Its even pallor, its quiet level regard, there in the faint dusk . . . It hit his fine frenzy like a blow, got his breath, so that he stood like one stricken to an intolerable poise.

'Maggie!' He cleared his throat. He shifted his weight from one foot to the other. 'Eh – you're – you're finished your milking?' A forced smile creased uncertainly.

'Yes,' she said.

'Maggie – I want to – to say to you –' He looked at her with a propitiatory effort at frank directness. 'Look here, Maggie; I was thinking – I was saying to the old man – he was saying you – you liked the smell of this tobacco aboot the place. I was saying to him that there was no reason why you shouldn't have it always. Eh? What do ye say, Maggie? Eh?'

Her eyes moved from his face and stared past him.

'Come on now, Maggie!' He took a step nearer her. 'Tullach is no' a bad little croft. What?' A movement of his arm towards her brought her eyes back to his face for a moment. The tentative arm-movement wavered uncertainly. 'We've known each other a gey long time.' The arm-movement stiffened; fingers touched her waist. 'Eh?'

She did not draw back. He edged closer, his hand spreading along her waist, beginning to press downwards against the curve of her hip. 'Eh?' She was so near. His breathing was getting choked. In the name o' Gode what was she staring like that for? He had her. What did it matter aboot her face? . . . It was clayey, as though the last drop of blood had been wrung out of it. . . . 'Eh, Maggie!' he whispered, his hand pressing more firmly, the fingers clawing her towards him, slowly, persuasively. 'Eh?' He stooped to take the pail from her hand, but her fingers would not open their hold, as though they could not. 'Let it go!' he whispered. His clothes brushed her face, left the imminence of him in her nostrils – and instantly her face winced in a pinched quickening, her eyes dilated. She gripped at the pail spasmodically.

'No, no!'

The sudden sound of her voice startled him to a letting go of the pail-handle, and, straightening himself, he met her eyes. But he hung on to his smile of intimacy, of invitation.

'Come on, Maggie! Eh!' But his smile gradually fixed before those eyes, and as it fixed it hardened and the intimacy died.

For Maggie's eyes were on him as though she had never seen him before, and were not so much shocked at his apparition as startled into round-eyed incredulity at it, into pinched, questing dismay, a faint horror.

'No,' she said.

Eyes to eyes.

'No!' he echoed. Then the smile breaking out again in little hard lines, 'Why no?'

'No.'

'So it's no, is it?' His head nodded. 'It's no, eh?'

The startled note passed from Maggie's expression, leaving it once more level but now indescribably hostile. To Tullach it was not a flattering expression; it was anything but a flattering expression; and the truth of it, its elemental hostility, was beyond all doubt, all possibility of conjuring away.

Tullach's eyeballs hardened, glistened.

'Why – no?' he repeated, with a horrible softness.

'No.' And now her breathing was audible, her breast rose and fell.

'So it's no, eh? Ye think it can be no – what?'

She saw the brute in him stiffening, hovering.

'Let me go.'

'Let ye go, eh? Go.'

Gradually all his body began to come at her. She did not break away or shout wildly. Her flesh froze, her lips and face narrowed in a cold deadliness. Suddenly he enveloped her, snatched her bodily with a fierce grunt, so that the milk-pail smashed against his leg; crushed her, crushed her, as though each constriction were a gluttonous oath. 'Let you go, eh!'

Then he let her go, and stood back a pace, gloating, glowering. . . .

She never wavered nor spoke. Through the blood mist in his eyes and the darkling atmosphere of the byre, her face blazed whitely at him like a lit-up corpse face. Her body had been a pillar of ice. His husky grunt of triumph, of further intention, wavered and broke. His glower wavered. He stooped and slashed the milk from his trousers-leg. 'That bluidy milk has wet me through!'

And while yet he stooped she walked past him. He could have grabbed her at the first step, at the second, but communication between brain and fist had got disordered; another step and she was clear of him, going out at the door. She was gone.

He gazed at the door-opening with a blankness which was a contorted, fist-clenching rigidity of the flesh. It broke on a flood of oaths. He choked himself, cloyed his brain, with the gushing blackness; raised his fists in a grotesque pantomime of gnashing and pulverising; thick laughter. . . . But wary, devilish laughter as he escaped from the byre and made his way over the fence into his own field. Now and then he stooped and slashed his leg. 'That bluidy milk!' . . . But all the time at the back of his mind the great whorls of rage gathered in face-shapes that gibbered and gnashed. Gode, he would pulverise them! Choked, cloyed by his rage: for not yet could he face the far bitterer madness of defeat, of inexorable loss, nor stare into that look of Maggie's with its subtle disintegration of him. Such exquisite torture, with whatever might spring from it, was cunningly waiting on the spent, unavoidable moments of vision.

CHAPTER NINETEEN

MAGGIE entered the back-place; busied herself there until the children came. The old man listened to her comings and goings, could scarce contain himself in his chair. Why wasn't she coming into the kitchen? Couldn't he go out on some pretext or other? Mightn't he call her and tell her to put on peats? But the fire didn't need peats. What would he be wanting peats for at this hour? . . . Ah, perhaps Tullach was waiting for her outside – to complete things!

Her voice to the children was quite in its usual! She was cute, too; able! There they went! What in the world could she be having to say to them like that! . . . Ah, she was going!

But Maggie's footsteps re-entered immediately she had seen the children over the doorstep. The back door clicked shut. Was that the bolt going home? The old man's head lifted in intensity of speculation; the flesh gathered in puckers round his eyes, slitting them. Gode, could she have undone everything!

He made no show of indifference to her entry. His crafty eyes immediately raked her. She was as normal as ever he had seen her, except for something about her that was meant for danger, a kind o' leave-me-or-I'll-sting! Sting, would she? Hoity-toity, uh? An' their world in smash!

'Did ye see Tullach?'

'Yes.'

'An' did he speak to ye?'

'He did.'

'He did, did he?'

She turned to the bed and began clearing the counterpane of its odds and ends.

'Will ye answer me?' His voice rose shrilly.

She paused, and, unhurriedly turning, faced him.

'I did answer ye.'

'Don't ye dare answer me like that!'

She waited.

'An' – an' what did he say to ye?'

'I don't quite remember now.' It was suddenly not danger, but a far more deadly polite indifference. Facing her, he began a spluttering that ended in a fit of coughing. He was choking. She waited.

He wiped his eyes; he got to his feet. He was trembling.

'What did he say to ye?'

'I don't quite remember.'

He took an involuntary step nearer her.

'Ye hussy! Did he – ask ye?'

'Ask me what?'

'Did he – ask ye?'

She turned away.

'Maggie!'

She paused.

'I think,' she said, 'he was meaning something like that.'

'Meaning – something – like that!'

'Yes, I think so.'

He took a moment.

'An' what did ye answer?'

' "No!" '

'Ye said "no"!' The shrillness faded to an incredulous whisper.

She began moving about again. His eyes followed her, fascinated.

'Ye said "no"!'

Silence.

'So ye said "no"? "No!" Ye said "no"!' At last the intelligence penetrated, and his expression gathered an intense malevolence.

'Ye dared say that to him?'

'Yes.'

'Ye dared! Did ye know what ye were saying?'

She suddenly stared back. Was there some horrible something in his tone she didn't understand? Had Tullach got him in some way? . . .

'D'ye no' know it means ruin? Ruin!'

Her stare broke, giving way to a dourness. Dourness can hide insecurity in its folds of dumb defiance.

'What are we – withoot him? What's the croft? What's going to come o' us? What – what – what have ye done?'

Her dourness held, but the thought that they were entangled by Tullach, who would have no mercy – now, was a terrible thought, and she involuntarily stammered –

'Do ye owe him –?' and stopped.

His eyes opened. He absorbed her meaning slowly. She surreptitiously watched him. He tore the stillness with a fiercely ironic:

'Owe him! Don't we owe him for everything?'

He had penetrated her meaning. She had spoken

273

too quickly. He could lie now by cunning implications. And yet he might not be lying.

'Owe him! What's he been doing all these years? Do ye think he's the sort to be doing things for nothing? To keep on at doing them for nothing? Would any man? Is he a fool?'

Her dourness held.

'An' ye who – who could have paid him – no, but paid yoursel' an' me an' everyone an' everything, who could have settled everything for ever, ye – ye – "no"! Gode, have ye no' sense at all? Are ye clean by yersel'? Canno' ye see what ye have done? Canno' ye see?'

She did not affect to see anything, but a dull, round spot of red was forming on each cheek bone.

'Surely it's no' too late yet! No, it's no' too late. I'll see to that! When ye could have everything, everything by – by –'

'By selling mysel'.'

The silence was instantly stark as though the Word of God had been spoken. The silence was haunted by vague evocations of painted Jezebel faces. Through the silence she walked into the backplace, pulling the door to behind her.

His mouth had come adrift; his eyes were goggling on the door.

He stirred, the irritation of coarse laughter tickling his throat. He lit the candle. His old hand shook. The laughter was instantly becoming more defined, more contorted. It got a grip of him. It ripped his throat with a thick hilarity. Mutterings and cursings; then laughter again. Selling hersel' was such a – a – hell o' a joke! The brazen limmer! Such a – a bluidy bit o' nonsense! That she could dare! . . . A purple anger choked him. On the surge of it, clip-clop went his slippers ben the house.

But not immediately to bed. Some sort of realisation first, some sort of definiteness. He humped down on the chair by the bed, and gradually his eyes got fixed on nothing, though his head kept just perceptibly nodding, his flesh just perceptibly shaking, as in an insidious paralysis agitans. But his eyes could make nothing of it. His brain seemed full of windy echoes, and all that would move in it of any immediate significance was a querulousness which was wanting more and more to become peevish. Sweeping, condemnatory thought evaded him. Irritation wormed in his brain in short, red-hot spirals. He began to feel how life was conspiring against him. No one had any thought for him. No, not one. An access of self-pity troubled his breathing, which was already thick enough. He clawed at his breast in a half-conscious gesture. Yet irritation remained, bafflement. It was terrible the way life could smash an old done man! Selling hersel'!

He got to his feet; took off his jacket. Let them say what they liked, do what they liked: he was not done yet! No, he was not done! They might think it, but he was not! Everything might join against him, but yet and on! . . .

In bed, the restlessness of his mind continued, the one moment self-pitying, the next defiant with a flickering of cuteness along the bone. Out of this weak interplay was gradually borne a sense of

275

essential loneliness, a realisation of his age – not as a mere wordy mumbling concerning an old man, but as the finality that is near dissolution – death.

The starkness of the involuntary imaging gripped him. It was the final picture of himself, however they carry on. He felt the loneliness about him like the coldness on a dead moor. He saw himself an image set in the void expanse. . . .

He moved. At once the loneliness became earthy and crawled over him. He needed something to hold on to. His mind twisted, trying to grip at something. He was not done yet. He thought of his money, and instantly a warm comforting flowed about his heart.

The desire to see his money became ungovernably strong. The craving itself was tonic, and in no time all the cutenesses of the flesh were playing in the mind. He would go now. Was she in bed? . . . Yes. Better wait a little though. It was not so late that everyone would be in bed. What if anyone ever saw him? What if anyone ever robbed him of the whole thing? His flesh stiffened in a convulsion of fear. Appalling thought! He glared at it and saw, beyond any questioning, that it would kill him. He would die under it.

But no, there was little chance of that. No one on earth could ever guess. Even if anyone ever broke in, even if the place was burnt down, there would be nothing to show. . . . No fear!

He had to be comforted; and in truth there was little fear. He let the minutes pass over him in bearable impatience.

Later, in the kitchen, he felt about for his boots. He did not think much of the girl in the bed from which no sound came. His earlier fierce angers were given logical continuance in a satiric grunt, a pech, a throat-clearing, for the benefit of all whom it should concern. Roy's paws padded in soft impatience. Presently the night wrapped them about, the secret, companionable night.

Maggie heard the footsteps fading out and continued to lie still, though an urge came on her to go secretly forth into the night, too. But the urge was prompted by no conscious desire other than a physical one for breath. Life was too confined in the box-bed; beat back on her in wearying pulsations to an infinite exhaustion. She lay flat on her back, staring eyes finding, between the flowered curtains, the greyness of the blind.

But beyond being choked by this weariness she felt little. The depth of her mind had become a place of evenness like the grey coast, and in its still desolation no whorl of feeling moved at all. It was also like a place on which a door had closed; an empty, uninhabited place. The desolation would continue, the emptiness would know only the still changes of decay. Above the desolation and the emptiness her life would be lived and words would be spoken. . . . As the weariness of lying there suffocated the pores of her flesh, tossing it now and then restlessly, as surface eddies of feeling swirled and faded, as vague humours and vague self-pityings disturbed the wearinesses to faint chokings as of tears, deep down the mind looked on the grey places with grey eyes. And in the grey places it was as though a word had been spoken long, long ago, and everything lay under the spell of the word, and the word was *Forevermore*.

Tullach and the scene in the byre had now no meaning, were touched by no vitality. Her mind did not question what she had done. It was surely strange that it could ever have been worried by any such possible happenings at all. It was not worried now. The lifelessness of it all was – no, not curious, but evenly incurious.

She would not think yet of what she would do, of how she would have to plan life so that existence would become possible for her uncle and herself. She was too weary to think about anything now. But somehow she would do, she would manage; only, she would think about it all again. She had better just try to go to sleep.

But when she closed her eyes her mind became so still that it hearkened to the words telling of the passing of Ivor, and the words had strange tragic echoes to them, like trailing sounds of the birth of death. The whole day was a day of birth and a day of death, like a story remote from her but with this clear, terrible power of changing all the days coming after forevermore. And possibly the strangeness and the remoteness were there because the life in her dared not think of Ivor himself, lest her strength crumple up and her mind collapse, clinging frantically to the shadow of him, and there be an end to everything. . . . Fortitude, the dour will, and the days would go on. She must just go to sleep. Her uncle would be out yonder after the rabbits, and to-morrow or next day she would be going for fish. And he would be cursing her yet, and thinking cunningly in his own mind how he could change things. . . .

But, as it happened, at the moment her uncle was neither thinking of rabbits nor yet cursing her. His eyes and his fingers, body and soul, were seduced by the glittering pile on the bench before him. The golden light was a golden warmth moving in all his veins like nights of old Jamaica rum. And as his fingers clawed slowly in around the pile, thought ran in fine tumultuous riot to a muttering, gloating accompaniment of fragmentary, husky sound, that broke now and then in husky laughter. A golden warmth that thawed chill miserliness and brought to relief not so much an essential duality of character as distinct mental opposites that were yet capable of being transfused in this golden over-existence. Here he could gloat and give basic craftiness or cunning its utterance of power, undeterred by thought of the practical considerations of existence, undeterred even by the thought of ever having to use, to spend, to destroy, one of these everlasting circles of golden magic. Spend it! Not only did the thought not arise: it could not; any more than could considerations of the morning after have affected any remote night of the past given over to the golden gods of Jamaica.

The dark vision of Tullach loomed in his mind, conjured up by inscrutable, involuntary ironies. He could point his thought with a sort of oblique direct-ness, shaft upon shaft, at it; or ignore it in a contem-

plation or side-issue that was yet most subtly privy
to its dark presence; a chequer game, with triumph
moving and disposing.

He leant over the bench, face crawling with his
thought.

'So she said "no" til him!'

Ay, it was a joke that; it was the hell o' a joke
altogether! An' she would say 'no' til him – wi' her
face like yon! Gode, it was wonderful! He laughed
with suppressed huskiness that seemed to break out
through an obstructed throat. He cleared his throat
in a raw harshness that resulted in a mouthful of
phlegm on the floor. The horrible expectoration was
like a gesture to his spirit. He would have attempted
a still greater clearance were it not that sound
travelled. As it was the spittle could easily have
gone through the dark vision, right through its face –
without the vision being absolutely certain of
positiveness in the intention. He squawked again,
and, bending still lower, brought his hands to the
gold, the cool, living gold.

'Wi' her face like yon! – an' him – him –' The
gold slid and tinkled. The dark vision began to fade.
Slid and tinkled; into a confused richer tinkling;
into a music that hypnotised; into a deepening of
colour, gold into red. . . .

Rumbling and throaty came Roy's sudden growl,
deliberate and stiff-necked. It caught the pulse of
the hut with the fingers of terror; caught the old man
as though the iron fingers were at his throat. His
fists remained clenched among the gold pieces, his
eyes glared horribly. The iron fingers were choking

280

him. The double fear could be seen in the eyes. Not merely fear of the night without; but now the actual physical throes of choking. He began to gasp. His hands left the gold, his will forcing them to leave it without a tinkle. They caught at his neck. He needed breath. In a paroxysm of asphyxiation he clawed at the neck-band of his shirt; his body doubled up; he reached the floor the better to wrestle; stretched himself; stiffened; mouth wide, trying to gasp. And all the time his ears listened; his brain thought, 'They'll never get in!' with a venomous vindictiveness.

But there came no further growling from without, and presently the breathless fit passed. He knew what these spasms meant — a weak heart. It was the worst one he had had yet. But the fits were not dangerous — if he was careful. He got up, and with a shaking hand wiped the beads of sweat from his forehead. His face had a ghastly pallor, and the furrows in it were deep. But it was what informed the pallor that arrested: a sort of startled decrepitude of the flesh that was like a listening to a sound from the abyss.

He began to put the pieces back in the bags without stacking or counting them and with as little sound as possible, though his weakness was such that every muscle trembled in exhaustion and shook the pieces to a smothered chattering. For all he knew, too, there might be an ear against the wooden wall fornent him, listening with full understanding; perhaps peering through a sun-shrunken slit or nail-hole, a malignant, greedy eye.

Yet it was panic foolishness to let the walls and the dark corners get studded with eyes, when Roy was out there. And now the bags were full. He lifted them by the necks into the box and, stepping as quietly as his fumbling legs could, reached the earth-hole. There, on hands and knees, he hastily scratched a thin layer of earth over the wood, raking it with his nails to look of an undisturbed agedness, pieces of old brown bracken and dried dung helping him out. Then gathering the last remnants of his strength, and with an effort of will that brought the sweat out afresh, he lifted back the litter and junk.

By the candle again, he leant heavily on the bench, head lifted, ears listening intensely in the moments between his gasping. No other sound had come from the night. Of that he felt certain. He must get out of here. The strain of hiding the gold was lifted from him. He felt lighter.

Blowing out the candle, he stepped to the door. In the darkness his legs seemed to come high up, then scarcely to feel the ground. He knew himself staggering from a light-headedness. The bar swung round with an alarming clack. The night met him in a cool swishing of trees. At the door was Roy, inclined to twist and fawn a little as though glad to see him – and conscious of that growl.

'What is it, Roy?'

The twisting was like a half-grovelling apology. The old man looked about him; got the chain in position and padlocked it securely; then he walked round the hut. Nothing. No sign of anything.

'What was it?'

The dog grovelled perceptibly.

'Ye ould fool!' Plainly the dog was uncertain, equally plainly nothing had come near the hut. There may have been some strange sound or other from the wood. Suddenly heartened that it could be no more, Jeems turned homeward, a hand grabbing unconsciously at his chest. The sooner he got lying down the better. Some little way from the hut he paused on a new thought.

'Seek him oot! Seek him oot! Sst!' Roy gave an aimless turn here and there and came back. 'Ah, ye!' and Jeems went on, trying to hold the earth steady. The old dog had merely missed his fun with the rabbits. . . .

But the crack of the twig had come upwind to the dog's ears, and though plainly denoting the passing presence of a foreign body, yet a body without scent or visible substance. Then – silence. When the master appeared there was slight self-consciousness allied to the still-springing hope of rabbits.

From the wood the black figure of a man now crossed over to the hut with noiseless caution, fingered the padlock, the chain; felt the staples. For a long time he remained there, motionless. It would be a simple matter to break in. But what could there be in there more than rabbit snares and trock? Yet what in the name . . . was driving the ould devil . . . at this time o' night . . . here? What? If not to poach, then what?

Tullach's fierce, half-crazed eyes searched the night about him, his cunning whispering that to break in now would be to give the show away . . .

when with caution . . . biding his time . . . eh?
Teeth crunched.

He passed away into the wood again, the scrambling of his feet in the brae-face like the scattering steps of an animal.

CHAPTER TWENTY

THE next three days saw the old man wandering about in a mood of dumb aimlessness that seemed daring anyone to scratch it, that could contain itself only by occasional harsh outbursts of irritability. Once when he stubbed his toe on a stone by the byre door, Maggie heard his language clearly in the back-place. The curses were unusual and shocking. Her flesh shuddered. The voice was a gibbering, momentary madness of rage. She avoided him as much as she could without appearing to do so, for even to herself she did not wish to appear to avoid anyone.

Neither, however, did she wish to precipitate a second argument, though she felt it had to come, was certain that all his mind was seething with it, all his body even. Hence the curses, the suppressed rage. But she was not going to work herself into a state over that! It would be so easy to work herself into a state. But it would also be fatal. She must keep cool command, not think, see the grey indifference. There were sufficient unreasoning forces in herself, pressing up; forces that might passionately overwhelm for the mere sake of an outburst, that would lead to nothing, would mean nothing. A mere passionate woman's craving for some sort of relief. And all the time this suppressed rage of his was keeping her on edge. It wasn't fair.

But every time she got to the stage of thinking it wasn't fair, she had to choke things back. She mustn't think about it at all.

285

And mostly she succeeded; yet the state of suspense was a rarefied atmosphere in which consciousness must constantly breathe, and now and then the traitorous gust would come perilously near an outburst.

But he persisted in his aimlessness, his animal wanderings and mutterings, until in the end the cry rose in her mind: Couldn't he say what had to be said, and be done with it!

But no, no, he had to keep on. . . .

And then into a hollow of silence in her mind came the frightful thought: Would he always keep on like this now, – go on like this forevermore?

It was an appalling thought, a horrible, paralysing thought. It took the strength from her, drained her utterly, and left her staring at it.

Perhaps it was natural enough that she should have been misled by the old man's behaviour into thinking the wrong thoughts for him, for she could hardly know that a new and terrible idea had been begotten in his brain. This idea he wrestled with in the loneliness that knows no communion, that is caught up from life into the grey forewastes of eternity.

The idea had first begun to torment him when, having returned from the hut and got into bed, the memory of Roy's growl assumed significant proportions, working up into alarming proportions. Once or twice only by a severe exercise of will had he kept himself from a second and hurried trip to make sure that no attempts at robbery were going on. The loss of his money would be a worse calamity than any conceivable thing else; it even dwarfed death, gave it in some way an empty meaninglessness that was frightful to contemplate, gave it a cold, clayey nakedness. His golden wealth, the warmth of it, the strength, the near companionableness. . . .

Then into his alarm, in amongst the warmth of his love, had crept this snake of an idea coupling Maggie to his gold (once he himself was dead) in a last mocking despite of Tullach.

The mockery was there, the final, gloating triumph over Tullach. But what an echoing emptiness the mockery, what a husk the triumph! It wrung his soul in a slow agony, there in the lonely forewastes. To be robbed of his golden fire during life might have to be borne; to be robbed of it in death was a conception excruciatingly intolerable.

The night passed like a fevered nightmare, until exhaustion claimed him some three hours before breakfast, so that he had to be called twice. With daylight-wakefulness came a rush of confused thought, startling him into an obscure sense of something lacking, lost. . . . Remembering Roy's growl and its implications, he was himself in a moment; presently getting through breakfast with a dumb irritability that hid a stealthy haste; going out and around the barn-end with the usual morning leisureliness; and ultimately making Matthew's Woodie and the hut by way of an inspection of Nance and her tether.

The hut was intact. Relief rushed about his heart. He could afford to jeer at his fears.

He jeered at them, and not until he had exhausted

the humours of his relief did he discover that they jeered back. Most subtly they jeered back, their needle lances expert and poisoned, getting his very soul in the raw. The contest was long and utterly brutal. Crush them and pash them in the mire as he might, they would rally and come at him, slyly, subtly, remorselessly. In due course and in quite a clear vocal moment, they said: 'So ye'll make a will – leaving it all to her!'

At that he had tottered from the cairn of stones by the barn-end and in crossing the yard by the byre door, had stubbed his toe. The torrent of curses had been a sweet outpouring. But he had not entered the back-place; did not want to see Maggie, to look on her robber's face. By Gode, they were not getting him as easy as that! . . .

Until the third day and the evening of the third day.

During the afternoon he had secreted ben the house pen and ink and the penny packet of stationery. A certain quietism had come on his spirit, of exhaustion, of the inevitabilities, rather than the quietism of acceptance, as though suppressed irritability had deepened into dourness. He would sit silently for a long time, to all appearance lost in profoundest thought; then spasmodically fingers would clutch, a flicker would pass over hardening eyes, a movement of the body, breath audible in the nostrils, and he had shifted his position – to settle down once more.

The evening came and went without his opening his mouth. So profound was his preoccupation that more than once Maggie had searched him with her eyes, only to be baffled into a sense of intangible insecurity. Insecurity of what, of whom? She could not definitely know; and felt that it might be as well not to risk the discovery of the knowledge openly; yet could not say why she felt it; as though in some way the inscrutability of the depth of his preoccupation connoted an unknown strength, a grim man-power that might in some unthinkable way make her cave in, submit. Though even then – submit to what? Yet she knew herself moving about softly, unprovocatively. And when at last he went with his candle, she found in the empty kitchen a sudden freedom.

She was holding her own. She would weather it. The fight was good for her. It kept her mind occupied. Though there was no need to think why it should be necessary to keep her mind occupied. There was no need, and she didn't do it. Her thought blew about superficially, avoiding definition; she busied herself leaving everything tidy for the morning. She finally looked round on the kitchen and nodded, satisfied; blew out the lamp, knelt to her prayers, and slipped into bed. She was able to manage her own affairs, to hold her own; decidedly able. She had to watch things, watch herself, at every point. But she could do it. Suddenly in a black rush all thought was blotted out, her face was in the pillow, her body was racked by gusts of emotion. Tears came and choking sobs. Her hands clawed into the pillow. A mad, insensate desire to cry out, to cry out aloud, not to care for anything, to give way utterly. . . . She dug into the pillow, clung to it as to something that would choke her. . . . Oh, she mustn't, she mustn't cry out . . . ah, she mustn't. . . .

Utterly spent she lay, small tremors passing over her body every now and then like dying waves on a worn shore. And in her mind sat the clear, terrible knowledge that this was only the beginning of such nights. . . .

But no sound had penetrated to the old man ben the house, whose body lay stiff-stretched on top of the bed-clothes. There was no need for hurry in what he had to do. He could wait. He did not want to be disturbed. She would be asleep by this time most like, anyway. He would get up in a little and put a match to the candle.

Moreover, there was this subtle comfort in Scots law that if a man wrote his will in his own hand and signed it – it would be enough, it would be valid, without witnesses. He knew that for a certainty. So that a man could make his will and carry it about with him and no one be a bit the wiser. Furthermore, if at any time he wished to destroy it, he could destroy it. There was, it could not be denied, a good deal of comfort in that.

A lot of comfort, of raw, ironic satisfaction, the Scots metaphysic declaring itself in the letter of its law. He could carry the will in his inside breast-pocket, and should the whim move him he could take it out and drop it in the fire. It would be like watching the burning of a cheque drawn on the sum total of gold in the hut!

A satisfactory visualisation. His face wrinkled grimly in the dark and his tongue came moistening his dry lips. One thing was certain, that had there been any necessity for witnesses there would be no will. And if there were no will? Then the hoard would have remained his own for ever.

The Scots law had him there! It was knowing; it had the devilish cunning of the mind. It gave the way out, the simple, tempting way. . . .

He got off the bed as noiselessly as he could and lit the candle. Its flame sent grotesque shadows flapping round the room as he moved with it to the circular, claw-legged table The old table creaked and tilted as in the uncertain light his hand came too heavily upon it. He hissed at the sound, steadied himself, then turning to the ancient chest of drawers with its peeling veneer, extracted therefrom pen, ink, and the packet of paper.

He sat down to the table, laying the packet of paper before him; and, fumbling in his pocket, produced the long, ragged leather case which contained his glasses. He gave the lenses a wipe with the edge of the table cover, and tried them. The result was dissatisfying. He wiped them again, wiped and tried and breathed upon and peered through and over them. In the end he kept them on, fumbling about with the packet of paper in a peering and side-tilting of the face that expressed a mounting irascibility. The pen-nib he wiped between his lips, then inserting it in the ink-bottle, he shook with a splashing rattle what fluid there might be. He was ready.

Ready enough, yet cramped, not set to it. He shifted about, irascibility still mounting. It was nonsense all this, just mad blethers and trock. There was not only no need for it; but, far worse, it was tempting Providence. Was he mad that he could have thought about it at all! To put down on paper where – where all yon was! in black and white! Gode, it was asking for a judgment! So it was. In black and white – on paper! He was getting dottled. That was it – dottled. People got dottled without knowing it. When he was young they always saw the old folk getting dottled. He was one of the old now, going dottled!

He glowered upon the white paper, knowing in his own mind that the irascibility was a surface manifestation, yet holding to it as to something tonic and crushing; giving in to it, aiding and abetting it, till finally it blotted out all other considerations. Curse them, all of them! They weren't getting him! Not likely! As if it wasn't all his own, every shining round coin of it! Why should he give it away, sign it away in black and white! They were mad to think it, to expect it! They were clean mad! It was his, all his, would be his forever! To sign it away – in black and white – on paper – so that sooner or later it would be taken from him, would not be his! . . . Gode, what were they thinking!

His eyes narrowed behind the greasy lenses, which now and then flashed vacuously. The thin wisps of grizzled hair stuck up and out in a lank dishevelment. A peering, cross-grained, drawn face, with the blood-vessels showing in the eyeballs when they steadied in a glower; a tormented, persecuted face that fought grimly back, with irony, with sweeping, raucous dismissals, hiding cunning in their folds.

And the white paper remained before him, and all the time he knew, deep down, that on the white paper he was going to write his will.

He peered at the pen-nib, bunching his eyebrows, madder than ever at thus being driven. He squared himself to the paper, curses forming in his throat in the beginning of a real anger. He had worked out the opening sentence. It was to run: 'I, James Sutherland, hereby bequeath to my niece, Margaret, all of which I die possessed.' He knew that was the way the law expected it to run. He could begin writing it at any time – at once. And suddenly he started.

It was a laborious, intolerably teasing business. When at last he had got the pen-nib to flow, the ink had come in a blot. There was no blotting paper. By the time he got the sentence down on a clean sheet of paper, sweat beads gleamed on his temples, were caught in a glistening dew in the furrows of his forehead. A murderous feeling cried for relief by way of doing smashing violence to a pen-nib which had persisted in sticking. He wiped his forehead, breathing thickly, shifting on his chair; then finally squaring to it again.

'In a corner of the shed down at Mathew's Wood . . .'

His hand shook; he paused, listening. The still night was about him. Not a sound. He looked at what he had written as a man might look at the beginning of some frightful confession. His breathing began to quicken, to thicken. He felt the thudding of his heart. There were no eyes watching him. Steady a bit, steady!

'. . . the far corner next to the strath is a heap. Take away the heap and in below is a box of money. . . .'

He had to stop writing. He was going to have a 'turn' with his heart. What if he died now, here, on this chair, leaving this sheet of paper! . . . Panic threatened, sent clawing fingers at the sheet, left eyes glaring wildly, breath stertorous. The hand drew back, collapsed, fell heavily on the table. An inexplicable previsioning told him that, however he died, it would not be on account of a heart turn.

He would take his time. He would finish it now, though the doing it killed him. Tullach! – ha, he could spit through Tullach! Tullach thought he was wonderful smart! . . . She looked at him like yon! . . . He had to hang on now to the central reality of his mind through a whirling and slipping in his head. He fought the dizziness with flying scraps of defiant ironies, ejected his spleen like venom into it, even while his mouth hung open and dry in the laboured passing of his breath.

Then the surge ebbed, and presently his mind stilled. He squared himself once more to the table. The pen now shook perceptibly in his hand. All over his body his flesh trembled. But that was merely the faint and passing weakness of reaction. . . .

'I likewise hereby bequeath what is in the bags in the sum of £371 (three hundred and seventy-one) to the aforesaid Margaret at my death.'

After a breathing space, he squared himself for the final adhibiting of signature, place and date.

That was that. He looked upon it to find that in some unaccountable way the wonder, the fear, had gone out of it. He was tired, utterly wearied, exhausted. The sheet fascinated him, but with a fascination of coldness. He lifted it gingerly, held it to the candle flame, drawing it to and fro shakily. Perhaps it was dry now. He laid it down anyway, and pushed himself to his feet, the table tilting and creaking as it might.

Slowly he got his clothes off until at last he stood in his dark-grey flannel shirt, white flannel undershirt showing at his scraggy, hairy chest and against the sinewy shanks of his legs. He read the will over, folded it, put it in an envelope. Later on he would gum it down and address it to Maggie; meantime, into the breast-pocket of his jacket with it.

Blowing out the candle, he scrambled into bed, under the clothes. Gode, he was tired, he was done. Feeling he was going to faint, his mind went groping. . . . Tullach – fauch – spit! . . . The limmer, she wouldn't. . . . No one cared what happened to him. No one. . . . None. . . . Till thought found the unfathomed ways of oblivion.

CHAPTER TWENTY-ONE

Ivor cormack staggered down the brae-face on the far edge of Matthew's Woodie, stumbled, fell, lay for a second or two, then doggedly got to his feet again. The old well should be thereabouts. He could do with a drink. But the darkness was treacherous, so many hollows and blacknesses, and his feet were not quite reliable, not heavy enough. The ground slid from them, or came and hit them too soon, in a way that might have been remotely curious had the mind been capable of making any speculative effort at all. But the mind had become one with the body in its persistent animal direction-ing towards the well. And there it was – that flattish blackness in front, if he knew anything about the ground.

These feet of his kicked into a grassy tussock and he fell again. He lay for a few seconds, then gathered himself on hands and knees and crawled to the flattish blackness.

His hot palm came on the flat stone that was the well's lip. Good enough! He got both hands on it and tried to lower his head, but his hands knuckled under him and he fell flat, breast to the stone.

His mouth found the cold water, exquisitely cold; his face found it; a caressing coldness; a desire to let his head droop down, down, came over him in a craving for cool revivifying sleep. He suddenly became aware of the buzz of water in his ears. With an effort he pulled himself back, and, rolling over, lay still, his eyes wide to the stars.

The water was cool on his face, trickling over it, dripping from his hair. A hand came up and wiped the drops that were tickling his eyes. Lying there, extended, the earth a soft cushion under him, his brain cleared to the lightness of a puff of thistledown drifting down the daylight. As clear as daylight, too. No pain, nor ache; not unpleasant – if only he would be left to lie there, if only no one, no thought, would intrude! But the completion of his journey from Stornoway to Matthew's Woodie, strange nightmare effort, was the merest first step, was less than nothing, compared with what lay ahead in the way of personal shame. Skulking back home like this, he who had waved his arm, pointing to Glasgow and the world! Oh, he wasn't going back to Balriach; nothing for him yonder! Skulking back home like this now! . . .

And now he could break his oath not to think, not to debate with himself, not to wander from the compass point of Balriach, until Balriach was reached; for was not this Balriach at last, with its grey, poverty-stricken soil under him like a feather bed! The same, by heaven! Balriach. This was about where ould Jeems would tether Nance when he wanted her to trim the edges of Tullach's ditch! It was funny! He had managed what he had set his mind on, and he was here, arrived, free to make the bluidiest fool o' himself before creation!

He had known of the bitterness that would come at him like this, had known it every step he had taken, yet the knowledge had been a black under-knowledge that he had ignored, had trodden over, had not allowed to exist – till the task should be doggedly completed.

And now here was Balriach, and here the under-knowledge jeering and whispering already. He should never have taken the first step. Fool and laughable fool! What did he think? Because of a bit of moonshine on peat-moss and too much whisky in his head. . . .

He lay very still, muscles stiffening a trifle, fists clenching.

The peat-moss and the moonlight – and the white moment of vision and certainty! It was clear yet, stark clear; now, indeed, possessing this additional clarity that he could see himself from the outside as that figure on the moor; see the scene objectively, and yet know the inner thrill, too.

Gode, he had been drunk that night! And yet – he had not been drunk. The whisky had not made him drunk; on the contrary, had given an extra-ordinary reality, a quickening, to the inner loneliness that was himself. Round this inner, withdrawn self, how his flesh and his mouth and his words had swaggered and fought! He could see them at it now – from the outside; then he had seen them only from the inside. Easy in his body, saying this and that, laughing, not giving a damn for anyone, in black joviality . . . with the inner lonely thing watching, jealous, ready. How he had worked up through laughter and swagger, when the veiled jeer from yon Stornoway bastard had got at him, getting nearer the realities of the fool, nearer and nearer, swaggering through the swagger of the fool – till he had stopped him stiff! He had been swaggering when the fellow, swearing through spittle at the mouth, had leapt for him. The cold deadliness of the watching inner spirit then, the devilish thrill as he had let out! He hadn't been drunk, they all found! And he had known, coldly, that he could kill the fellow, and the inner spirit in its colder pride had whispered no restraint, might never have whispered it. . . . They had torn him from his game. . . .

He hadn't started it. One or two of them had been getting at a Skyeman. But how he had elbowed in with his joviality, disliking the dark visage of the fellow who had been trying to use his wit in baiting the Skyeman, John Macdonald, a decent man; the inner spirit egging him on, ready, whispering: 'You're cut adrift – for good! Why not let out – damwell to celebrate!' curling its thin lips.

He had let out all right. Served them damwell right! Only, he had been denied making a clean sweep of them; for a time he had felt maddeningly baffled at this to the point that he would have made a special effort, with all his cunning, to catch up with his game again, had not John Macdonald hung on to him. Curse John Macdonald! But John Macdonald wouldn't take a cursing. John had hung about him like an older brother – and an audience. He had played his part before the decent John and that Lewsach who had lived on a croft house outside the town. He had allowed them to prevail on him, to smooth him, to reassure him. Nor had their hurried Gaelic asides been altogether lost on his pride. Not that he had caught every word, but the tenor had been clear enough: if they did not hang on to the lad he might do murder yonder! In tones of the starkest belief!

They had pulled him round a corner into some place where a bottle was produced. He had taken a lengthy pull at it. For half-a-spittle he would have swallowed the whole lot – without turning a hair, to show anyone whom it might concern that he was himself! . . .

Swagger, eh! The black surge of it in his blood, and the inner loneliness watching with the thin curl on its lips. Cut adrift – for good!

He had taken the bottle from his mouth with a generous arm-sweep that had shaken some of the spirit from the neck. 'Ay, ay, loachain! that's you!' they had whispered, patting him and praising him and forcibly detailing the swinish characteristics of their recent antagonists. And the inner spirit had watched and twisted its thin lips in more pronounced approval than ever, saying: 'What the hell does it matter anyway!'

Thereafter a road out of the town, the three of them on it, bumping into one another. The bumps had been devilish funny! He had felt that the others could not help themselves; he had pretended that he could not help himself, and yet had found himself bumping when he had a mind to try not to. A rollicking game! A slap on decent John's shoulder, a dramatic pause to enquire the cause of John's stumbling, followed by extinguishment in laughter!

In the croft house there had been food, the woman

of the house, a young lad with a crutch who had played the fiddle. . . .

Ah, the fiddle – that was it! The playing on the fiddle. That was the beginning of it. It had brought him back through his mind, past the swagger, to the last innermost loneliness, to the bleak grey stretches that could only hunger dumbly for God knew what. And he had no desire to be brought back there . . . But the fiddle had gone on, and in the roundest joviality he must praise the fiddler! So that from reels the fiddle went to songs, and voices were lifted up, from something about *Lennan mo chridhe* to *O, till, a leannain*. Lennan mo chridhe – the one of my heart. Great songs, for certain! He had applauded mightily! Oh, their damned songs, with the dirge to them and the heart twisted! He had gone out – for a minute, by the way. Had walked away from the house on to the moor. Lennan mo chridhe. Haunted and bedamned!

The moor lay under the waning last quarter of the moon. He had stumbled on blindly, missing the pathway from the house, missing the road; had got bogged in a sweet-smelling myrtle marsh to emerge on a rounded knoll. There he had paused to take breath, his brain a ravelment of fiddle music and the twisting flames of meaningless, defiant cursings. He was sodden to the knees. . . .

When suddenly the world lay at his feet.

The black shape of him staring on that world! A queer, silent, listening world at first; but gathering to itself quickly a witchery, a pallor, a loveliness that was uncanny, a remembered strangeness – without words but known to something of the long ago; swimming nearer, in about him, till it went over his body in a shiver, and started a sudden gulp of emotion that choked him in the throat.

O utter fool! A wild desire to throw his arms at it, to jeer aloud, just stopped short of fulfilling itself. And then in an instant he was dead sober, his forehead cold, his flesh shivering in upon his bones.

It was a strange mood of cold exaltation that followed, with its eyes seeing himself, life, everything, in a stark clarity, seeing beauty with a vision that was remorseless. The moon and the dim night and the loneliness about him, swimming in about him in swirls, like swirls from the secret, invisible passing of Beauty's self. . . . And remorseless vision could see only the beckoning loveliness.

His manhood came upon him then, and he shivered before it, and felt his breath cold on his lips. He saw himself, and he saw Maggie, and he saw his desires. The moment of realisation was absolute.

The strength was in him too, the driving power of his manhood, which had fought and smashed that very night. It came upon him again in an access of exultation. He would see Maggie, he would speak to her, he would tell her. Manhood required it of him, life required it. He had been running away, and covering himself in his own eyes by drinking and swaggering and fighting. He would go back, and he would speak to Maggie, come of it what might. Then if he took the road again – why, God help him, he had not played coward.

The logical moment was one of quivering revelation. No doubting upon such a peak, no foreseeing of shame, and he had lifted his fist to that waning moon and cried: 'God, I will go!' An oath that thrilled to an ecstasy, and thrilled the night . . . upon whose pale beauty he had thereupon whispered a name; and a great wave of joyousness had flooded over him, and the foam of it had burst on his lips in wild laughter.

What a night with its visioning and its certainty! Such utter certainty! And the laughter that was ecstasy and the knoll that was enchanted ground! To go back, though all the powers in hell or on earth should try to prevent him! He would stick to his oath. . . . And suddenly his imagination had embodied Maggie, and together they had walked on the moor. . . .

Honest John Macdonald had run him to Portree, though John's own home was nearer Staffin. From Portree, nothing offering by sea, he had tramped to Kyleakin, where a decent ferryman had given him a lift to Kyle. At Kyle his last penny went in food, and then, quite destitute, he had faced the trek across Scotland for the east coast and the north road.

How many days he had been on the journey he could not be quite sure; how he had managed to live was not altogether clear. For the shame of it and the shame of himself he could not beg. But folk in the lonely places had been kind and twice a caravan of tinkers had offered him the freedom of their pot. Somehow he had gotten something to keep him going, except that day and yesterday, when he had avoided everyone.

But all that – what had been the use of it? Plainly the use of it had been that he would end like this, like a thrashed cur slinking home with its tail between its legs! Folk would laugh at him slyly, gossip and laugh. 'Did ye hear that Ivor Cormack's come hom'?' 'No!' 'Oh ay!' 'But I thought he was off to Glasgow!' 'Ay, just that!' Eyes meeting; the dry smile; the jalousing that the making o' a fortune was maybe no' just so simple, as ye might say!

Bitter enough. And the pale light of the moment of revelation on the moor could seem pretty thin now. . . .

He stirred in a half shiver. His face felt cold. It was time he was making a move. What had to be said to his mother he knew: He had found, after all, that there had been no berth for him on the Glasgow boat, but he had fixed up all about going to Glasgow in a few days' time; felt he might as well take the chance to come home and say good-bye . . . And so on; that very night before going to bed, so that he would not have to meet the full, impossible burden of it in the morning. A light tap on the kitchen window and his mother would wake and let him in. Sitting by the smoored fire, and she in her bed again, he could say it easily enough, and she would know somehow in that queer, silent way o' hers . . . ah, what would she know? . . . A warmth moved about his heart, a stirring of instinct towards her, a dumb acknowledgment.

And then, when he had seen Maggie – the long road again. What else? But he would see Maggie.

For days and days she had got mixed up with his consciousness in a way there was no unravelling. But he would see her and tell her, perhaps to-morrow evening by Matthew's Woodie, for there would be little chance of anyone disturbing them there, if she would be out that way for the cow; but sometime and in such a way that she would know. And then he would know.

Up in the darkness of the brae-face behind him something was moving; a cattle beast, maybe. He could hear the hoof-thuds coming down; began listening with aimless intentness to them. Queer thuds, too, for a beast. . . . Or were they footsteps? His body quickened in listening suspicion. There was no need for anyone to come on him now – yet was he fair in the way of the well. But surely, at this time of night. . . . Another second or two and doubt became impossible. Moreover, the footsteps, heavy human stridings, were coming straight at the well.

He lay very still, instinctively gathering himself to the ground. He might be passed by, whereas if he moved discovery was made certain. His blood was up and pounding away again, telling of his weakness. Nearer and nearer came the steps; a violent kick on his legs and a body went headlong over him. And not in silence. Daun Tullach's oaths were spat out with guttural fierceness.

Ivor Cormack managed to his feet – to find Tullach already stiffened, head and shoulders hunched forward, peering at him. The darkness was deep enough, perhaps, to make peering necessary, and such an apparition rising from the well's mouth must have been startling enough in any case; but Ivor knew that the hunched head and shoulders, the peering eyes, betokened an incredulity that could hardly breathe; and that when it did breathe, whispered:

'Ye!'

Moments passed in which the very air about them became electric with passion.

'Ye!'

'Yes, me.'

'Eh? Ye!' The whisper hardened into a harsh, half-strangled mockery. 'So ye've come back!'

Ivor swayed. This on-rushing of the primal passions affected his flesh in dissolving tremblings, made his brain spin. But his body hunched up, too; fists clenched.

'Ay, I've come back.'

Tullach straightened himself, laughed; and in the thick barkings was something unclean.

'So ye've come back!' he repeated. 'Ye weren't long making yer fortune. No, begod, ye didn't take long!'

'No, not that long.' And it seemed to Tullach that Ivor swayed nearer him. His nostrils flexed, sniffing at him.

'An' now ye're back on a visit!'

Silence.

'Nosing aboot in the dark like – like a damn thief!' The laugh again. Then: 'Maybe ye'll have been going to pay her a visit in her bed!'

Ivor came at him, but it was the onwhirling of a spent leaf against a wall. Tullach's fist smashed into

306

his face. He dropped in a tangled heap. There was a fading consciousness of a boot in his back with the words trailing afar off: 'I'll bluidy weel settle *ye*. . . .'

Consciousness trickled back uncertainly. He sat up, hands and then eyes groping about him. There was the slimy stickiness of blood in his throat. His nose was bleeding from a blow; his hand went up to make sure. But it was not bleeding, he found; the blood lay congealed and caked about his nostrils. Then consciousness became complete, and for a long time he sat staring at realisation; sat staring until what he saw, what he felt, could be no more endured, and his body, jerking spasmodically, snapped the tension. He would keep his mind off everything till he got strength; he must go to the well and wash his face. . . . But he did not move. Presently great tears fell from his drooping head on to his fists. Shame was upon him with the bitterness of nothing else on earth.

In a little he stirred, two knotted fists uprising, his face turned to the paling stars:

'O God, I'll kill him! I'll kill him!'

CHAPTER TWENTY-TWO

THE blustering wind and rain of the early morning and forenoon had died out. The earth lay in a sodden plentitude, infused with scents that touched the senses to an awakening of age-old instincts.

From the gable-end, ould Jeems got the heavy rottenness of the corn-patch in a sudden whiff. He sniffed it deliberately, and the heaviness did not repel him. On the contrary, it called to mind the progress of the year, the forming of the fruits of the earth, and the growing of living things; did it vaguely by way of creating a background for the clearer visualising of his first snaring experience of last year.

It must have been at this very time, for he remembered so vividly getting this smell in the early morning as he returned home with a whole haul, a great catch. The grass had been wet and the bracken hanging with rain drops. A queer freshness about Matthew's Woodie had appealed very strongly, and his feet, squelching about in his boots, had felt soft and warm. He had put it down to being the first snaring raid since before the spring breeding; yet there had been something hauntingly attractive about it which had not gone out of his head for a long time, which came back into it now with relish.

Not but that now and then, about Matthew's Woodie, in the evening loneliness, with his ears and senses alert, sudden fancies struck him, vague feelings of indescribable knowingness, of age-old familiarities, sending his eyes quickly this way and that, as he

308

hammered home a 'backie' (snare-stake), or walked from rabbit-run to rabbit-run. Only, the memory of that first raid held something curiously fragrant and sappy, of a green everlastingness.

But the evening was getting on and he would soon be starting. His snares were all ready in the hut. He must see that that lassie went for the cow, so that there would be no chance of interference. This evening was to be enjoyed, and, as things were, the setting of snares along Tullach's ground was an operation to be undertaken with all due caution. Ay, with all due caution, as things were!

What Tullach might not do if he found him! Yet, looking at it all round, what could he do? Have him up before the sheriff for poaching? Would he risk it? Jeems thought along the line of the question for a moment. If he did that, with everyone knowing how he had been out and in of his, Jeems's, house, helping with the croft and the peats, would not everyone wink and laugh, saying that he was showing his spite because the lassie had thrown him over? Would Tullach be too blind to see that?

And if he didn't do it that way, how then?

The old man felt uncomfortable, experienced an uneasiness that he might laugh at but could not quite dissipate. For in Tullach he sensed a dark force, a dark brutality, that would find its own way, its own outlet, when the moment came. Tullach was the sort of man that, maddened into unreason, would be capable of following him up and strangling him mockingly over his very money as it lay spread before him on the bench.

Jeems involuntarily glanced about him, as though his horrible thought had made itself audible; then glanced again at the visualisation, the spread money, the clawed, choking paws of Tullach, the contorted face. . . .

His tongue came between his lips, his eyes brightened. 'The b –!' he said. His old eyes grew stormy. 'I have seen the day!' he thought. Then his face folded in a canny, withered laugh. He would poach his ground, whateverway! Looking about him, he sniffed the heavy rottenness of the corn, sniffed and nodded. It was about time to move.

He entered the house by the front door, having been taking the air from the gable-end opposed to the yard. In the kitchen he lifted his voice:

'Is it no' aboot time for the coo?'

There was no reply.

'Maggie! Is the coo in?'

He went through to the back-place to find it empty. She must have gone for the cow. At the back door he heard movements in the byre. Perhaps the cow was in and Maggie was at the milking already. He had been in the barn whittling three new backies and might have missed her. About to lift his voice to make sure – he paused. He might as well go quietly.

Coming out at the byre door, Maggie saw him disappearing round the house towards the Woodie. He would be going for the cow, she thought. She had been bedding the stall, and now crossed quickly into the back-place, examined herself, sniffed her clothes, could not sit down. His going for the cow would save her wetting her feet, anyway. The night was before her. She was expecting no one, nothing. But she could not sit down, even though the thin excitement moving at its own inexorable will in her body was as a faintness. Three hours before, she had learned of Ivor's return.

Meantime, Jeems held on his way with every appearance of shauchling normality. At a certain point, before dipping to the wood, he paused and cast about him with leisurely unconcern, at the sky, at the land. 'The rain's no' done yet,' he muttered, instinctively covering, as though even from himself, his object in spying out the possible intrusion of the human. 'No, not done yet,' and continued on his way, a subtle pleasure in his acting disturbing the deeps. There was no one about. He would have time and place to himself. He held straight for the shed.

Roy would be with Maggie in the byre. He did not need him at the moment; would not need him until the small hours for the rounding up. After a look about Matthew's Woodie, partially covered by an apparently practical consideration of the condition of the hut, he mumbled, 'Ay, could do wi' a lick o' paint'; then, unlocking the padlock, entered. The door closed behind him.

The close, stuffy smell in the hut affected him with that pleasure which is born of illicit secrecies and is not cumbered by shame. The secrecies of the earth and the body gathered and concentrated; an alert, furtive smile in the eyes with the ears listening.

He did not sniff the smell: it invaded him, passed

all over him, and standing with his back to the door, he listened. Then moving to the bench, he groped for a contrivance in the wall which permitted the sliding to one side of a short piece of planking. To waste a candle in the daylight could hardly occur to him. And, in any case, the daylight served his purpose better.

From a shelf to the right of this aperture, he lifted down a bundle of hazel twigs, each about the length and thickness of a new pointed lead pencil, with the blunt end slit. He examined them carefully, counting and making a little heap of those he would require. From a nail below the shelf he lifted a heap of rabbit snares, and, holding them by their gleaming brazen nooses to the slot of light, examined them critically.

Nodding, he laid them on the bench, and set about separating snare from snare. From the backie up along the four or five inches of string, to the interwoven strands of the noose, to the final eye, he went methodically, testing knots, stressing, peching, and finally laying on one side; snare after snare, opening eyes, affixing a new backie here, a new string there, until finally satisfied. Then, stowing snares and hazel 'stickies' about his person, he slid back the panel, and, going to the door, listened, before finally emerging on an evening of gathering dusk and shadowy silences.

As he made for the foot of the brae-face with its clearing of sward, the blood flowed warmly through his flesh. Every sense was on the alert, his brain alive, his body shauchling in correspondences of muscle and nerve that were only so far faulty as to make efforts at exaggerated lightness of poise grotesque; otherwise, plainly knit to its job and slavering a trifle at the mouth when an unexpected stumbling brought the breath whistling.

On the last two inspections of this clearing below the brae he had been in doubt as to the faint beginnings of a new rabbit-run. The deep-bedded steps of the old run had yielded nothing last autumn. The clearing had been altogether deserted. This evening he paused, doubt at last cast out: they had come back to form here a new run altogether. A small pulse of excitement beat up for a moment and he nodded. They had come back. A new run, a virgin 'roadie,' a certainty! A yard from it, he followed its faint course until he came on some droppings which he examined for freshness. There could be no question of doubt now.

He selected the spot for his snare with due care, even though there could not be much trouble from a new moon (barring the headlong run, rabbits had a way of hopping round a yellow wire glistening in clear moonlight). An old dead clump of bronze bracken appealed to him, the more so as a draggled offshoot inclined to the middleway between two rabbit steps. He sunk the backie by the edge of the clump, thumping the head of it well home. The slim hazel stickie was now pushed an inch or two into the soil and the inner end of the wire, out beyond which was the running noose, was notched firmly in the slit on the head of the stickie. With careful fingers he cunningly smoothed the noose into a slightly flattened circle the distance of his closed fist from the ground, and exactly midway in the rabbit's leap from step to step.

He stood back from his handiwork admiringly, eyebrows and forehead puckering, head atilt. It was a well-set snare; it was all but a certainty. He gave a wide spang over the roadie so that no human scent should linger upon it, and began to scrutinise the ground for further signs.

In all he set three in this short brae-face, the *thud*, *thud* of grey stone to wooden backie sounding hollow and mysterious in the evening silence. Every now and then he would look up as though he feared that long-eared faces might be slanting a look at him, with malevolent intent; watchful, grinning faces. He had had snares stolen and rabbits. And a face could easily enough peer round a hump of grey rock or through a darkling tuft of scrub.

Moreover, he had often noted this still, listening quietude of twilight, this hollow in which he moved as with unnameable expectancies. The smell of the grassy turf was quite different, too, from any smell of the croft land. The trees on the brae-face leant out and over a little, their interlacings and contortions arrested to a curious attention. The slightest sound – and he was round on it.

He liked it. Sometimes he dreamed about it. And even at the worst, when nightmare turned the writhing birch branches into snakes and their wintry, tufted excrescences to tree'd devil faces, he was of the company of it: devil faces, branches, snakes, night-torches, and blood-red Jamaica rum. The world of the croft and the money was the reality, of course. This was the unreality, but made possible of pursuit because of the two saving points of contact in rabbit flesh and Beel-the-Tink.

He worked his way up through the trees and presently seated himself on a bare patch. The greenish, elfin silver of the moon's sickle was gathering substance in a fading sky. What dead colours there were about him came to life and glared a little on his sight. Of all moments this was the one holding the deepest unreality, the most hushed unreality, the moment that cut him off from earth-digging and money-scraping and a jealous God as in a magical circling of the unchancy, the immemorial, the inscrutably delectable.

Not that he consciously divined it so, but, more, he had the feel of it about him. This listening hollow of evening that slipped into the night shadows – old, older than the remote fireside stories of child-hood which were stories of infinitely old things, of men and women and mornings and nights going back to the dawn of time itself and the first blowing of wind down the green world. A kinship to it, a quality of visioning it. For untold ages to come evenings would die like this. . . .

A relish for it all moved over him, crinkled along his skin. To visit it through the years to come! To steal back from the places *beyond*, to steal back. . . . And the money down in the shed there – to visit that! . . .

Lifting his head, he suddenly glanced about him furtively, his tongue coming out between his lips.

A hand went to the inner breast-pocket where the letter, the will, lay; felt the letter. Then his mouth closed, the lips meeting tightly. And slowly his mind called up the figures of Tullach, of Maggie, of that young fellow who was going to the sea. They came round about him, their faces watching him, while his glance moved from one to the other, knowingly, reading them, a laugh in his throat.

But he did not know that even as he called them the three figures were gathering in about him – Tullach and Maggie and Ivor Cormack – to a point in time, to a moment in destiny, that was as surely of his own creating as though his old wrinkled face were a satyr force compelling the final issue; and compelling it with the inexorability that knows no coincidence, that is built out of inevitable step by step with a stark simplicity.

For Tullach was up in the whin-patch with its old quarry waiting for him, his mind dark and gluttonous, full of suspicions and half-baffled guessings, gleaned of the night, of the old man's mysterious midnight visits to the hut, of the poaching, waiting on certainty the better to command calamity; while, down by the burn, Ivor had seen Maggie, grown impatient of Nance's return, pass along the hollow below the hut towards the bracken patch that sloped downwards from the well. All three of them gathering round the wrinkled satyr face in the wood, 'taking his breath' to read them knowingly, a hidden laugh in the throat.

Jeems started and shivered. The dusk was

316

decidedly creeping in about, and there were a good few snares to set yet. This dwauming about of his thought was hardly the thing. He got to his feet with an odd smile and passed up over the brow of the brae.

There the smile faded, for Tullach land lay before him nakedly. In on this land he must set the body of his snares, so that in the early hours Roy would reach far out and round, sending the white scuts helter-skelter into the invisible nooses. And the snares must be set in such a disposition that he would infallibly come on them in the dark.

The perfect spot for the first snare proved to be on a slight declivity where a grass tuft bordered the run. A fine, well-trodden run. When he came on it, he paused to look about him, far up into Tullach land and down the old clearing in the wood to his own shed. Seeing no living danger, he stooped to his work.

He found he had left his hammer-stone behind, but just his own length below him was a small cairn of grey stones. Considering himself lucky, he selected one twice the size of his fist.

But he had trouble with the backie. The first time it went in altogether too easily. The second time it took a firmer hold, yet, pulling strongly on the cord, he felt it come a little. Dissatisfied, he eased the backie once more. The third time he struck a firmer spot, and, indeed, the wood was in danger of splitting at the head from the thudding of the stone. 'That'll hold a whale!' he grunted, as he pulled on the rock-like fixity.

He dug in the stickie and stuck the wire-end in the notch. Then he smoothed out to a flattened circle the golden noose. Because of the declivity, however, and the shape of and distance between the steps, he saw that the rabbits were in the habit of taking this particular bit of ground at leaping speed, so he raised the noose higher than his closed fist by the thickness of two fingers.

It was all done neatly, carefully, and yet with a smoothing of finger-tips on wire, a final slightest tilting of the noose, a covering over of the turf abrasions with plucked grass, that was not unlike an artist's care for his effect. Even as he got erect again and moved upwards, he studied the result, head sideways, as though from the unconscious rabbit's point of view. Then he lifted his head – and beheld his niece, Maggie, and the young fisherman, Ivor Cormack, side by side, faces in front of them, walking like two figures out of a dream from the direction of the bracken patch where the cow had been tethered, walking across the level bare patch and disappearing behind the hut.

Stiffened he stood, like one who had looked upon the slow, fateful passing of figures in an old legend; figures not speaking to each other, caught up in a dumb suspense becoming momentarily more intolerable; slow, awkward figures, surcharged with an emotion that would presently burst and engulf.

A sudden crafty fear that this thing might have been seen by others sent his head jerking quickly around – and there, bearing down on him from the whin bushes about the disused quarry, came Daun Tullach.

His old mind was no more nimble than his old limbs, and it was pure instinct that made him swerve from the advancing figure (though as he swerved a half thought began whispering involuntarily that he could pretend later, if need be, he had not seen anyone . . .), when in a moment the swerve and the sudden step and the declivity combined to throw him a little forward off his balance. Normally, he would just have sat down, but now, whipped on by the instinctive urge to get clear, he tried to race the short declivity so that beyond the foot of it he could overtake his balance. He never reached the foot of it, for the snare, so perfectly set, caught over the toe of his right boot and he was flung forward in a crashing dead weight towards the little mound of grey boulders.

Tullach came up at a heavy run, a fiery redness in his darting eyes, breath heaving in thick gulps. The cunning that might have kept him lying low until a richer, more informative, more damning moment should arise, had been dimmed by gnashings of madness and impotence when he had caught a glimpse of Maggie crossing from the croft and of Ivor Cormack circling warily up the burnside as though to intercept her. Too much! By Gode, too much! . . .

So that now he stood heaving over the still figure, ugly words tearing from his throat, stood gulping, waiting for the figure to move. But the figure made no movement at all. And presently Tullach stooped, caught it at the shoulder, hesitated for a moment, then slowly, slowly turned it half-round. The head fell loosely to one side, exposing a forehead which

319

had been smashed in, in that spot he had always seen the butcher select for his pole-axe. His fingers let go the shoulder and the body fell limply back.

His breath came now in short hissing gasps between his teeth, a chalkiness crept in about his stiffened features, his restless eyes fixed fascinatedly on the body.

Then he drew back one step – two.

'My Gode!' His teeth snapped shut, his fists clenched in a muscular spasm. 'My Gode!'

Thought surged back with a memory of the two figures down by the bracken patch, and on the instant he turned wildly for the clearing in the wood.

A few yards, and he drew up in a hunched, dreadful stiffening. Down through the clearing in the trees his glaring eyes were fastened on the two by the hut, on the passion that had at last burst intolerable suspense and swept body to body.

An appalled moment of realisation for Tullach that was to become for ever after a moment of pure vision, to become an unpredictable series of maniacal moments when the inner eye would glare down a clearing in the shadow-show of the mind at a picture etched to a searing clarity.